The Sturdy Oak

Edited by Elizabeth Jordan

This edition is published in 2023 by Flame Tree 451

The text for *The Sturdy Oak* is based on the original
edition serialized in *Collier's Magazine*, 1917 and published
as a novel by Henry Holt & Company, 1917.
All other text © copyright 2023 Flame Tree Publishing Ltd

Flame Tree 451
6 Melbray Mews,
Fulham, London SW3 3NS
United Kingdom
www.flametree451.com

Flame Tree 451 is an imprint of Flame Tree Publishing Ltd
www.flametreepublishing.com

A CIP record for this book is available from the British Library

ISBN 978-1-80417-269-8

© 2023 Flame Tree Publishing Ltd

Cover image was created by Flame Tree Studio, based
on images courtesy Madame Tatillonne.

Printed and bound in the UK

MIX
Paper from
responsible sources
FSC® C018072

The Sturdy Oak

Edited by Elizabeth Jordan

FOUNDATIONS OF FEMINIST FICTION

With an introduction by June Purvis

Contents

A Taste for the Fantastic

From mystery to crime, supernatural to horror, fantasy to utopian, dystopian and the foundations of modern speculative fiction, the terrific range of paperbacks and ebooks from Flame Tree 451 offers a healthy diet of werewolves and mechanical men, bloodlusty vampires, dastardly villains, mad scientists, secret worlds, lost civilizations and escapist fantasies. Discover a storehouse of tales gathered specifically for the reader of the fantastic.

Great works by H.G. Wells and Bram Stoker stand shoulder to shoulder with gripping reads by titans of the gothic novel (Algernon Blackwood, Charles Brockden Brown, Arthur Machen), and individual novels by literary giants (Jane Austen, Gustave Flaubert, Charles Dickens, Emily Brontë) mingle with the intensity of H.P. Lovecraft and the pure psychological magic of Edgar Allan Poe.

Of course there are classic Conan Doyle adventures, Wilkie Collins mysteries and the outlandish fantasies of Robert E. Howard, Edgar Rice Burroughs and Mary Shelley, but there are so many other tales to tell: *The White Worm, Black Magic, The Murder Monster, When the World Screamed, The Centaur* and more.

Check our website for regular updates and new additions to our incredible, curated range of speculative fiction at flametreepublishing.com

FANTASTIC TALES

The Sturdy Oak

Edited by Elizabeth Jordan

Series Foreword

What did feminism – in fiction and in reality – mean at the turn of the twentieth century? This series of reprints of rare and often forgotten texts from that period answers this question in the widest possible way. For some of its authors, it meant the representation of the New Woman, the sometimes hostile term applied to women who sought the vote, the opportunity for higher education, access to the professions (or just to jobs), or who just wanted their independence from the stifling conventions of the nineteenth century where a woman's place was definitely 'in the home' and where venturing out meant chaperonage or else a risk to reputation. So, some of our chosen texts (for example, *The Job* by Sinclair Lewis) show those women achieving a measure of independence. In the spirit of the realism which was his hallmark, Lewis also shows that getting a job is actually an illusory form of freedom. The daily grind of the office or factory is not the utopian dream that some seekers after female emancipation had hoped. In other terms, and for other reasons, Kate Chopin's *The Awakening* also shows that women could not easily free themselves from standards of sexual propriety: sexual choice is not the route to utopia any more than earning capacity is. Her heroine briefly tastes the pleasure of sexual liberation but cannot escape the judgement of her society: her story does not end well.

For other writers (Charlotte Perkins Gilman, for instance), the representation of *life as it is* that realism demands was also problematic. Realism permitted only the diagnosis of social ills: it could not manage the process of prescribing solutions for the problems it uncovered in the world as it was then constituted. The construction of fantasy worlds, in which current imbalances between the sexes could be redressed in an imagined future was Gilman's solution in *Herland*. This is a speculative fiction, a 'what if?' world rather than a 'what is' world, though in common with all fantasy, it also speaks of the limitations of its own moment of production.

Long ago, Elaine Showalter pointed out, in *A Literature of their Own* (1977), that focusing purely on representation whether realistic or fantastic can be a kind of dead end. If readers only look at false pictures of reality or at impossible visions of futurity, they get stuck: despair or dreamscapes. A third possibility is to look at the woman writer herself, what she does, often slyly and obliquely, with genre and form. Francis Stevens (Gertrude Barrows Bennett), a woman writer cloaked by a male pseudonym, offers another potential meaning for the first wave of feminism: the professional woman writer, using man-made genres for her own ends, both aesthetic and financial. She belongs to a category that frighteningly often overtakes the woman writer – the forgotten novelist. In recovering and reprinting her work, the series shows both her indebtedness to, and her distinctiveness from, the male models of the adventure fiction genre and the weird tale which, along with romance and crime, were the mainstays of the pulp magazines of the early twentieth century. She also made money – an important consideration for the woman who wants independence – in her chosen domain.

If Stevens stands for 'pulp' and popularity, Virginia Woolf is the highbrow novelist par excellence (though she also sold pretty well and was also very interested in the money she could make from her pen as her extended essay *A Room of One's Own* makes clear). Her works span a massive range of reviews, short fiction, novels and polemics, and she often returns to the figure of the woman artist and/or writer to demonstrate the ways in which women can be denied their creativity ('Women can't paint, women can't write', Mr Tansley says dismissively to the artist Lily Briscoe in *To the Lighthouse*) and opportunity ('Why are women poor?' she asks in *A Room of One's Own*).

For this series, we have brought together texts which showcase women's talents and their frustrations in a historical moment that is not so very long ago. The battles that the New Woman, the Suffragists and Suffragettes, and the founders of women's colleges and union members fought on our behalf may all seem to be won. But they only seem that way. Count the women politicians in the House of Representatives and the House of Commons. Check how much an average woman earns over her lifetime and compare it to the average man's earning capacity. Ask yourself who cleans the bathroom in your house and who does the double shift at work and home. And pay attention to how easily some rights can be lost by the flick of a legislator's pen and a minor political shift.

The feminism of the early years of the twentieth century had its own blind spots: it was not inclusive of women of colour, nor of women from working-class backgrounds, nor of those women for whom heterosexual romance was not their choice, nor of those women who lived at the intersections of multiple disadvantages. Early feminists were also very often conflicted about the 'sex' part of sexual liberation. Nonetheless, those early struggles for white middle-class women's rights have resonance and lessons to teach for the broader struggles for all women, and for other dis-privileged groups. And representation in its broadest sense (of characters, but also of the women writers we might read) is one of our routes to understanding, action and – let us hope – change.

Ruth Robbins

A New Introduction

Early Campaigning for Women's Suffrage

The struggle for the parliamentary vote for women in Britain was long and hard fought. It is usually dated from 1865, when John Stuart Mill ran a successful campaign to be elected to Parliament with votes for women forming part of his election address. The following year three influential members of the early women's movement – Barbara Bodichon, Emily Davies and Bessie Parkes – asked Mill if he would present to Parliament a petition in favour of women's enfranchisement, which he agreed to do. Although the petition was unsuccessful, it did encourage interested women to form small suffrage committees. Lydia Becker and Millicent Garrett Fawcett became central figures in the Victorian women's movement.

Both Becker and Fawcett were what we might call 'constitutional suffragists'; they advocated legal and peaceful means of campaigning, such as presenting an annual petition to Parliament, lobbying MPs and holding public meetings (Elizabeth Crawford 1999 and Jane Robinson 2018). After Becker died in 1890 Fawcett became the key figure in the movement, especially after 1897 when the National Union of Women's Suffrage Societies (NUWSS) was formed from an amalgamation of the small suffrage groupings. Its membership included both men and women and its aim was to win the parliamentary vote for women on equal terms with men – that is, on the ownership or occupation of property of a certain value. While only about one-third of men had the vote at this time, all women were excluded because of their sex.

Founding of the Suffragette Movement in Early Edwardian Britain

Emmeline Pankhurst and her eldest daughter Christabel, both based in Manchester, were members of the NUWSS. However, these two women had become increasingly dissatisfied with tactics that were bearing no fruit. Women's suffrage bills were regularly debated in Parliament but never passed. Nor were they happy with the Independent Labour Party (ILP), of which they were also members. The ILP claimed to be supportive of sexual equality, but refused to give priority to the issue.

The compassionate, fiery Emmeline, fuelled by her passion to end the oppressed conditions of her sex, decided that women had to form an independent women's movement in order to raise themselves from their secondary status. On 10 October 1903 she called a small group of local socialist women to her home at 62 Nelson Street, Manchester. There, together with Christabel, she formed the Women's Social and Political Union (WSPU). In 1914 Emmeline Pankhurst recollected:

> We resolved to limit our membership exclusively to women, to keep ourselves free from affiliation to any of the political parties of the day and to be satisfied with nothing but action on our question. Deeds, not words, was to be our permanent motto.

Although the WSPU was to campaign primarily for the parliamentary vote for women, its aims were much broader – as Emmeline and the charismatic Christabel, its Chief Organiser and strategist, made clear (June Purvis 2002, 2018 and 2021). A radical transformation of women's role in society was necessary to ensure equality with men in all walks of life, freed from all their 'disabilities', as the oppressive conditions were termed. Members of the WSPU soon became known as 'suffragettes', a term that was coined by the *Daily Mail* as an insult but was readily embraced.

Early WSPU Tactics and the 1905 Free Trade Hall Protest

In its early days the WSPU engaged in peaceful campaigning, but all to no effect. There was no newspaper coverage of the women's cause, nor did the issue grab the eye of politicians. Christabel decided that more assertive, less ladylike tactics were necessary. Instead of asking politely for the vote, women had to demand their democratic right. Further, since so many MPs, with no success, had individually presented women's suffrage bills to Parliament, in a form known as Private Members' bills, it was necessary to push for a government sponsored measure. The autumn of 1905 was the time to act, since the Liberal Party was expected to form the next government.

On 13 October 1905 Christabel and Annie Kenney, a recent working-class recruit to the WSPU, attended a meeting at the Free Trade Hall in Manchester where a leading Liberal politician was speaking. Annie rose and asked the question that Christabel had prepared in advance: 'Will the Liberal government, if returned, gives votes to women?' When no answer was given Christabel jumped up, repeating the question. In the disturbance that ensued, both young women were roughly ejected from the hall. Once outside Christabel, who was studying for a law degree at Owen's College (later Manchester University), deliberately committed the technical offence of spitting at a policeman in order to be arrested. Charged with disorderly conduct, both women chose, as they had prearranged, to receive short prison sentences rather than pay a fine. Such so-called 'militant' action had the desired effect. Suddenly, women's suffrage attracted the attention of the press and MPs. Many more women joined the WSPU or wrote letters of sympathy (Antonia Raeburn 1973). From then until the outbreak of war in August 1914, heckling of parliamentary candidates became a common tactic. So was a willingness among members to go to prison and join deputations to Parliament.

Women of all Parties and Social Classes Join the WSPU

The Liberal Party won a landslide victory in the general election of January 1906. Since it would not support votes for women, the WSPU had decided to oppose all Liberal candidates standing for election. In the event 29 Labour candidates were also returned to Parliament, among them Keir Hardie, a keen supporter of women's enfranchisement. However, hopes of support from Labour MPs were soon dashed. When five of the 29 drew places for a Private Member's bill and one place remained in doubt Emmeline demanded, without success, that it should be given to women's suffrage.

For Christabel, such an outcome confirmed her belief that working men could be as unjust to women as men in other social classes. In her view gender was the key obstacle facing women gaining the franchise, not social class. The WSPU, she argued, had to separate itself from class politics; rather than remain merely 'a frill on the sleeve of any political party', it must 'rally' women of all parties and those who belonged to none, bringing them together 'as one independent force' (Christabel Pankhurst 1959).

The call succeeded. Women of all political parties and none, and from all social classes, joined the WSPU. Working-class pupil teachers, women factory workers, domestic servants and shop girls worked side by side with titled ladies, housewives, artists, writers and novelists. All shared a common link in that, irrespective of their station in life, no woman could exercise the parliamentary vote.

WSPU Headquarters Move from Manchester to London

The two leaders of the WSPU came to the conclusion that their campaign would stand a better chance of success if the centre of activity was based in London. In September 1906 the WSPU took over some of the lower floors in 4 Clement's Inn as its headquarters. Emmeline and Fred Pethick-Lawrence, a socialist, wealthy, radical couple who lived in a large apartment in the same building, were keen supporters of the WSPU and Mrs Pethick-Lawrence had recently been appointed its Honorary Treasurer. She had a genius for raising money and was a generous donor herself, soon putting the WSPU on a firm financial footing. The

Pethick-Lawrences invited Christabel to come and live with them. She did so in the summer of 1906, after being awarded a first class honours degree in Law at Owen's College. However, Emmeline Pankhurst did not move to London until the spring of 1907. From then on she had no settled home but travelled with her belongings packed in a few suitcases, staying in hotels, rented flats or the homes of friends and supporters. Although she was the WSPU's key speaker, a spellbinder applauded on the public stage, Emmeline was often lonely.

Rapid Expansion

By early 1907 the WSPU had rapidly expanded; it then possessed 47 branches and nine paid organisers. Meetings were held on Monday afternoons in the large office at headquarters where members and prospective members gathered to hear announcements about deputations, buy suffragette literature and listen to talks, often about strategy and given by Christabel. All this activity, over the next seven years of the WSPU's campaigning, could not have taken place without the work both of volunteers and paid employees. Over 150 full-time workers were employed. Some worked in London, but the majority were based in local branches throughout Britain (Krista Cowman 2007).

The 'Dishonourable Double-faced' Herbert Asquith

Despite the expansion of suffragette activity, things took a turn for the worse when, in April 1908, the ailing prime minster Henry Campbell-Bannerman resigned. He was succeeded by another Liberal, Herbert Asquith, who proved a staunch opponent of votes for women. Since Asquith proclaimed himself a supporter of democracy but excluded women from their democratic right to exercise the parliamentary vote, the WSPU took particular exception to the new prime minister, denouncing him as 'dishonourable double-faced Asquith' (Diane Atkinson 2018). When Asquith failed to be moved by a colourful procession of over 40,000 suffragettes in Hyde Park in June 1908, an event that drew a crowd of about half a million, Emmeline Pankhurst decided that she had exhausted argument. Her decision was supported by both Christabel and Mrs Pethick-Lawrence. From now on, militancy that had largely involved peaceful tactics began to include law-breaking deeds, such as undirected and uncoordinated window breaking (Sandra Stanley Holton 1996).

On 1 July 1908 Mary Leigh and Edith New, two former schoolteachers, became the first window smashers when they went to Downing Street and threw stones at Asquith's official residence. They were protesting against the way in which their comrades had been treated by the police the evening before. Suffragettes in twos and threes had ventured into the dense crowd gathered in Parliament Square which was cordoned by 2,000 police, some mounted and others on foot. Those who had volunteered for prison attempted to make speeches as they clung precariously to the iron railings of Palace Yard until the police pulled them down, flinging them into the swaying crowd. Mary and Edith were arrested and sentenced to two months in the Third Division in prison, alongside common criminals.

Such violence against the protesters was not unusual. Later that year in December, David Lloyd George, Chancellor of the Exchequer, was speaking at a Women's Liberal Federation meeting at the Albert Hall. At the event men in the audience and stewards trying to keep order refused to tolerate any interruption, even it if meant physically attacking protesters. As Sylvia Pankhurst (1931) recollected, the hecklers arrived back at Clement's Inn

> bruised and dishevelled, hatless, with hair dragged down and clothing torn: some had their corsets ripped off, false teeth knocked out, faces scratched, eyes swollen, noses bleeding.

Forms of Militancy in the Suffrage Campaign

Although 'militancy' is often identified with the more violent illegal forms of suffrage protest engaged in from 1912, such as mass window smashing, it also covered a wide range of deeds that were constitutional and neither violent nor illegal. In a famous speech, Emmeline Pankhurst invited her followers to be 'militant in your own way' – in other words, suffragettes could choose which type of action they might engage in. This might include doing valuable secretarial work at headquarters or engaging in eye-catching stunts such as posting themselves as 'human letters' to Downing Street, selling the WSPU newspapers, *Votes for Women* and *The Suffragette* in the street, or saying prayers for Emmeline Pankhurst during a Church of England service. Such 'militant' tactics, which made women's enfranchisement visible in public places, cannot be divorced from the gender of the participants, regarded as the 'gentle sex' engaging in 'inappropriate' behaviour.

Conciliations Bills, 'Black Friday' and Mass Window Smashing

Militancy was suspended for much of 1910 to order to allow a cross-party group of MPs, called the Conciliation Committee, to draft a Private Member's women suffrage bill. The bill, narrowly drawn up to order to obtain Tory support, was to extend the parliamentary vote to women who were heads of households or occupied property worth ten pounds annually. However, Asquith was determined not to allow this First Conciliation Bill to pass beyond its Second Reading, and so it was killed off.

On 18 November 1910 the WSPU responded to the bill's failure by sending to Parliament a deputation of over 300 women, divided into detachments of 12. Unprecedented violence was inflicted on the women, much of it of a sexual nature, as the police tried to push them back from reaching their goal. Legs were kicked, arms were twisted, breasts were grabbed and pinched, knees thrust between legs. The violence experienced on 'Black Friday', as it became known, was frequently cited as justification for the more extreme forms of militancy adopted from March 1912. What was the point of women's bodies being battered in their demand for their democratic rights if damage to property brought about a quicker and painless method of securing arrest?

Two further Conciliation Bills, in 1911 and 1911–12, also failed to be passed. The lack of progress on a women's suffrage measure led a minority of suffragettes, from March 1912, to engage in attacks on private and public property. These included mass window smashing of shops in London's West End, setting fire to empty buildings, destroying letters in postboxes, pouring acid on men's golf courses and cutting telephone wires.

Throughout the campaign, both Emmeline and Christabel Pankhurst insisted that the aim was never to endanger human life, which they regarded as sacred. As the aged Mary Leigh remembered in the 1960s, 'Mrs. Pankhurst gave us strict instructions...not a cat or a canary to be killed: no life'. However, the Pethick-Lawrences did not agree with this more extreme form of militancy. Emmeline Pankhurst thus ousted them from the WSPU and took over the position of Honorary Treasurer herself.

Christabel by this time was living in Paris. In March 1912, when the police raided WSPU offices to arrest the leaders, she managed to escape to France, from where she attempted, with her mother, to lead the WSPU.

Hunger Striking and Force Feeding

The hunger strike as a political tool had been introduced in July 1909 not by the WSPU leadership but by a member of the rank and file, Marion Wallace-Dunlop. A sculptor and illustrator, she had been sent to HM Prison Holloway for printing an extract from the Bill of Rights on the wall of St Stephen's Hall, the House of Commons. Marion went on hunger strike as a protest against the authorities' refusal to recognise her as a political offender and, as such, entitled to be placed in the First Division in prison, where political prisoners enjoyed considerable privileges. After 91 hours of fasting, she was released. Other imprisoned suffragettes also adopted the strategy of hunger strike, believing that they could also avoid serving their sentences. However, the authorities soon responded by force-feeding them, arguing that it was 'ordinary hospital treatment' necessary to save life. Thus began a vicious circle of events that has shaped our portrayal of the suffragette movement to the present day.

The image of the individual suffragette, voluntarily on hunger strike in her isolated prison cell, held a particular cultural resonance – she appropriated a form of protest that had been adopted by some male dissidents in the past and made it her own. Wishing to retain control of her own body, she used the hunger strike as a form of passive resistance to challenge the injustice of an all-male Liberal government.

Forcible feeding was a brutal, life-threatening and degrading procedure, undertaken by male doctors on struggling female bodies. The prisoner was usually held down on a bed by wardresses or tied to a chair which was tipped back. Two male doctors then performed the operation, one pushing a rubber tube up a nostril or down the throat into the stomach. The latter was the most painful method since a steel gag that cut into soft tissue was inserted into the mouth and screwed into place. The other doctor then poured a mixture of milk, bread and brandy through the rubber tube. Although suffragettes did not use the word 'rape' to describe their experiences, the instrumental invasion of the body, accompanied by overpowering physical force, suffering and humiliation, was akin to such an assault and was commonly described as an 'outrage'.

Emily Wilding Davison

A well-known suffragette who was forcibly fed was Emily Wilding Davison. She died on 8 June 1913, four days after sustaining terrible injuries trying to grab the reins of the king's horse at the Derby. A former governess and graduate with a first class honours degree in English, Emily was a deeply committed Christian. She believed that the true militant would willingly sacrifice friendship, good report, love and even life itself to win the 'Pearl of Freedom' for her sex. She was imprisoned eight times, went on hunger strike seven times and was forcibly fed 49 times.

The 'Cat and Mouse Act', April 1913

On 14 June 1913, 5,000 women marched in the solemn funeral procession for Emily Wilding Davison, an event that drew large crowds. The circumstances leading to her death were covered in all the newspapers and caught on Pathe News so that many people across the world knew about it. Emily's death proved to be a turning point in public opinion in Britain, with the majority of the population feeling that it was time to end the struggle for votes for women.

Some two months earlier in April 1913, the Liberal government had rushed 'The Prisoners' Temporary Discharge for Ill-Health Bill', usually known as the 'Cat and Mouse Act', through Parliament. Under this act, suffragette 'mice' in a poor state of health could be released into the community on a licence; there they were to be nursed back to good health, in order to be clawed back by the state 'cat' to complete their sentence. A widely circulated WSPU poster of a large ginger cat showing his bloodied teeth, with the limp injured body of a small suffragette in his mouth portrayed the brutality of such an approach. Many released 'mice' suffered prolonged but interrupted sentences as they tried to avoid re-arrest by staying in safe houses, watched by detectives.

By 1914 the Liberal government's response to hunger strikers had become more brutal. Stories emerged of women being drugged to make them more docile, as well as more accounts of accidents when prisoners were fed by tube. Ethel Moorhead, a daughter living at home, developed double pneumonia in Carlton Jail in Edinburgh after her eighth forcible feeding when some food entered her lungs. Kitty Marion, an actress and arsonist, experienced such pain during the 232 times that she was fed that she thought she was going mad and begged the doctor to give her some poison. The situation could not continue. Increasing numbers of doctors as well as members of the general public were speaking out against forcible feeding. They declared that it contravened the rules of medical practice and that those doctors who performed the operation were punishing prisoners rather than treating patients.

Outbreak of the First World War, August 1914

The outbreak of the First World War in August 1914 allowed both the WSPU and the Liberal government to retreat. Once all suffragette prisoners were released, Emmeline Pankhurst called a temporary suspension of militancy while the government granted an amnesty to all suffrage prisoners. Both Emmeline Pankhurst and Millicent Garrett Fawcett supported the war effort, encouraging their followers to engage in war work. Their stand caused splits in both the WSPU and the NUWSS, but the issue of women's suffrage could no longer be ignored.

Representation of the People Act, 1918

On 6 February 1918 the Representation of the People Act granted the parliamentary vote to certain categories of women aged 30 and over – householders, wives of householders, occupiers of property of a yearly value of not less than £5 and university graduates. The 8,4000,000 million women who were enfranchised were disproportionately middle-class housewives, however, rather than the young working-class single women who had been employed in the munition factories. Although women were not granted the vote on equal terms with men – the issue on which the WSPU had campaigned so strongly – the principle of sex discrimination had at last been broken. Equal voting rights were not granted until 1928.

Cultural Forms Such as Plays, Novels and Poetry

Given the dedication, commitment, drama and passion in the women's suffrage movement it is not surprising that many plays, novels and poetry were written about it. Often the authors were women who had participated in the events they describe. Or the literature was written and published to sway readers politically, as in the case of *The Sturdy Oak,* which was a response to the 1916–17 New York campaign for suffrage.

Plays

Through their words as deeds, suffrage playwrights – not all of whom were members of the WSPU – helped to organise many actresses to join the women's movement. As Naomi Paxton (2018) notes, the constitutional work undertaken by playwrights and actresses in collaboration with other suffrage societies served to blur the lines between militant and non-militant. In particular, it is the work of the Women's Writers' Franchise League (WWFL), founded in 1908, and the Actresses' Franchise League (AFL), established in the same year, that has received considerable attention from present-day scholars.

Women playwrights in the WWFL explored various feminist themes, including the exploitation and subjection of women, the double sexual standard and arguments for and against women's suffrage. One particularly influential figure was WSPU member Elizabeth Robins, an American-born actress, novelist and playwright. She was close to both Emmeline and Christabel Pankhurst and, for a time, a member of the WSPU's central committee. For years Elizabeth Robins had been frustrated by male domination of the theatre and the lack of female directors and playwrights. Her popular 1907 play *Votes for Women* formed the basis for her later successful novel, *The Convert*. In the play, Vida Levering is a deeply committed suffragette who encounters her former lover Geoffrey Stoner, now a Conservative MP, and his upper-class fiancée Jean. It transpires that some ten years earlier Vida and Stoner had had an affair; when she became pregnant, rather than marry her, he advised her to have an abortion, to which she had reluctantly agreed. Robins creates in Vida a new type of heroine – a woman with a supposedly 'immoral past' who uses her experience to transform herself into a powerful advocate for the women's cause (Carolyn Christensen Nelson 2004). In the play, Vida even blackmails her former lover into supporting

women's suffrage in order to bring political freedom for herself
and other women. As the first play to bring the women's suffrage
movement to the stage, *Votes for Women* had a powerful impact,
highlighting how the conditions of women's lives made their
enfranchisement essential.

Cecily Hamilton, a founding member of the WWSL, was another
successful suffrage playwright. More temperamentally suited to
the suffragist wing of the movement than to the militancy of the
WSPU, she left the latter in 1907 and joined the Women's Freedom
League. Hamilton's *A Pageant of Great Women*, which first opened
in London in November 1909, was performed all over the country.
It showed how gifted women in the past – learned women, artists,
saintly women, heroic women, rulers and warriors – had been
excluded from political life not through lack of talent but through
the presence of male prejudice and blind justice.

Earlier in 1909, Hamilton had written *How the Vote was Won*,
together with Christopher St. John, a member of both the AFL and
the WWSL. Perhaps the most successful of the suffrage plays, it was
first performed in London in April of that year. The scene is set in
the home of Horace and Ethel Cole in Brixton, south London, on
the day of a women's strike called by suffragettes in protest against
a government announcement that women did not need the vote
since they were looked after by their menfolk. All the women who
had previously supported themselves leave their jobs and insist
that their nearest male relative support them. Horace's female
relatives arrive at his house, forcing him to confront the reality
of their lives. The play ends with Horace and all the other men
in London rushing to parliament demanding 'Votes for Women'
(Naomi Paxton 2013).

How the Vote was Won had a running time of approximately 45 minutes. However, the Actresses' Franchise League also had a Play Department that produced much shorter, one-act dramas; these works served as propaganda that could easily be fitted into a performance. One such contribution was *The Mother's Meeting*, written by Mrs. Harlow Phibbs, the wife of a Church of England curate, and published in 1913. It consists of a comic monologue spoken by a working-class woman, Mrs Puckle, who accidently went to an anti-suffrage meeting, met some suffragettes and joined the WSPU. In the play Mrs Puckle, wearing a hat in the WSPU colours of purple, white and green, exposes inconsistencies in the anti-suffrage argument.

Novels

Suffrage novels, like suffrage plays, are frequently mentioned by scholars today. They were avidly read by suffragettes themselves, only too conscious of the ways in which their actions and motives were vilified by the press (Maroula Joannou, 1998). Some of the themes found in the plays re-appear in suffrage novels, including the comradeship and webs of friendship between women and the necessity for women's enfranchisement as a means of ending the evils of prostitution and poverty. Perhaps the two best-known suffrage novels that were popular when written and still read today are *Suffragette Sally* by Gertrude Colmore (1911) and *No Surrender* by Constance Elizabeth Maud (1912). Both works dispel the myth that women's suffrage was only of interest to middle-class women.

Suffragette Sally tells the story of three women from differing social backgrounds – the working-class maid Sally Simmonds, the middle-class Edith Carstairs and the aristocrat Lady Geraldine Hill – who form cross-class allegiances in campaigning for the vote. Sally and Geraldine, as members of the WSPU, supported militant action but Edith did not, favouring instead the constitutional methods of NUWSS.

No Surrender focuses on the strong support for women's suffrage in the North of England among women factory workers, as well as the prejudice they faced from many men in the Labour movement. It features Jenny Clegg, a young working-class mill worker who, after her first imprisonment, decides not to return to the mill but to devote all her time to the WSPU. After holding a protest meeting outside a Midlands county jail in which some of her comrades are held, she is imprisoned again. Placed in a Second Division cell, among ordinary criminals, she takes a hairpin and uses her own blood to paint on the wall 'Votes for Women'.

Poetry

Unlike suffrage plays and novels, suffrage poetry is rarely referred to in critical work today; it plays very much a secondary role to prose. This relative neglect of suffrage poems may be because they are scattered in various publications rather than presented in one or several volumes. One of the few available collections is *Holloway Jingles* (1912), published by the Glasgow Branch of the WSPU.

Many of the women who wrote poems in this collection were window breakers, as was Emily Wilding Davison. Her verse reveals not only the bonds of love and friendship that bound Emily to her comrades, but also her deep commitment to the women's just cause (Collette 2013).

L'Envoi

Stepping onwards, oh my comrades!
Marching fearless through the darkness,
Marching fearless through the prisons,
With the torch of freedom guiding!

See the face of each is glowing,
Gleaming with the love of freedom;
Gleaming with a selfless triumph,
In the cause of human progress!

Like the pilgrim in the valley,
Enemies may oft assail us,
Enemies may close around us,
Tyrants, hunger, horror, brute force.

But the glorious dawn is breaking,
Freedom's beauty sheds her radiance:
Freedom's clarion call is sounding,
Rousing all the world to wisdom.

28 April, 1912

Although some scholars claim that such poems are of only limited literary merit, we must remember that they gave women a voice – a way to tell the world outside the lonely prison cell about the injustice of their treatment (Glenda Norquay 1995). The prison poems capture the triumph of the spirit over physical assault, a way for women to retain control over their own bodies now being brutalised by all-male prison authorities, at the request of an all-male Liberal government.

Conclusion

Suffrage plays, novels and poetry were part of the rich cultural heritage of the votes for women campaign. Together with the cry of the WSPU leaders 'Rise Up Women!', they helped to rouse thousands of women across the social and political spectrum in a mass movement unparalleled in British history. Suffragette militancy, in all its various forms, was critical for women gaining their enfranchisement although this is a subject of debate among historians (Purvis, Crawford and Holton 2019). Militant tactics, which embodied rebellion against the submissive and inferior status of women, expected to ask politely for their democratic right to the vote, was a form of consciousness raising that changed women's perceptions of themselves. Yet, although the vote was won, the wider issue of sex equality continued to elude women in the Edwardian era – as it does today.

June Purvis

Further Reading

Atkinson, Diane, *Rise Up Women The Remarkable Lives of the Suffragettes* (London: Bloomsbury, 2018)

Collette, Carolyn P., *The Writing of Emily Wilding Davison, Militant Suffragette* (Ann Arbor: University of Michigan Press, 2013)

Cowman, Krista, *Women of the Right Spirit: Paid Organisers of the Women's Social and Political Union (WSPU) 1904–18* (Manchester: Manchester University Press, 2007)

Crawford, Elizabeth, *The Women's Suffrage Movement: A Reference Guide 1866–1928* (London: UCL Press, 1999)

Holton, Sandra Stanley, *Suffrage Days* (London: Routledge, 1996)

Joannou, Maroula, 'Suffragette fiction and the fictions of suffrage', in *The Women's Suffrage Movement: New Feminist Perspectives*, edited by Maroula Joannou and June Purvis (Manchester: Manchester University Press, 1998 and 2009), pp. 101–116

Nelson, Carolyn Christensen, ed., *Literature of the Women's Suffrage Campaign in England* (Ontario: Broadview Press, 2004)

Norquay, Glenda ed., *Voices & Votes: a Literary Anthology of the Women's Suffrage Campaign* (Manchester: Manchester University Press, 1995)

Paxton, Naomi, ed., *The Methuen Drama Book of Suffrage Plays* (London: Bloomsbury, 2013)

Paxton, Naomi, *Stage Rights: The Actresses' Franchise League, Activism and Politics 1908–58* (Manchester: Manchester University Press, 2018)

Pankhurst, Christabel, *Unshackled: The Story of How We Won the Vote* (London: Hutchinson, 1959)

Pankhurst, Emmeline, *My Own Story* (London: Eveleigh Nash, 1914)

Pankhurst, E. Sylvia, *The Suffragette Movement: An Intimate Account of Persons and Ideals* (London: Longmans, 1931)

Purvis, June, *Emmeline Pankhurst: A Biography* (London: Routledge, 2002)

Purvis, June, *Christabel Pankhurst: A Biography* (London: Routledge, 2018)

Purvis, June, Crawford, Elizabeth and Stanley Holton, Sandra, 'Did Militancy Help or Hinder the Granting of Women's Suffrage in Britain?', *Women's History Review*, December 2019, pp. 1200–1234

Purvis, June, 'Emmeline Pankhurst (1858–1928): The Making Of A Militant', in *The British Women's Suffrage Campaign: National and International Perspectives*, edited by June Purvis and June Hannan (London: Routledge, 2021), pp. 25–42

Raeburn, Antonia, *The Militant Suffragettes* (London: Michael Joseph, 1973)

Robinson, Jane, *Hearts and Minds: The Untold Story of the Great Pilgrimage and How Women Won the Vote* (London: Doubleday, 2018)

The Sturdy Oak

Edited by Elizabeth Jordan

Preface

At a certain committee meeting held in the spring of 1916, it was agreed that fourteen leading American authors, known to be extremely generous as well as gifted, should be asked to write a composite novel.

As I was not present at this particular meeting, it was unanimously and joyously decided by those who were present that I should attend to the trivial details of getting this novel together.

It appeared that all I had to do was:

First, to persuade each of the busy authors on the list to write a chapter of the novel.

Second, to keep steadily on their trails from the moment they promised their chapters until they turned them in.

Third, to have the novel finished and published serially during the autumn Campaign of 1917.

The carrying out of these requirements has not been the childish diversion it may have seemed. Splendid team work, however, has made success possible.

Every author represented, every worker on the team, has gratuitously contributed his or her services; and every dollar realized by the serial and book publication of *The Sturdy Oak* will be devoted to the Suffrage Cause. But the novel itself is first of all a very human story of American life today. It neither unduly nor unfairly emphasizes the question of equal suffrage, and it should appeal to all lovers of good fiction.

Therefore, pausing only to wipe the beads of perspiration from our brows, we urge every one to buy this book!

Elizabeth Jordan
New York, November, 1917

* * *

"Nobody ever means that a woman really can't get along without a man's protection, because look at the women who do."

It was hard on the darling old boy to come home to Miss Emelene and the cat and Eleanor and Alys every night!

"You mean because she's a suffragist? You sent her away for *that*! Why, really, that's *tyranny*!"

Across the way, Mrs. Herrington, the fighting blood of five generations of patriots roused in her, had reinstated the Voiceless Speech.

Principal Characters

George Remington... Aged twenty-six; newly married. Recently returned to his home town, New York State, to take up the practice of law. Politically ambitious, a candidate for District Attorney. Opposed to woman suffrage.

Genevieve... His wife, aged twenty-three, graduate of Smith. Devoted to George; her ideal being to share his every thought.

Betty Sheridan... A friend of Genevieve. Very pretty; one of the first families, well-to-do but in search of economic independence. Working as stenographer in George's office; an ardent Suffragist.

Penfield Evans... Otherwise "Penny," George's partner, in love with Betty. Neutral on the subject of Suffrage.

Alys Brewster-Smith... Cousin of George, once removed; thirty-three, a married woman by profession, but temporarily widowed. Anti-suffragist. One Angel Child aged five.

Martin Jaffry... Uncle to George, bachelor of uncertain age and certain income. The widow's destined prey.

Cousin Emelene... On Genevieve's side. Between thirty-five and forty, a born spinster but clinging to the hope of marriage as the only career for women. Has a small and decreasing income. Affectedly feminine and genuinely incompetent.

Mrs. Harvey Herrington... President of the Woman's Club, the Municipal League, Suffrage Society leader, wealthy, cultured and possessing a sense of humor.

Percival Pauncefoot Sheridan... Betty's brother, fifteen, commonly called Pudge. Pink, pudgy, sensitive; always imposed upon, always grouchy and too good-natured to assert himself.

E. Eliot... Real estate agent (added in Chapter VI by Henry Kitchell Webster).

Benjamin Doolittle... A leader of his party, and somewhat careless where he leads it (added in Chapter VII by Anne O'Hagan).

Patrick Noonan... A follower of Doolittle.

Time... The Present.

Place... Whitewater, N.Y. A manufacturing town of from ten to fifteen thousand inhabitants.

Chapter I
Samuel Merwin

Genevieve Remington had been called beautiful. She was tall, with brown eyes and a fine spun mass of golden-brown hair. She had a gentle smile, that disclosed white, even teeth. Her voice was not unmusical. She was twenty-three years old and possessed a husband who, though only twenty-six, had already shown such strength of character and such aptitude at the criminal branch of the law that he was now a candidate for the post of district attorney on the regular Republican ticket.

The popular impression was that he would be elected hands down. His address on Alexander Hamilton at the Union League Club banquet at Hamilton City, twenty-five miles from Whitewater (with which smaller city we are concerned in this narrative), had been reprinted in full in the Hamilton City *Tribune*; and Mrs. Brewster-Smith reported that former Congressman Hancock had compared it, not unfavorably, with certain public utterances of the Honorable Elihu Root.

George Remington was an inch more than six feet tall, with sturdy shoulders, a chin that gave every indication of stubborn strength, a frank smile, and a warm, strong handclasp. He was connected by blood (as well as by marriage) with five of the eight best families in Whitewater. Mr. Martin Jaffry, George's uncle and sole inheritor of the great Jaffry estate (and a bachelor), was known to favor his candidacy; was supposed, indeed, to be a large contributor to the Remington campaign fund. In fact, George Remington was a lucky young man, a coming young man.

George and Genevieve had been married five weeks; this was their first day as master and mistress of the old Remington place on Sheridan Road.

Genevieve, that afternoon, was in the long living-room, trying out various arrangements of the flowers that had been sent in. There were a great many flowers. Most of them came from admirers of George. The Young Men's Republican Club, for one item, had sent eight dozen roses. But Genevieve, still a-thrill with the magic of her five-weeks-long honeymoon, tremulously happy in the cumulative proof that her husband was the noblest, strongest, bravest man alive, felt only joy in his popularity.

As his wife she shared his triumphs. "For better or worse, for richer or poorer, in sickness and health..." the ancient phrases repeated themselves so many times in her softly confused thought, as she moved about among the flowers, that they finally took on a rhythm—

> *"For better or worse,*
> *For richer or poorer,*
> *For richer or poorer,*
> *For better or worse—"*

* * *

On this day her life was beginning. She had given herself irrevocably into the hands of this man. She would live only in him. Her life would find expression only through his. His strong, trained mind would be her guide, his sturdy courage her strength. He would build for them both, for the twain that were one.

She caught up one red rose, winked the moisture from her eyes, and gazed – rapt, lips parted, color high – out at the close-clipped lawn behind the privet hedge. The afternoon would soon be waning – in another hour or so. She must not disturb him now.

In an hour, say, she would run up the stairs and tap at his door. And he would come out, clasp her in his big arms, and she would stand on the tips of her toes and kiss away the wrinkles between his brows, and they would walk on the lawn and talk about themselves and the miracle of their love.

The clock on the mantel struck three. She pouted; turned and stared at it. "Well," she told herself, "I'll wait until half-past four."

The doorbell rang.

Genevieve's color faded. The slim hand that held the rose trembled a very little. Her first caller! She decided that it would be best not to talk about George. Not one word about George! Her feelings were her secret – and his.

Marie ushered in two ladies. One, who rushed forward with outstretched hand, was a curiously vital-appearing creature in black – plainly a widow – hardly more than thirty-two or thirty-three, fresh of skin, rather prominent as to eyeballs, yet, everything considered, a handsome woman. This was Alys Brewster-Smith. The other, shorter, slighter, several years older, a faded, smiling, tremulously hopeful spinster, was Genevieve's own cousin, Emelene Brand.

"It's so nice of you to come—" Geneviève began timidly, only to be swept aside by the superior aggressiveness and the stronger voice of Mrs. Brewster-Smith.

"My *dear*! Isn't it perfectly delightful to see you actually mistress of this wonderful old home. And" – her slightly prominent eyes swiftly took in furniture, pictures, rugs, flowers, –" how wonderfully you have managed to give the old place your own tone!" "Nothing has been changed," murmured Genevieve, a thought bewildered.

"Nothing, my dear, but yourself! I am *so* looking forward to a good talk with you. Emelene and I were speaking of that only this noon. And I can't tell you how sorry I am that our first call has to be on a miserable political matter. Tell me, dear, is that wonderful husband of yours at home?"

"Why – yes. But I am not to disturb him."

"Ah, shut away in his den?"

Genevieve nodded.

"It's a very important paper he has to write. It has to be done now, before he is drawn into the whirl of campaign work."

"Of course! Of course! But I'm afraid the campaign is whirling already. I will tell you what brought us, my dear. You know of course that Mrs. Harvey Herrington has come out for suffrage – thrown in her whole personal weight and, no doubt, her money. I can't understand it – with her home, and her husband – going into the mire of politics. But that is what she has done. And

Grace Hatfield called up not ten minutes ago to say that she has just led a delegation of ladies up to your husband's office. Think of it – to his office! The first day!... Well, Emelene, it is some consolation that they won't find him there."

"He isn't going to the office today," said Genevieve. "But what can they want of him?"

"To get him to declare for suffrage, my dear."

"Oh – I'm sure he wouldn't do that!"

"Are you, my dear? Are you *sure*?"

"Well—"

"He has told you his views, of course?"

Genevieve knit her brows. "Why, yes – of course, we've talked about things—"

"My dear, of course he is *against suffrage*."

"Oh yes, of course. I'm sure he is. Though, you see, I would no more think of intruding in George's business affairs than he would think of intruding in my household duties."

"Naturally, Genevieve. And very sweet and dear of you! But I'm sure you will see how very important this is. Here we are, right at the beginning of his campaign. Those vulgar women are going to hound him. They've begun already. As our committee wrote him last week, it is vitally important that he should declare himself unequivocally at once."

"Oh, yes," murmured Genevieve, "of course. I can see that."

The doors swung open. A thin little man of forty to fifty stood there, a dry but good-humored man, with many wrinkles about his quizzical blue eyes, and sandy hair at the sides and back of an otherwise bald head. He was smartly dressed in a homespun Norfolk suit. He waved a cap of homespun in greeting.

"Afternoon, ladies! Genevieve, a bachelor's admiration and respect! I hope that boy George has got sense enough to be proud of you. But they haven't at that age. They're all for themselves."

"Oh no, Uncle Martin," cried Genevieve, "George is the most generous—"

Mr. Martin Jaffry flicked his cap. "All right. All right! He is." And slowly retreated.

Mrs. Brewster-Smith, an eager light in her eyes, moved part way across the room. "But we can't let you run away like this, Mr. Jaffry. Do sit down and tell us about the work you are doing at the Country Club. Is it to be bowling alley *and* swimming pool—"

"Bowling alley *and* swimming pool, yes. Tell me, chick, might a humble constituent speak to the great man?"

Genevieve hesitated. "I'm sure he'd love to see you, Uncle Martin. But he *did* say—"

"Not to be disturbed by *any*body, eh?"

"Yes, Uncle Martin. It's a very important statement he has to prepare before—"

"Good day, then. You look fine in the old house, chick!"

Mr. Jaffry donned his cap of homespun, ran down the steps and out the front walk, hopped into his eight-cylinder roadster, and was off down the street in a second. There was a sharp decisiveness about his exit, and about the sudden speed of his machine; all duly noted by Mrs. Brewster-Smith, who had gone so far as to move down the room to the front window and watch the performance with narrowed eyes. The Jaffry Building stands at the southwest corner of Fountain Square. It boasts six stories, mosaic flooring in the halls, and the only passenger elevator in Whitewater. The ground floor was given over to Humphrey's drug store; and most of Humphrey's drug store was given over to the immense marble soda fountain and the dozen or more wire-legged tables and the two or three dozen wire chairs that served to accommodate the late afternoon and evening crowd.

At the moment the fountain had but one patron – a remarkably fat boy of, perhaps, fifteen, with plump cheeks and drooping mouth.... The row of windows across the second floor front of the building, above Humphrey's, bore, each, the legend – *Remington and Evans, Attorneys at Law.*

The fat boy was Percival Sheridan, otherwise Pudge. His sister, Betty Sheridan, worked in the law offices directly overhead and possessed a heart of stone.

Betty was rich, at least in the eyes of Pudge. For more than a year (Betty was twenty-two) she had enjoyed a private income. Pudge definitely knew this. She had money to buy out the soda fountain. But her character, thought Pudge, might be summed up in the statement that she worked when she didn't have to (people talked about this; even to him!) and flatly refused to give her brother money for soda.

As if a little soda ever hurt anybody. She took it herself, often enough. Within five minutes he had laid the matter before her – up in that solemn office, where they made you feel so uncomfortable. She had said: "Pudge Sheridan, you're killing yourself! Not one cent more for wrecking your stomach!"

She had called him "Pudge." For months he had been reminding her that his name was Percival. And he wasn't wrecking his stomach. That was silly talk. He had eaten but two nut sundaes and a chocolate frappé since luncheon. It wasn't soda and candy that made him so fat. Some folks just were fat, and some folks were thin. That was all there was *to* it!

Pudge himself would have a private income when he was twenty-one. Six years off... and Billy Simmons in his white apron, was waiting now, on the other side of the marble counter, for his order – and grinning as he waited. Six years! Why, Pudge would be a man then – too old for nut sundaes and chocolate frappés, too far gone down the sober slope of life to enjoy anything!

Pudge wriggled nervously, locked his feet around behind the legs of the high stool, rubbed a fat forefinger on the edge of the counter, and watched the finger intently with gloomy eyes.

"Well, what'll it be, Pudge?" This from Billy Simmons.

"My name ain't Pudge."

"Very good, Mister Sheridan. What'll it be?"

"One of those chocolate marshmallow nut sundaes, I guess, if – if—"

"If what, Mister Sheridan?"

"—if, oh well, just charge it."

Billy Simmons paused in the act of reaching for a sundae glass. The smile left his face.

Pudge, though he did not once look up from that absorbing little operation with the fat forefinger, felt this pause and knew that Billy's grin had gone; and his own mouth drooped and drooped. It was a tense moment.

"You see, Pudge," Billy began in some embarrassment, only to conclude rather sharply, "I'll have to ask Mr. Humphrey. Your sister said we weren't—"

"Oh, well!" sighed Pudge. Getting down from the stool he waddled slowly out of the store.

It was no use going up against old Humphrey. He had tried that. He went as far as the fire-plug, close to the corner, and sank down upon it. Everybody was against him. He would sit here awhile and think it over. Perhaps he could figure out some way of breaking through the conspiracy. Then Mr. Martin Jaffry drove up to the curb and he had to move his legs. Mr. Jaffry said, "Hello, Pudge," too. It was all deeply annoying.

Meantime, during the past half-hour, the law offices of Remington and Evans were not lacking in the sense of life and activity. Things began moving when Penny Evans (christened Penfield) came back from lunch. He wore an air – Betty Sheridan noted, from her typewriter desk within the rail – of determination. His nod toward herself was distinctly brusque; a new quality which gave her a moment's thought. And then when he had hung up his hat and was walking past her to his own private office, he indulged in a faint, fleeting grin.

Betty considered him. She had known Penny Evans as long as she could remember knowing anybody; and she had never seen him look quite as he looked this afternoon.

The buzzer sounded. It was absurd, of course; nobody else in the office. He could have spoken – you could hear almost every sound over the seven-foot partitions.

She rose, waited an instant to insure perfect composure, smoothed down her trim shirtwaist, pushed back a straying wisp of her naturally wavy hair, picked up her notebook and three sharp pencils, and went quietly into his office.

He sat there at his flat desk – his blond brows knit, his mouth firm, a light of eager good humor in his blue eyes.

"Take this," he said... Betty seated herself opposite him, and was instantly ready for work.

"... Memorandum. From rentals – the old Evans property on Ash Street, the two houses on Wilson Avenue South, and the factory lease in the South Extension, a total of slightly over $3600.

"New paragraph. From investments in bonds, railway and municipal, an average the last four years of $2800.

"New paragraph. From law practice, last year, over $4500. Will be considerably more this year. Total—"

"New paragraph?"

"No. Continue. Total, $10,900. This year will be close to $12,000. Don't you think that's a reasonably good showing for an unencumbered man of twenty-seven?"

"Dictation – that last?"

"No, personal query, Penny to Betty."

"Yes, then, it is very good. You want this in memorandum form. Any carbons?"

"One carbon – in the form of a diamond – gift from Penny to Betty." Miss Sheridan settled back in her chair, tapped her pretty mouth with her pencil, and surveyed the blond young man. Her eyes were blue – frank, capable eyes.

"Penny, I like my work here—"

"I should hope so—"

"And I don't want to give it up."

"Then don't."

"I shall have to, Penny, if you don't stop breaking your word. It was a definite agreement, you know. You were not to propose to me, on any working day, before seven P.M. This is a proposal of course—"

"Yes, of course, but I've just—"

"That makes twice this month, then, that you've broken the agreement. Now I can go on and put my mind on my work, if you'll let me. Otherwise, I shall have to get a job where they *will* let me."

"But, Betty, I've just this noon sat down and figured up where I stand. It has frightened me a little. I didn't realize I was taking in more than ten thousand a year. And all of a sudden it struck me that I've been an imbecile to wait, or make any agreement—"

"Then you broke it deliberately?"

"Absolutely. Betty – no fooling now; I'm in earnest—"

Studying him, she saw that he was intensely in earnest.

"You see, child, I've tried to be patient because I know how you were brought up, what you're used to. Why, I wouldn't dream of asking you to be my wife unless I could feel pretty sure of being able to give you the comforts you've always had and ought to have. But hang it, Betty, I *can* do it right! I can give you a home that's worthy of you. Any time! This year, even!"

"Penny, do you think I care what your income is – for one minute?"

"Why – why—"

"When I'm earning twenty dollars a week myself and prouder of it than—"

"But that's absurd, Betty – for you to be working – as a stenographer, of all things! A girl with your looks and your gifts and all that's back of you."

"You mean that I should make marriage my profession?"

"Well – well—"

"Probably that's why we keep missing each other, Penny. I've pinned my flag to the principle of economic independence. You're looking for a girl who will marry for a living. There are lots of them. Pretty, attractive girls, too. Your difficulty is, you want that sort. You really believe all girls are that sort at heart, and you think my independence a fad – something I shall get over. Don't you, now?"

"Well, I'll confess I can't see it as the normal thing. Yes, I believe – I hope – you will get over it."

"Well—" Miss Sheridan slammed her book shut and stood up— "I won't."

She stepped to the door.

"And the agreement stands. I want to keep on working. And I want to keep on being fond of you. That agreement is necessary to both desires." She opened the door, hesitated and a hint of mischief flashed across her face. "I'll tell you just the person for you, Penny. Really. Marriage is her profession. She's very experienced. Temporarily out of a job – Alys Brewster-Smith."

He snatched a carnation from the glass on his desk and threw it at her. It struck a closed door.

* * *

The outer door opened just then, and Mr. Martin Jaffry stepped in. He nodded, with his little quizzical smile, to the composed young woman who stood within the railing.

"Anybody here, Betty?"

A slight movement of her prettily poised head indicated the door marked "Mr. Evans." And she said, "Penny's there."

"Is he shut up, too? His partner is too important to be seen today."

"Oh no," Betty replied, inscrutably sober, "he's not important."

Mr. Jaffry wrinkled up his eyes, chuckled softly, then stepped to the door of the unimportant one. Before opening it, he turned. "Mrs. Harvey Herrington been in?"

"Twice with a committee."

"Any idea what she wanted?"

Betty was aware that the whimsical and roundabout Mr. Jaffry knew everything about everybody in Whitewater. She was further aware that he had, undoubtedly, reasons of his own for questioning her. He was always asking questions, anyway. Worse than a Chinaman. And for some reason – perhaps because he was Martin Jaffry – you always answered his questions.

"Yes," said Betty. "She wants to pledge him to suffrage."

"Umm! Yes, I see! You wouldn't be against that yourself, would you?"

"Naturally not. I'm secretary of the Second Ward Suffrage Club."

"Umm! Yes, yes!" With which illuminating comment, Mr. Jaffry tapped on Penny Evans' door, opened it and entered.

"Spare a minute?" he inquired.

"Sure," said Penny; "two, ten! Take a chair."

"No," replied Mr. Jaffry, "I won't take a chair. Think better on my feet. I'm in a bit of a quandary. Suppose you tell me what this important paper is that George is drawing up. Do you know?"

"I do."

"Is he coming out against suffrage?"

"Flatly."

"Umm!" Mr. Jaffry flicked his cap about. "I want to see George. He mustn't do that."

"Say, Mr. Jaffry, you haven't swung over—"

"Not at all. It's tactics. I ought to see him."

"Why not run out to his house—"

"Just been there. Ran away. Some one there I'm afraid of."

"Telephone?"

Mr. Jaffry shook his head and lowered his voice.

"With Betty hearing it at this end, and the committee from the Antis sitting it out down there – the telephone's on the stair landing—"

He pursed his lips, waved his cap slowly to and fro and observed it with a whimsical expression on his sandy face, then glanced out of the window. He stepped closer, looking sharply down. A very fat boy with pink cheeks and a downcast expression was sitting on a fire-plug. Mr. Jaffry leaned out.

"Pudge," he called, "come up here a minute."

On the Remington and Evans stationery he penciled a note, which he sealed. Then he scribbled another – to Mrs. George Remington, asking her to hand George the inclosure the moment he appeared from his work. The two he slipped into a large envelope. The very fat boy stood before him.

"Want to make a quarter, Pudge? Take this letter, right now, to Mrs. George Remington. Give it to her personally. It's the old Remington place, you know."

He felt in his change pocket. It was empty. He hesitated, turned to Evans, then, reconsidering, produced a dollar bill from another pocket and gave it to the boy.

"Now run," he said.

The boy, speechless, turned and moved out of the office. His sister spoke to him, but he did not turn his head. He rolled down the stairs to the street, stood a moment in front of Humphrey's, drew a sudden breath that was almost a gasp, waddled into the store, advanced directly on the soda fountain, and with a blazing red face and angrily triumphant eyes confronted Billy Simmons.

"I'll take a chocolate marshmallow nut sundae," he said. "And you needn't be stingy with the marshmallow, either!"

* * *

At ten minutes past four, the anxious Antis in the Remington living-room heard the candidate for district attorney running down the stairs, and even Mrs. Brewster-Smith was hushed. The candidate stopped, however, on the landing. They heard him lift the telephone receiver. He called a number. Then—

"*Sentinel* office?... Mr. Ledbetter, please.... Hello, Ledbetter! Remington speaking. I have that statement ready. Will you send a man around?... Yes, right away. And I wish you'd put it on the wires. Display it just as prominently as you can, won't you?... Thanks. That's fine! Good-by."

He ran back upstairs.

But shortly he appeared, wearing the distrait, exalted expression of the genius who has just passed through the creative act. He looked very tall and strong as he stood before the mantel, receiving the congratulations of Mrs. Brewster-Smith and the timid admiration of Cousin Emelene. His few words were well chosen and were uttered with dignity.

"And now, dear Mr. Remington, I'm sure I don't need to ask you if you are taking the right stand on suffrage." This from Mrs. Brewster-Smith.

The candidate smiled tolerantly.

"If unequivocal opposition is 'right'—"

"Oh, you dear man! I was sure we could count on you. Isn't it splendid, Geneviève!"

The reporters came.

* * *

It was a busy evening for the young couple. There were relatives for dinner. Other relatives and an old friend or two came later. Throughout, George wore that quietly exalted expression, and carried himself with the new dignity.

To the adoring Genevieve his chin had never appeared so long and strong, his thought had never seemed so elevated, his quiet self-respect had never been so commanding. He was no longer merely her George, he was now a public figure. Soon he would be district attorney; then, very likely, Governor; then – well, Senator; and finally – it was possible – some one had to be – President of the United States. He had begun, this day, by making a great decision, by stepping boldly out on principle, on moral principle, and announcing himself a defender of the home, of the right.

At midnight, the last guest departed. George and Genevieve stepped out into the summer moonlight and strolled arm in arm down the walk.

Waddling up the street appeared a very fat boy.

"Why, Pudge," cried Geneviève, "what on earth are you doing out at this time of night!"

"I'm going home, I tell you!" muttered the boy, on the defensive. He carried a large bag of what seemed to be chocolate creams, from which he was eating.

As he passed, a twinge of memory disturbed him. He fumbled in his pockets.

"I was to give you this," he said then; and leaving a crumpled envelope in Genevieve's hand, he walked on as rapidly as he could.

A few minutes later, standing under the light in the front hall, George Remington read this penciled note:

"I stood ready to contribute more than I promised – any amount to put you over. But if you give out a statement against suffrage you're a damn fool and I withdraw every cent. A man with no more political sense and skill than that isn't worth helping. You should have advised me.

"M.J."

Chapter II
Harry Leon Wilson

It may have been surmised that our sterling young candidate for district attorney had not yet become skilled in dalliance with the equivocal; that he was no adept in ambiguity; that he would confront all issues with a rugged valiance susceptible of no misconstruction; that, in short, George Remington was no trimmer.

If he opposed an issue, one knew that he opposed it from the heart out. He said so and he meant it. And, being opposed to the dreadful heresy of equal suffrage, no reader of the Whitewater *Sentinel* that morning could say, as the shrewd so often say of our older statesmen, that George was "side-stepping."

Not George's the mellow gift to say, in effect, that of course woman should vote the instant she wishes to, though perhaps that day has not yet come. Meantime the speaker boldly defies the world to show a man holding woman in loftier regard than he does, or ready to accord her a higher value in all true functions of the body politic. Equal suffrage, thank God, is inevitable at some future time, but until that glorious day when we can be assured that the sex has united in a demand for it, it were perhaps as well not to cloud the issues of the campaign now opening; though let it be understood, and he cannot put this too plainly, that he reveres the memory of his gray-haired mother without whose tender ministrations and wise guidance he could never have reached the height from which he now speaks. And so let us pass on to the voting on these canal bonds, the true inwardness of which, thanks to the venal activities of a corrupt opposition, even an exclusively male constituency has thus far failed to comprehend. And so forth.

Our hero, then, had yet to acquire this finesse. As we are now privileged to observe him, he is as easy to understand as the multiplication table, as little devious and, alas! as lacking in suavity. Yet, let us be fair to George. Mere innocence of guile, of verbal trickery, had not alone sufficed for his passionate bluntness in the present crisis. At a later stage in his career as a husband he might have been equally blunt; yet never again, perhaps, would he have been so emotional in his opposition to woman polluting herself with the mire of politics.

Be it recalled that but five weeks had elapsed since George had solemnly promised to cherish and protect the fairest of the non-voting sex – at least in his State – and he was still taking his mission seriously. As he wrote the words that were now electrifying, in a manner of speaking, the readers of the *Sentinel*, and of neighboring journals with enough enterprise to secure them, he had beheld his own Genevieve, fine, flawless, tenderly nourished flower that she was, being dragged from her high place with the most distressing results.

He saw her rushed from the sacred shelter of her home and made to attend primaries; he saw her compelled to strive tearfully with problems that revolted all her finer instincts; he saw her insulted at polling booths; saw her voting in company with persons of both sexes whom one could never know.

He saw her tainted, bruised, beaten down in the struggle, losing little by little all sense of the holy values of Wife, Mother, Home. As he wrote he heard her weakening cries for help as she perished, and more than once his left arm instinctively curved to shield her.

Was it not for his wife, then; nay, for wifehood itself, that he wrote? And so, was it quite fair for unmarried Penfield Evans, burning at his breakfast table a cynical cigarette over the printed philippic, to murmur, "Gee! old George *has* spilled the beans!"

Simple words enough and not devoid of friendly concern. But should he not have divined that George had been appalled to his extremities of speech by the horrendous vision of his fair young bride being hurled into depths where she would be obliged, if not to have opinions of her own, at least to vote with the rabble as he might decide they ought to vote?

And should not other critics known to us have divined the racking anguish under which George had labored? For one, should not Elizabeth Sheridan, amateur spinster, have been all sympathy for one who was palpably more an alarmed bridegroom than a mere candidate?

Should not her maiden heart have been touched by this plausible aspect of George's dilemma, rather than her mere brain to have been steeled to a humorous disparagement tinged with bitterness?

And yet, "What rot!" muttered Miss Sheridan,—" silly rot, bally rot, tommy rot, and all the other kinds!"

Hereupon she creased a brow not meant for creases and defaced an admirable nose with grievous wrinkles of disdain. "Sacred names of wife and mother!" This seemed regrettably like swearing as she delivered it, though she quoted verbatim. "Sacred names of petted imbeciles!" she amended.

Then, with berserker fury, crumpling her *Sentinel* into a ball, she venomously hurled it to the depths of a waste basket and religiously rubbed the feel of it from her fingers. As she had not even glanced at the column headed "Births, Deaths, Marriages," it will be seen that her agitation was real. And surely a more discerning sympathy might have been looked for from the seasoned Martin Jaffry. A bachelor full of years and therefore with illusions not only unimpaired but ripened, who more quickly than he should have divined that his nephew for the moment viewed all womankind as but one multiplied Genevieve, upon whom it would be heinous to place the shackles of suffrage?

Perhaps Uncle Martin did divine this. Perhaps he was a mere trimmer, a rank side-stepper, steeped in deceit and ever ready to mouth the abominable phrase "political expediency." It were rash to affirm this, for no analyst has ever fathomed the heart of a man who has come to his late forties a bachelor by choice. One may but guess from the ensuing meager data.

Uncle Martin at a certain corner of Maple Avenue that morning, fell in with Penfield Evans, who, clad as the lilies of a florist's window, strode buoyantly toward his office, the vision of his day's toil pinkly suffused by an overlaying vision of a Betty or Sheridan character. Mr. Evans bubbled his greeting. "Morning! Have you seen it? Oh, *say*, have you seen it?"

The immediate manner of Uncle Martin not less than his subdued garb of gray, his dark gloves and his somber stick, intimated that he saw nothing to bubble about.

"He has burned his bridges behind him." The speaker looked as grim as any bachelor-by-choice ever may.

"Regular little fire-bug," blithely responded Mr. Evans, moderating his stride to that of the other.

"Can't understand it," resumed the gloomy uncle. "I sent him word in time; sent it from your office by messenger. It was plain enough. I told him no money of mine would go into his campaign if he made a fool of himself – or words to that effect."

"Phew! Cast you off, did he? Just like that?"

"Just like that! Went out of his way to overdo it, too. Needn't have come out half so strong. No chance now to backwater – not a chance on earth to explain what he really did mean – and make it something different." "Quixotic! That's how it reads to me."

Uncle Martin here became oracular, his somber stick gesturing to point his words.

"Trouble with poor George, he's been silly enough to blurt out the truth, what every man of us thinks in his heart—"

"Eh?" said Mr. Evans quickly, as one who has been jolted.

"No more sense than to come right out and say what every one of us thinks in his secret heart about women. I think it and you think it—"

"Oh, well, if you put it *that* way," admitted young Mr. Evans gracefully. "But of course—"

"Certainly, of *course!* We all think it – sacred names of home and mother and all the rest of it; but a man running for office these days is a chump to say so, isn't he? Of course he is! What chance does it leave him? Answer me that."

"Darned little, if you ask me," said Mr. Evans judicially. "Poor old George!"

"Talks as if he were going to be married tomorrow instead of its having come off five weeks ago," pursued Uncle Martin bitterly. Plainly there were depths of understanding in the man, trimmer though he might be.

Mr. Evans made no reply. Irrationally he was considering the terms "five weeks" and "married" in relation to a spinster who would have professed to be indignant had she known it.

"Got to pull the poor devil out," said Uncle Martin, when in silence they had traversed fifty feet more of the shaded side of Maple Avenue.

"How?" demanded the again practical Mr. Evans.

"Make him take it back; make him recant; swing him over the last week before election. Make him eat his words with every sign of exquisite relish. Simple enough!"

"How?" persisted Mr. Evans.

"Wiles, tricks, subterfuges, chicanery – understand what I mean?"

"Sure! I understand what you mean as well as you do, but – come down to brass tacks."

"That's an entirely different matter," conceded Uncle Martin gruffly. "It may take thought."

"Oh, is that all? Very well then; we'll think. I, myself, will think. First, I'll have a talk with the sodden amorist. I'll grill him. I'll find the weak spot in his armor. There must be something we can put over on him."

"By fair means or foul," insisted Uncle Martin as they paused at the parting of their ways. "Low-down, underhanded work – do you get what I mean?"

"I do, I do!" declared young Mr. Evans and broke once more into the buoyant stride of an earlier moment. This buoyance was interrupted but once, and briefly, ere he gained the haven of his office.

As he stepped quite too buoyantly into Fountain Square, he was all but run down by the new six-cylinder roadster of Mrs. Harvey Herrington, driven by the enthusiastic owner. He regained the curb in time, with a ready and heartfelt utterance nicely befitting the emergency.

The president of the Whitewater Women's Club, the Municipal League and the Suffrage Society, brought her toy to a stop fifteen feet beyond her too agile quarry, with a fine disregard for brakes and tire surfaces. She beckoned eagerly to him she might have slain. She was a large woman with an air of graceful but resolute authority; a woman good to look upon, attired with all deference to the modes of the moment, and exhaling an agreeable sense of good-will to all.

"Be careful always to look before you start across and you'll never have to say such things," was her greeting to Mr. Evans, as he halted beside this minor juggernaut.

"Sorry you heard it," lied the young man readily.

"Such a flexible little car – picks up before one realizes," conceded Whitewater's acknowledged social dictator. "But what I wanted to say is this: that poor daft partner of yours has mortally offended every woman in town except three, with that silly screed of his. I've seen nearly all of them that count this morning, or they've called me by telephone. Now, why couldn't he have had the advice of some good, capable woman before committing himself so rabidly?"

"Who were the three?" queried Mr. Evans.

"Oh, poor Genevieve, of course; she goes without saying. And you'd guess the other two if you knew them better – his cousin, Alys Brewster-Smith, and poor Genevieve's Cousin Emelene. They both have his horrible school-boy composition committed to memory, I do believe.

"Cousin Emelene recited most of it to me with tears in her weak eyes, and Alys tells me his noble words have made the world seem like a different place to her. She said she had been coming to believe that chivalry of the old true brand was dying out, but that dear Cousin George has renewed her faith in it.

"Think of poor Genevieve when they both fall on his neck. They're going up for that particular purpose this afternoon. The only two in town, mind you, except poor Genevieve. Oh, it's too awfully bad, because aside from this medieval view of his, George was probably as acceptable for this office as any man could be."

The lady burdened the word "man" with a tiny but distinguishable emphasis. Mr. Evans chose to ignore this.

"George's friends are going to take him in hand," said he. "Of course he was foolish to come out the way he has, even if he did say only what every man believes in his secret heart."

The president of the Whitewater Woman's Club fixed him with a glittering and suddenly hostile eye.

"What! you too?" she flung at him. He caught himself. He essayed explanations, modifications, a better lighting of the thing. But at the expiration of his first blundering sentence Mrs. Herrington, with her flexible little car, was narrowly missing an aged and careless pedestrian fifty yards down the street.

* * *

"George come in yet?"

For the second time Mr. Evans was demanding this of Miss Elizabeth Sheridan who had also ignored his preliminary "Good morning!"

Now for a moment more she typed viciously. One would have said that the thriving legal business of Remington and Evans required the very swift completion of the document upon which she wrought. And one would have been grossly deceived. The sheet had been drawn into the machine at the moment Mr. Evans' buoyant step had been heard in the outer hall, and upon it was merely written a dozen times the bald assertion, "Now is the time for all good men to come to the aid of the party."

Actually it was but the mechanical explosion of the performer's mood, rather than the wording of a sentiment now or at any happier time entertained by her.

At last she paused; she sullenly permitted herself to be interrupted. Her hands still hovered above the already well-punished keys of the typewriter. She glanced over a shoulder at Mr. Evans and allowed him to observe her annoyance at the interruption.

"George has not come in yet," she said coldly. "I don't think he will ever come in again. I don't see how he can have the face to. I shouldn't think he could ever show himself on the street again after that – that—"

The young woman's emotion overcame her at this point. Again her relentless fingers stung the blameless mechanism— "to come to the aid of the party. Now is the time for all good—" She here controlled herself to further speech. "And *you!* Of course you applaud him for it. Oh, I knew you were all alike!"

"Now look here, Betty, this thing has gone far enough—"

"Far enough, indeed!"

"But you won't give me a chance!"

Mr. Evans here bent above his employee in a threatening manner.

"You don't even ask what I think about it. You say I'm guilty and ought to be shot without a trial – not even waiting till sunrise. If you had the least bit of fairness in your heart you'd have asked me what I really thought about this outbreak of George's, and I'd have told you in so many words that I think he's made all kinds of a fool of himself."

"No! Do you really, Pen?"

Miss Sheridan had swiftly become human. She allowed her eyes to meet those of Mr. Evans' with an easy gladness but little known to him of late. "Of course I do, Betty. The idea of a candidate for office in this enlightened age breaking loose in that manner! It's suicide. He could be arrested for the attempt in this State. Is that strong enough for you? You surely know how I feel now, don't you? Come on, Betty dear! Let's not spar in that foolish way any longer. Remember all I said yesterday. It goes double today – really, I see things more clearly."

Plainly Miss Sheridan was disarmed.

"And I thought you'd approve every word of his silly tirade," she murmured. Mr. Evans, still above her, was perilously shaken by the softer note in her voice, but he controlled himself in time and sat in one of the chairs reserved for waiting clients. It was near Miss Sheridan, yet beyond reaching distance. He felt that he must be cool in this moment of impending triumph.

"Wasn't it the awfullest rot?" demanded the spinster, pounding out a row of periods for emphasis.

"And he's got to be made to eat his words," said Mr. Evans, wisely taking the same by-path away from the one subject in all the world that really mattered.

"Who could make him?"

"I could, if I tried." It came in quiet, masterful tones that almost convinced the speaker himself.

"Oh, Pen, if you could! Wouldn't that be a victory, though? If you only could—"

"Well, if I only could – and if I do?" His intention was too pointed to be ignored.

"Oh, *that*!" He winced at the belittling "that." "Of course I couldn't promise – anyway I don't believe you could ever do it, so what's the use of being silly?"

"But you will – will you promise, if I *do* convert George? Answer the question, please!" Mr. Evans glared as only actual district attorneys have the right to.

"Oh, what nonsense – but, well, I'll promise – I'll promise to promise to think very seriously about it indeed, if you bring George around."

"Betty!" It was the voice of an able pleader and he half arose from his chair, his arms eloquent of purpose. "'Now is the time for all good men to come to the aid of the party. Now is the time for'—" wrote Miss Sheridan with dazzling fingers, and the pleader resumed his seat.

"How will you bring him 'round," she then demanded.

"Wiles, tricks, stratagems," replied the rising young diplomat moodily, smarting under the moment's defeat.

"Serve him right for pulling all that old-fashioned nonsense," said Miss Sheridan, and accorded her employer a glance in which admiration for his prowess was not half concealed.

"The words of a fool wise in his own folly," went on the encouraged Mr. Evans, and then, alas! a victim to the slight oratorical thrill these words brought him,—" honestly uttering what every last man believes and feels about woman in his heart and yet what no sane man running for office can say in public – here, what's the matter?"

The latter clause had been evoked by the sight of a blazing Miss Sheridan, who now stood over him with fists tightly clenched. "Oh, oh, oh!" This was low, tense, thrilling. It expressed horror. "So that's what your convictions amount to! Then you do applaud him, every word of him, and you were deceiving me. Every man in his own heart, indeed. Thank heaven I found you out in time!"

It may be said that Mr. Evans now cowered in his chair. The term is not too violent. He ventured to lift a hand in weak protest.

"No, no, Betty, you are being unjust to me again. I meant that that was what Martin Jaffry told me this morning. It isn't what I believe at all. I tell you my own deepest sentiments are exactly what yours are in this great cause which – which—"

Painfully he became aware of his own futility. Miss Sheridan had ceased to blaze. Seated again before the typewriter she grinned at him with amused incredulity.

"You nearly had me going, Pen."

Mr. Evans summoned the deeper resources of his manhood and achieved an easier manner. He brazenly returned her grin. "I'll have you going again before I'm through – remember that."

"By wiles, tricks and stratagems, I suppose."

"The same. By those I shall make poor George recant, and by those, assuming you to be a woman with a fine sense of honor who will hold a promise sacred, I shall have you going. And, mark my words, you'll be going good, too!"

"Silly!"

She drew from the waste basket the maltreated *Sentinel*, unfurled it to expose the offending matter, and smote the column with the backs of four accusing fingers.

"There, my dear, is your answer. Now run along like a good boy."

"Silly!" said Mr. Evans, striving for a masterly finish to the unequal combat. He arose, dissembling cheerful confidence, straightened the frame of a steel-engraved Daniel Webster on the wall, and thrice paced the length of the room, falsely appearing to be engaged in deep thought.

Miss Sheridan, apparently for mere exclamatory purposes, now reread the fulmination of the absent partner. She scoffed, she sneered, flouted, derided, and one understood that she was including both members of the firm. Then her listener became aware that she had achieved coherence.

"Indeed, yes! Do you know what ought to happen to him? Every unprotected female in this county ought to pack her trunk and trudge right up to the Remington place and say, 'Here we are, noble man! We have read your burning words in which you offer to protect us. Save us from the vote! Let your home be our sanctuary. That's what you mean if you meant anything but tommy-rot. Here and now we throw ourselves upon your boasted chivalry. Where are our rooms, and what time is luncheon served.'"

"Here! Just say that again," called Mr. Evans from across the room. Miss Sheridan obliged. She elaborated her theme. George should be taken at his word by every weak flower of womanhood. If women were nothing but ministering angels, it was "up to" George to give 'em a chance to minister.

So went Miss Sheridan's improvisation and Mr. Evans, suffering the throes of a mighty inspiration, suddenly found it sweetest music.

When Miss Sheridan subsided, Mr. Evans appeared to have forgotten the cause of their late encounter. Whistling cheerily he bustled into his own office, mumbling of matters that had to be "gotten off." For some moments he busied himself at his desk, then emerged to dictate three business letters to his late antagonist.

He dictated in a formal and distant manner, pausing in the midst of the last letter to spell out the word "analysis," which he must have known would enrage her further. Then, quite casually, he wished to be told if she might know the local habitat of Mrs. Alys Brewster-Smith and a certain Cousin Emelene. His manner was arid.

Miss Sheridan chanced to know that the ladies were sheltered in the exclusive boarding-house of one Mrs. Gallup, out on Erie Street, and informed him to this effect in the fewest possible words. Mr. Evans whistled absently a moment, then formally announced that he should be absent from the office for perhaps an hour. Hat, gloves and stick in hand, he was about to nod punctiliously to the back of Miss Sheridan's head when the door opened to admit none other than our hero, George Remington. George wore the look of one who is uplifted and who yet has found occasion to be thoughtful about it. Penfield Evans grasped his hand and shook it warmly.

"Fine, George, old boy – simply corking! Honestly, I didn't believe you had it in you. You covered the ground and you did it in a big way. It took nerve, all right! Of course you probably know that every woman in town is speaking of your young wife as 'poor Genevieve,' but you've had the courage of your convictions. It's great!"

"Thanks, old man! I've spoken for the right as I saw it, let come what may. By the way, has Uncle Martin been in this morning, or telephoned, or sent any word?"

Miss Sheridan coldly signified that none of these things had occurred, whereupon George sighed in an interesting manner and entered his own room.

Mr. Evans had uttered his congratulations in clear, ringing tones and Miss Sheridan, even as she wrote, contrived with her trained shoulders to exhibit to his lingering eye an overwhelming contempt for his opinions and his double-dealing.

In spite of which he went out whistling, and dosed the door in a defiant manner.

Chapter III
Fannie Hurst

Destiny, busybody that she is, has her thousand irons in her perpetual fires, turning, testing and wielding them.

While Miss Betty Sheridan, for another scornful time, was rereading the well-thumbed copy of the *Sentinel*, her fine back arched like a prize cat's, George Remington in his small mahogany office adjoining, neck low and heels high, was codifying, over and over again, the small planks of his platform, stuffing the knot holes which afforded peeps to the opposite side of the issue with anti-putty, and planning a bombardment of his pattest phrases for the complete capitulation of his Uncle Jaffry.

While Genevieve Remington in her snug library, so eager in her wifeliness to clamber up to her husband's small planks, and if need be, spread her prettily flounced skirts over the rotting places, was memorizing, with more pride than understanding, extracts from the controversial article for quotation at the Woman's Club meeting, Mr. Penfield Evans, with a determination which considerably expanded his considerable chest measurement, ran two at a bound up the white stone steps of Mrs. Gallup's private boarding-house and pulled out the white china knob of a bell that gave no evidence of having sounded within, and left him uncertain to ring again.

A cast-iron deer, with lichen growing along its antlers, stood poised for instant flight in Mrs. Gallup's front yard.

While Mr. Evans waited he regarded its cast-iron flanks, but not seeingly. His rather the expression of one who stares into the future and smiles at what he sees.

Erie Street, shaded by a double row of showy chestnuts, lay in summer calm. A garden hose with a patent attachment spun spray over an adjoining lawn and sent up a greeny smell. Out from under the striped awning of Hassebrock's Ice Cream Parlor, cat-a-corner, Percival Pauncefort Sheridan, in rubber-heeled canvas shoes and white trousers, cuffed high, emerged and turned down Huron Street, making frequent forays into a bulging rear pocket.

Miss Lydia Chipley, vice-president of the Busy Bee Sewing and Civic Club, cool, starchy and unhatted, clicked past on slim, trim heels, all radiated by the reflection from a pink parasol, gay embroidery bag dangling.

"Hello, Lyd!"

"Hello, Pen!"

"What's your hurry?"

"It's my middle name."

"Why hurry, when the future is always waiting?"

"Why aren't you holding your partner's head since he committed political suicide in the *Sentinel*?"

"I'd rather hold your head, Lyd, any day in the week."

"Gaul," said Miss Chipley, passing on, her sharply etched little face glowing in the pink reflection of the parasol, "is bounded on the north by Mrs. Gallup's boarding-house, and on the south by—"

"By the Frigid Zone!"

Then the door from behind swung open. Mr. Penfield Evans stepped into Mrs. Gallup's cool, exclusive parlor of better days, and delivering his card to a moist-fingered maid, sat himself among the shrouded furniture to await Mrs. Alys Brewster-Smith and Miss Emelene Brand.

Mrs. Gallup's boarding-house was finishing its noonday meal. Boiled odors lay upon a parlor that was otherwise redolent of the more opulent days of the Gallups. A not too ostentatious clatter of dishes came through the closed folding-doors.

Almost immediately Mrs. Alys Brewster-Smith, her favorite Concentrated Breath of the Lily always in advance, rustled into the darkened parlor, her stride hitting vigorously into her black taffeta skirts. Even as she shook hands with Mr. Evans, she jerked the window shade to its height, so that her smoothness and coloring shone out above her weeds.

In the shadow of her and at her life job of bringing up the rear, with a large Maltese cat padding beside her, entered Miss Brand on rubber heels. She was the color of long twilight.

Mr. Evans rose to his six-feet-in-his-stockings and extended them each a hand, Miss Emelene drawing the left.

Mrs. Smith threw up a dainty gesture, black lace ruffles falling back from arms all the whiter because of them.

"Well, Penny Evans!"

"None other, Mrs. Smith, than the villain himself."

"Be seated, Penfield."

"Thanks, Miss Emelene."

They drew up in a triangle beside the window overlooking the cast-iron deer. The cat sprang up, curling in the crotch of Miss Emelene's arm.

"Nice ittie kittie, say how-do to big Penny-field-Evans. Say how-do to big man. Say how-do, muvver's ittie kittie." Miss Emelene extended the somewhat reluctant Maltese paw, five hook-shaped claws slightly in evidence.

"Say how-do to Hanna, Penfield. Hanna, say how-do to big man."

"How-do, Hanna," said Mr. Evans, reddening slightly beneath his tan. Then hitched his chair closer.

"To what," he began, flashing his white smile from one to the other of them, and with a strong veer to the facetious, "are we indebted for the honor of this visit? Are those the unspoken words, ladies?"

"Nothing wrong at home, Penfield? Nobody ailing or—"

"No, no, Miss Emelene, never better. As a matter of fact, it's a piece of political business that has prompted me to—"

At that Mrs. Smith jangled her bracelets, leaning forward on her knees.

"If it's got anything to do with your partner and my cousin George Remington having the courage to go in for the district attorneyship without the support of the vote-hunting, vote-eating women of this town, I'm here to tell you that I'm with him heart and soul. He can have my support and—"

"Mine too. And if I've got anything to say my two nephews will vote for him; and I think I have, with my two heirs."

"Ladies, it fills my heart with joy to—"

"Votes! Why what would the powder-puffing, short-skirted, bridge-playing women of this town do with the vote if they had it? Wear it around their necks on a gold chain?"

"Well spoken, Mrs. Smith, if—"

"I know the direction you lean, Penfield Evans, letting—"

"But, Miss Emelene, I—"

"Letting that shameless Betty Sheridan, a girl that had as sweet and womanly a mother as Whitewater ever boasted, lead you around by the nose on her suffrage string. A girl with her raising and both of her grandmothers women that lived and died genteel, to go traipsing around in her low heels in men's offices and addressing hoi polloi from soap boxes! Why, between her and that female chauffeur, Mrs. Herrington, another woman whose mother was of too fine feelings even to join the Delsarte class, the women of this town are being influenced to making disgraceful – dis— oh, what shall I say, Alys?"

Here Mrs. Smith broke in, thumping a soft fist into a soft palm.

"It's the most pernicious movement, Mr. Evans, that has ever got hold of this community and we need a man like my cousin George Remington to—"

"But, Mrs. Smith, that's just what I—"

"To stamp it out! Stamp it out! It's eating into the homes of Whitewater, trying to make breadwinners out of the creatures God intended for the bread-eaters – I mean bread-bakers."

"But, Mrs. Smith, I—"

"Woman's place has been the home since home was a cave, and it will be the home so long as women will remember that womanliness is their greatest asset. As poor dear Mr. Smith was so fond of saying, he – I can't bring myself to talk of him, Mr. Evans, but – but as he used to say, I – I—"

"Yes, yes, Mrs. Smith, I understa—"

"But as my cousin says in his article, which in my mind should be spread broadcast, what higher mission for woman than – than – just what are his words, Emelene?"

Miss Brand leaned forward, her gaze boring into space.

"What higher mission," she quoted, as if talking in a chapel, "for woman than that she sit enthroned in the home, wielding her invisible but mighty scepter from that throne, while man, kissing the hand that so lovingly commands him, shall bear her gifts and do her bidding. That is the strongest vote in the world. That is the universal suffrage which chivalry grants to woman. The unpolled vote! Long may it reign!"

Round spots of color had come out on Miss Emelene's long cheeks.

"A man who can think like that has the true – the true – what shall I say, Alys?"

"But, ladies, I protest that I'm not—"

"Has the true chivalry of spirit, Emelene, that the women are too stark raving mad to appreciate. You can't come here, Mr. Evans, to two women to whom womanliness and love of home, thank God, are still uppermost and try to convert us to—"

Here Mr. Evans executed a triple gyration, to the annoyance of Hanna, who withdrew from the gesture, and raised his voice to a shout that was not without a note of command.

"Convert you! Why women alive, what I've been bursting a blood vessel trying to say during the length of this interview is that I'd as soon dip my soul in boiling oil as try to convert you away from the cause. *My* cause! *Our* cause!"

"Why—"

"I'm here to tell you that I'm with my partner head-over-heels on the plank he has taken."

"But we thought—"

"We thought you and Betty Sheridan – why, my cousin Genevieve Remington told me that—"

"Yes, yes, Miss Emelene. But not even the wiles of a pretty woman can hold out indefinitely against Truth! A broad-minded man has got to keep the door of his mind open to conviction, or it decays of mildew. I confess that finally I am convinced that if there is one platform more than another upon which George Remington deserves his election it is on the brave and chivalrous principles he has so courageously come out with in the current *Sentinel*. Whatever may have been between Betty Sheridan and—"

"Mr. Evans, you don't mean to tell me that you and Betty Sheridan have quarreled! Such a desirable match from every point of view, family and all! It goes to show what a rattle-pated bunch of women they are! Any really clever girl with an eye to her future, anti or pro, could shift her politics when it came to a question of matri—"

"Mrs. Smith, there comes a time in every modern man's life when he's got to keep his politics and his pretty girls separate, or suffrage will get him if he don't watch out!"

"Yes, and Mr. Evans, if what I hear is true, a good-looking woman can talk you out of your safety deposit key!"

"That's where you're wrong, Mrs. Smith, and I'll prove it to you. Despite any wavering I may have exhibited, I now stand, as George puts it in his article, 'ready to conserve the threatened flower of womanhood by also endeavoring to conserve her unpolled vote!' If you women want prohibition, it is in your power to sway man's vote to prohibition. If you women want the moon, let man cast your proxy vote for it! In my mind, that is the true chivalry. To quote again, 'Woman is man's rarest heritage, his beautiful responsibility, and at all times his co-operation, support and protection are due her. His support and protection.'"

Miss Emelene closed her eyes. The red had spread in her cheeks and she laid her head back against the chair, rocking softly and stroking the thick-napped cat.

"The flower of womanhood," she repeated. "'His support and his protection.' If ever a man deserved high office because of high principles, it's my cousin George Remington! My cousin Genevieve Livingston Remington is the luckiest girl in the world, and not one of us Brands but what is willing to admit it. My two nephews, too, if their Aunt Emelene has anything to say, and I think she has—"

"Why, there isn't a stone in the world I wouldn't turn to see that boy in office," Mrs. Smith interrupted.

At that Mr. Evans rose.

"You mean that, Mrs. Smith?"

Miss Emelene rose with him, the cat pouring from her lap.

"Of course she means it, Penfield. What self-respecting woman wouldn't!"

Mr. Evans sat down again suddenly, Miss Emelene with him, and leaning violently forward, thrust his eager, sun-tanned face between the two women.

"Well, then, ladies, here's your chance to prove it! That's what brings me today. As two of the self-respecting, idealistic and womanly women of this community, I have come to urge you both to—"

"Oh, Mr. Evans!"

"Penfield, you are the flatterer!"

"To induce two such representative women as yourselves to help my partner to the election he so well deserves."

"Us?" "It is in your power, ladies, to demonstrate to Whitewater that George Remington's chivalry is not only on paper, but in his soul."

"But – how?"

"By throwing yourselves upon his generosity and hospitality, at least during the campaign. You have it in your power, ladies, to strengthen the only uncertain plank upon which George Remington stands today."

A clock ticked roundly into a silence tinged with eloquence. The Maltese leaped back into Miss Emelene's lap, purring there.

"You mean, Penfield, for us to go visit George – er – er—"

"Just that! Bag and baggage. As two relatives and two unattached women, it is your privilege, nay, your right."

"But—"

"He hasn't come out in words with it, but he has intimated that such an act from the representative antis of this town would more than anything strengthen his theories into facts. As unattached women, particularly as women of his own family, his support and protection, as he puts it, are due you, *due* you!"

Mrs. Smith clasped her plentifully ringed fingers, and regarded him with her prominent eyes widening.

"Why, I – unprotected widow that I am, Mr. Evans, am not the one to force myself even upon my cousin if—"

"Nor I, Penfield. It would be a pleasant enough change, heaven knows, from the boarding-house. But you can ask your mother, Penfield, if there ever was a prouder girl in all Whitewater than Emmy Brand. I—"

"But I tell you, ladies, the obligation is all on George's part. It's just as if you were polling votes for him. What is probably the oldest adage in the language, states that actions speak louder than words. Give him his chance to spread broadcast to your sex his protection, his support. That, ladies, is all I – we – ask."

"But I – Genevieve – the housekeeping, Penfield. Genevieve isn't much on management when it comes to—"

"Housekeeping! Why, I have it from your fair cousin herself, Miss Emelene, that her idea of their new little home is the Open House."

"Yes, but – as Emelene says, Mr. Evans, it's an imposition to—"

"Why do you think, Mrs. Smith, Martin Jaffry spends all his evenings up at Remingtons' since they're back from their honeymoon? Why, he was telling me only last night it's for the joy of seeing that new little niece of his lording it over her well-oiled little household, where a few extra dropping in makes not one whit of difference."

At this remark, embedded like a diamond in a rock, a shade of faintest color swam across Mrs. Smith's face and she swung him her profile and twirled at her rings.

"And where Genevieve Remington's husband's interests are involved, ladies, need I go further in emphasizing your welcome into that little home?"

"Heaven knows it would be a change from the boarding-house, Alys. The lunches here are beginning to go right against me! That sago pudding today – and Gallup knowing how I hate starchy desserts!"

"For the sake of the cause, Miss Emelene, too!"

"Gallup would have to hold our rooms at half rate."

"Of course, Mrs. Smith. I'll arrange all that."

"I – I can't go over until evening, with three trunks to pack."

"Just fine, Mrs. Smith. You'll be there just in time to greet George at dinner."

Miss Emelene fell to stroking the cat, again curled like a sardelle in her lap.

"Kitti-kitti-kitti—, does muvver's ittsie Hanna want to go on visit to Tousin George in fine new ittie house? To fine Tousin Georgie what give ittsie Hanna big saucer milk evvy day? Big fine George what like ladies and lady kitties!"

"Emelene, it's out of the question to take Hanna. You know how George Remington hates cats! You remember at the Sunday School Bazaar when—" A grimness descended like a mask over Miss Brand's features. Her mouth thinned.

"Very well, then. Without Hanna you can count me out, Penfield. If—"

"No, no! Why nonsense, Miss Emelene! George doesn't—"

"This cat has the feelings and sensibilities of a human being."

"Why of course," cried Penfield Evans, reaching for his hat. "Just you bring Hanna right along, Miss Emelene. That's only a pet pose of George's when he wants to tease his relatives, Mrs. Smith. I remember from college – why I've seen George *kiss* a cat!"

Miss Emelene huddled the object of controversy up in her chin, talking down into the warm gray fur.

"Was 'em tryin' to 'buse muvver's ittsie bittsie kittsie? Muvver's ittsie bittsie kittsie!"

They were in the front hall now, Mr. Evans tugging at the door.

"I'll run around now and arrange to have your trunks called for at five. My congratulations and thanks, ladies, for helping the right man toward the right cause."

"You're *sure*, Penfield, we'll be welcome?"

"Welcome as the sun that shines!"

"If I thought, Penfield, that Hanna wouldn't be welcome I wouldn't budge a step."

"Of course she's welcome, Miss Emelene. Isn't she of the gentler sex? There'll be a cab around for you and Mrs. Smith and Hanna about five. So long, Mrs. Smith, and many thanks. Miss Emelene, Hanna."

On the outer steps they stood for a moment in a dapple of sunshine and shadow from chestnut trees.

"Good-by, Mr. Evans, until evening."

"Good-by, Mrs. Smith." He paused on the walk, lifting his hat and flashing his smile a third time.

"Good-by, Miss Emelene."

From the steps Miss Brand executed a rotary motion with the left paw of the dangling Maltese.

"Tell nice gentleman by-by. Tum now, Hanna, get washed and new ribbon to go by-by. Her go to big Cousin George and piddy Cousin Genevieve. By-by! By-by!"

The door swung shut, enclosing them. Down the quiet, tree-shaped sidewalk, Mr. Penfield Evans strode into the somnolent afternoon, turning down Huron Street. At the remote end of the block and before her large frame mansion of a thousand angles and wooden lace work, Mrs. Harvey Herrington's low car sidled to her curb-stone, racy-looking as a hound. That lady herself, large and modish, was in the act of stepping up and in.

"Well, Pen Evans! 'Tis writ in the book our paths should cross."

"Who more pleased than I?"

"Which way are you bound?"

"Jenkins' Transfer and Cab Service."

"Jump in."

"No sooner said than done."

Mrs. Herrington threw her clutch and let out a cough of steam. They jerked and leaped forward. From the rear of the car an orange and black pennant – *Votes for Women* – stiffened out like a semaphore against the breeze.

Chapter IV
Dorothy Canfield

Genevieve Remington sat in her pretty drawing-room and watched the hour hand of the clock slowly approach five. Five was a sacred hour in her day. At five George left his office, turned off the business-current with a click and turned on, full-voltage, the domestic-affectionate.

Genevieve often told her girl friends that she only began really to live after five, when George was restored to her. She assured them the psychical connection between George and herself was so close that, sitting alone in her drawing-room, she could feel a tingling thrill all over when the clock struck five and George emerged from his office downtown.

On the afternoon in question she received her five o'clock electric thrill promptly on time, although history does not record whether or not George walked out from his office at that moment. With all due respect for the world-shaking importance of Mr. Remington's movements, it must be stated that history had, on that afternoon, other more important events to chronicle.

As the clock struck five, the front doorbell rang. Marie, the maid, went to open the door. Genevieve adjusted the down-sweeping, golden-brown tress over her right eye, brushed an invisible speck from the piano, straightened a rose in a vase, and after these traditionally bridal preparations, waited with a bride's optimistic smile the advent of a caller. But it was Marie who appeared at the door, with a stricken face of horror.

"Mrs. Remington! Mrs. Remington!" she whispered loudly. "They've come to stay. The men are getting their trunks down from the wagon."

"*Who* has come to stay? *Where?*" queried the startled bride.

"The two ladies who came to call yesterday!"

"*Oh!*" said the relieved Genevieve. "There's some mistake, of course. If it's Cousin Emelene and Mrs.—"

She advanced into the hall and was confronted by two burly men with a very large trunk between them.

"Which room?" said one of them in a bored and insolent voice.

"Oh, you must have come to the wrong house," Genevieve assured them with her pretty, friendly smile.

She was so happy and so convinced of the essential rightness of a world which had produced George Remington that she had a friendly smile for every one, even for unshaven men who kept their battered derby hats on their heads, had viciously smelling cigars in their mouths, and penetrated to her sacred front hall with trunks which belonged somewhere else.

"Isn't this G. L. Remington's house?" inquired one of the men, dropping his end of the trunk and consulting a dirty slip of paper.

"Yes, it is," admitted Genevieve, thrilling at the thought that it was also hers. "This is the place all right, then," said the man. He heaved up his end of the trunk again, and said once more, "Which room?"

The repetition fell a little ominously on Genevieve's ear. What on earth could be the matter?

She heard voices outside and craning her soft white neck, she saw Cousin Emelene, with her gray kitten under one arm and a large suitcase in her other hand, coming up the steps. There was a beatific expression in her gentle, faded eyes, and her lips were quivering uncertainly. When she caught sight of Genevieve's sweet face back of the bored expressmen, she gave a little cry, ran forward, set down her suitcase and clasped her young cousin in her arms.

"Oh Genevieve dear, that noble wonderful husband of yours! What have you done to deserve such a man... out of this Age of Gold!"

This was a sentiment after Genevieve's own heart, but she found it rather too vague to meet the present somewhat tense situation.

Cousin Emelene went on, clasping her at intervals, and talking very fast. "I can hardly believe it! Now that my time of trial is all over I don't mind telling you that I was growing embittered and cynical. All those phrases my dear mother had brought me to believe, the sanctity of the home, the chivalrous protection of men, the wicked folly of women who leave the home to engage in fierce industrial struggle."... At about this point the expressmen set the trunk down, put their hands on their hips, cocked their hats at a new angle and waited in gloomy ennui for the conversation to stop. Cousin Emelene flowed on, her voice unsteady with a very real emotion.

"See, dear, you must not blame me for my lack of faith... but see how it looked to me. There I was, as womanly a woman as ever breathed, and yet *I* had no home to be sanctified, *I* had never had a bit of chivalrous protection from any man. And with the New Haven stocks shrinking from one day to the next, the way they do, it looked as though I would either have to starve or engage in the wicked, unwomanly folly of earning my own living. Do you know, dear Genevieve, I had almost come to the point – you know how the suffragists do keep banging away at their points – I almost wondered if perhaps they were right and if men really mean those things about protection and support in place of the vote.... And then George's splendid, noble-spirited article appeared, and a kind friend interpreted it for me and told what it really meant, for *me*! Oh, Genevieve."... The tears rose to her mild eyes, her gentle, flat voice faltered, she took out a handkerchief hastily. "It seemed too good to be true," she said brokenly into its folds. "I've longed all my life to be protected, and now I'm going to be!"

"Which room, please?" said the expressman. "We gotta be goin' on."

Genevieve pinched herself hard, jumped and said "*ouch*." Yes, she was awake, all right!

"Oh, Marie, will you please get Hanna a saucer of milk?" said Cousin Emelene now, seeing the maid's round eyes glaring startled from the dining-room door. "And just warm it a little bit, don't scald it. She won't touch it if there's the least bit of a scum on it. Just take that ice-box chill off. Here, I'll go with you this time. Since we're going to live here now, you'll have to do it a good many times, and I'd better show you just how to do it right."

She disappeared, leaving a trail of caressing baby-talk to the effect that she would take good care of muvver's ittie bittie kittie.

She left Genevieve for all practical purposes turned to stone. She felt as though she were stone, from head to foot, and she could open her mouth no more than any statue when, in answer to the next repetition, very peremptory now, of "Which room?" a voice as peremptory called from the open front door, "Straight upstairs; turn to your right, first door on the left."

As the men started forward, banging the mahogany banisters with the corners of the trunk at every step, Mrs. Brewster-Smith stepped in, immaculate as to sheer collar and cuffs, crisp and tailored as to suit, waved and netted as to hair, and chilled steel and diamond point as to will-power.

"Oh, Genevieve, I didn't see *you* there! I didn't know why they stood there waiting so long. I know the house so well I knew of course which room you'll have for guests. *Dear* old house! It will be like returning to my childhood to live here again!" She cocked an ear toward the upper regions and frowned, but went on smoothly.

"Such happy girlhood hours as I have passed here! After all there is nothing like the home feeling, is there, for us women at any rate! We're the natural conservatives, who cling to the simple, elemental satisfactions, and there's a heart-hunger that can only be satisfied by a home and a man's protection! I thought George's description too beautiful ... in his article you know... of the ideal home with the women of the family safe within its walls, protected from the savagery of the economic struggle which only men in their strength can bear without being crushed."

She turned quickly and terribly to the expressmen coming down the stairs and said in so fierce a voice that they shrank back visibly, "There's another trunk to take up to the room next to that. And if you let it down with the bang you did this one, you'll get something that will surprise you! Do you hear me!"

They shrank out, cowed and tiptoeing. Mrs. Brewster-Smith turned back to her young cousin-by-marriage and murmured, "That was such a true and deep saying of George's... wherever does such a young man get his wisdom!... that women are not fitted by nature to cope with hostile forces!"

Cousin Emelene approached from behind the statue of Genevieve, still frozen in place with an expression of stupefaction on her white face. The older woman put her arms around the bride's neck and gave her an affectionate hug.

"Oh, dearest Jinny, doesn't it seem like a dream that we're all going to be together, all we women, in a real home, with a real man at the head of it to direct us and give us of his strength! It does seem just like that beautiful old-fashioned home that George drew such an exquisite picture of, in his article, where the home was the center of the world to the women in it. It will be to me, I assure you, dear. I feel as though I had come to a haven, and as though I *never* would want to leave it!"

The expressmen were carrying up another trunk now, and so conscious of the glittering eyes of mastery upon them that they carried it as though it were the Ark of the Covenant and they its chosen priests. Mrs. Brewster-Smith followed them with a firm tread, throwing over her shoulder to the stone Genevieve below, "Oh, my dear, little Eleanor and her nurse will be in soon. Frieda was taking Eleanor for her usual afternoon walk. Will you just send them upstairs when they come! I suppose Frieda will have the room in the third story, that extra room that was finished off when Uncle Henry lived here. Emelene, you'd better come right up, too, if you expect to get unpacked before dinner."

She disappeared, and Emelene fluttered up after her, drawn along by suction, apparently, like a sheet of paper in the wake of a train. The expressmen came downstairs, still treading softly, and went out. Genevieve was alone again in her front hall. To her came tiptoeing Marie, with wide eyes of query and alarm. And from Marie's questioning face, Genevieve fled away like one fleeing from the plague.

"Don't ask me, Marie! Don't *speak* to me. Don't you dare ask me what... or I'll..." She was at the front door as she spoke, poised for flight like a terrified doe. "I must see Mr. Remington! I don't know *what* to tell you, Marie, till I have seen Mr. Remington! I must see my husband! I don't know what to say, I don't know what to *think*, until I have seen my husband."

Calling this eminently wifely sentiment over her shoulder she ran down the front walk, hatless, wrapless, just as she was in her pretty flowered and looped-up bride's house dress. She couldn't have run faster if the house had been on fire.

The clicking of her high heels on the concrete sidewalk was a rattling tattoo so eloquent of disorganized panic that more than one head was thrust from a neighboring window to investigate, and more than one head was pulled back, nodding to the well-worn and charitable hypothesis, "Their first quarrel." The hypothesis would instantly have been withdrawn if any one had continued looking after the fleeing bride long enough to see her, regardless of passers-by, fling herself wildly into her husband's arms as he descended from the trolley-car at the corner.

Betty Sheridan was sitting in the drawing-room of her parents' house, rather moodily reading a book on the *Balance of Trade*.

She had an unconfessed weakness of mind on the subject of tariffs and international trade. Although when in college she had written a paper on it which had been read aloud in the Economics Seminar and favorably commented upon, she knew, in her heart of hearts, that she understood less than nothing about the underlying principles of the subject. This nettled her and gave her occasional nightmare moments of doubt as to the real fitness of women for public affairs. She read feverishly all she could find on the subject, ending by addling her brains to the point of frenzy.

She was almost in that condition now although she did not look it in the least as, dressed for dinner in the evening gown which replaced the stark linens and tailored seams of her office-costume, she bent her shining head and earnest face over the pages of the book.

Penfield Evans took a long look at her, as one looks at a rose-bush in bloom, before he spoke through the open door and broke the spell.

"Oh, Betty," he called in a low tone, beckoning her with a gesture redolent of mystery.

Betty laid down her book and stared. "What you want?" she challenged him, reverting to the phrase she had used when they were children together.

"Come on out here a minute!" he said, jerking his head over his shoulder. "I want to show you something."

"Oh, I can't fuss around with you," said Betty, turning to her book again. "I've got Roberts' *Balance of Trade* out of the library and I must finish it by tomorrow." She began to read again.

The young man stood silent for a moment. "Great Scott!" he was saying to himself with a sinking heart. "So *that's* what they pick up for light reading, when they're waiting for dinner!"

He had a particularly gone feeling because, although he had made several successful political speeches on international trade and foreign tariffs, he was intelligent enough to know in his heart of hearts that he had no real understanding of the principles involved. He had come, indeed, to doubt if any one had!

Now, as he watched the pretty sleek head bent over the book he had supposed of course was a novel, he felt a qualm of real apprehension. Maybe there was something in what that guy said, the one who wrote a book to prove (bringing Queen Elizabeth and Catherine the Great as examples) that the real genius of women is for political life. Maybe they *have* a special gift for it! Maybe, a generation or so from now, it'll be the *men* who are disfranchised for incompetence.... He put away as fantastic such horrifying ideas, and with a quick action of his resolute will applied himself to the present situation. "Oh Betty, you don't know what you're missing! It's a sight you'll never forget as long as you live... oh, come on! Be a sport. Take a chance!"

Betty was still suspicious of frivolity, but she rose, looked at her wrist-watch and guessed she'd have a few minutes before dinner, to fool away in light-minded society.

"There's nothing light-minded about this!" Penny assured her gravely, leading her swiftly down the street, around the corner, up another street and finally, motioning her to silence, up on the well-clipped lawn of a handsome, dignified residence, set around with old trees.

"Look!" he whispered in her ear, dramatically pointing in through the lighted window. "Look! What do you see?"

Betty looked, and looked again and turned on him petulantly:

"What foolishness are you up to now, Penfield Evans!" she whispered energetically. "Why under the sun did you drag me out to see Emelene and Alys Brewster-Smith dining with the Remingtons? Isn't it just the combination of reactionary old fogies you might expect to get together... though I didn't know Alys ever took her little girl out to dinner-parties, and Emelene must be perfectly crazy over that cat to take her here. Cats make George's flesh creep. Don't you remember, at the Sunday School Bazaar."

He cut her short with a gesture of command, and applying his lips to her ear so that he would not be heard inside the house, he said, "You think all you see is Emelene and Alys taking dinner *en famille* with the Remingtons. Eyes that see not! What you are gazing upon is a reconstruction of the blessed family life that existed in the good old days, before the industrial period and the abominable practice of economic independence for women began! You are seeing Woman in her proper place, the Home,... if not her own Home, somebody's Home, anybody's Home...

the Home of the man nearest to her, who owes her protection because she can't vote. You are gazing upon..."

His rounded periods were silenced by a tight clutch on his wrist. "Penfield Evans. Don't you dare exaggerate to me! Have they come there to stay! *To take him at his word!*"

He nodded solemnly.

"Their trunks are upstairs in the only two spare-rooms in the house, and Frieda is installed in the only extra room in the attic. Marie gave notice that she was going to quit, just before dinner. George has been telephoning to my Aunt Harriet to see if she knows of another maid...."

"Whatever... whatever could have made them *think* of such a thing!" gasped Betty, almost beyond words.

"I did!" said Penfield Evans, tapping himself on the chest. "It was *my* giant intelligence that propelled them here."

He was conscious of a lacy rush upon him, and of a couple of soft arms which gave him an impassioned embrace none the less vigorous because the arms were more used to tennis-racquets and canoe-paddles than impassioned embraces. Then he was thrust back... and there was Betty, collapsed against a lilac bush, shaking and convulsed, one hand pressed hard on her mouth to keep back the shrieks of merriment which continually escaped in suppressed squeals, the other hand outstretched to ward him off....

"No, don't you touch me, I didn't mean a thing by it! I just couldn't help it! It's too, *too* rich! Oh Penny, you duck! Oh, I shall die! I shall die! I never saw anything so funny in my life! Oh, Penny, take me away or I shall perish here and now!"

On the whole, in spite of the repulsing hand, he took it that he had advanced his cause. He broke into a laugh, more light-hearted than he had uttered for a long time. They stood for a moment more in the soft darkness, gazing in with rapt eyes at the family scene. Then they reeled away up the street, gasping and choking with mirth, festooning themselves about trees for support when their legs gave way under them.

"*Did* you see George's face when Emelene let the cat eat out of her plate!" cried Betty.

"And did you see Genevieve's when Mrs. Brewster-Smith had the dessert set down in front of her to serve!"

"How about little Eleanor upsetting the glass of milk on George's trousers!"

"Oh *poor* old George! Did you ever see such gloom!"

Thus bubbling, they came again to Betty's home with the door still open from which she had lately emerged. There Betty fell suddenly silent, all the laughter gone from her face. The man peered in the dusk, apprehensive. What had gone wrong, now, after all?

"Do you know, Penny, we're pigs!" she said suddenly, with energy. "We're hateful, abominable pigs!"

He glared at her and clutched his hair.

"Didn't you see Emelene Brand's face? I can't get it out of my mind! It makes me sick, it was so happy and peaceful and befooled! Poor old dear! She *believes* all that! And she's the only one who does! And its beastly in us to make a joke of it! She has wanted a home all her life, and she'd have made a lovely one, too, for children! And she's been kept from it by all this fool's talk about womanliness."

"Help! What under the sun are you..." began Penfield.

"Why, look here, she's not and never was, the kind any man wants to marry. She wouldn't have liked a real husband, either... poor, dear, thin-blooded old child! But she wanted a *home* just the same. Everybody does! And if she had been taught how to earn a decent living, if she hadn't been fooled out of her five senses by that idiotic cant about a man's doing everything for you, or else going without... why she'd be working now, a happy, useful woman, bringing up two or three adopted children in a decent home she'd made for them with her own efforts... instead of making her loving heart ridiculous over a cat...."

She dashed her hand over her eyes angrily, and stood silent for a moment, trying to control her quivering chin before she went into the house.

The young man touched her shoulder with reverent fingers. "Betty," he said in a rather unsteady voice, "its *true*, all that bally-rot about women being better than men. You *are*!"

With which very modern compliment, he turned and left her.

Chapter V

Kathleen Norris

Her first evening with her augmented family Genevieve Remington never forgot. It is not at all likely that George ever forgot it, either; but to George it was only one in the series of disturbing events that followed his unqualified repudiation of the suffrage cause.

To Genevieve's tender heart it meant the wreckage, not the preservation of the home; that lovely home to whose occupancy she had so hopefully looked. She was too young a wife to recognize in herself the evanescent emotions of the bride. The blight had fallen upon her for all time. What had been fire was ashes; it was all over. The roseate dream had been followed by a cruel, and a lasting, awakening.

Some day Genevieve would laugh at the memory of this tragic evening, as she laughed at George's stern ultimatums, and at Junior's decision to be an engineer, and at Jinny's tiny cut thumb. But she had no sense of humor now. As she ran to the corner, and poured the whole distressful story into her husband's ears, she felt the walls of her castle in Spain crashing about her ears.

George, of course, was wonderful; he had been that all his life. He only smiled, at first, at her news.

"You poor little sweetheart!" he said to his wife, as she clung to his arm, and they entered the house together. "It's a shame to distress you so, just as we are getting settled, and Marie and Lottie are working in! But it's too absurd, and to have you worry your little head is ridiculous, of course! Let them stay here to dinner, and then I'll just quietly take it for granted that they are going home—"

"But – but their trunks are here, dearest!"

Husband and wife were in their own room now, and Genevieve was rapidly recovering her calm. George turned from his mirror to frown at her in surprise. "Their trunks! They didn't lose any time, did they? But do you mean to say there was no telephoning – no notice at all?"

"They may have telephoned, George, love. But I was over at Grace Hatfield's for a while, and I got back just before they came in!"

George went on with his dressing, a thoughtful expression on his face. Genevieve thought he looked stunning in the loose Oriental robe he wore while he shaved.

"Well, whatever they think, we can't have this, you know," he said presently. "I'll have to be quite frank with Alys, – of course Emelene has no sense!"

"Yes, be quite frank!" Genevieve urged eagerly. "Tell them that of course you were only speaking figuratively. Nobody ever means that a woman really can't get along without a man's protection, because look at the women who *do*—"

She stopped, a little troubled by the expression on his face.

"I said what I truly believe, dear," he said kindly. "You know that!" Genevieve was silent. Her heart beat furiously, and she felt that she was going to cry. He was angry with her – he was angry with her! Oh, what had she said, what *had* she said!

"But for all that," George continued, after a moment, "nobody but two women could have put such an idiotic construction upon my words. I am certainly going to make that point with Alys. A sex that can jump headlong to such a perfectly untenable conclusion is very far from ready to assume the responsibilities of citizenship—"

"George, dearest!" faltered Genevieve. She did not want to make him cross again, but she could not in all loyalty leave him under this misunderstanding, to approach the always articulate Alys.

"George, it was Penny, I'm sure!" she said. "From what they said, – they talked all the time! – I think Penny went to see them, and sort of – sort of – suggested this! I'm so sorry, George—"

George was sulphurously silent.

"And Penny will make the most of it, you know!"

Genevieve went on quickly and nervously. "If you should send them back, tonight, I know he'd tell Betty! And Betty says she is coming to see you because she has been asked to read an answer to your paper, at the Club, and she might – she has such a queer sense of humor—"

Silence. Genevieve wished that she was dead, and that every one was dead.

"I don't want to criticize you, dear," George said presently, in his kindest tone. "But the time to *act*, of course, was when they first arrived. I can't do anything now. We'll just have to face it through, for a few days."

It was not much of a cloud, but it was their first. Genevieve went downstairs with tears in her eyes.

She had wanted their home to be so cozy, so dainty, so intimate! And now to have two grown women and a child thrust into her Paradise! Marie was sulky, rattling the silver-drawer viciously while her mistress talked to her, and Lottie had an ugly smile as she submitted respectfully that there wasn't enough asparagus.

Then George's remoteness was terrifying. He carved with appalling courtesy. "Is there another chicken, Genevieve?" he asked, as if he had only an impersonal interest in her kitchen. No, there was only the one. And plenty, too, said the guests pleasantly. Genevieve hoped there were eggs and bacon for Marie and Lottie and Frieda.

"I'm going to ask you for just a mouthful more, it tastes so delicious and homy!" said Alys. "And then I want to talk a little business, George. It's about those houses of mine, out in Kentwood...."

George looked at her blankly, over his drumstick.

"Darling Tom left them," said Tom's widow, "and they really have rented well. They're right near the factory, you know. But now, just lately, some man from the agents has been writing and writing me; he says that one of them has been condemned, and that unless I do something or other they'll all be condemned. It's a horrid neighborhood, and I don't like the idea, anyway, of a woman poking about among drains and cellars. Yet, if I send the agent, he'll run me into fearful expense; they always do. So

I'm going to take them out of his hands tomorrow, and turn it all over to you, and whatever you decide will be best!"

"My dear girl, I'm the busiest man in the world!" George said. "Leave all that to Allen. He's the best agent in town!"

"Oh, I took them away from Allen months ago, George. Sampson has them now."

"Sampson? What the deuce did you change for? I don't know that Sampson is solvent. I certainly would go back to Allen—"

"George, I can't!"

The widow looked at her plate, swept him a coquettish glance, and dropped her eyes again.

"Mr. Allen is a dear fellow," she elucidated, "but his wife is dreadful! There's nothing she won't suspect, and nothing she won't say!"

"My dear cousin, this isn't a question of social values! It's business!" George said impatiently. "But I'll tell you what to do," he added, after scowling thought. "You put it in Miss Eliot's hands; she was with Allen for some years. Now she's gone in for herself, and she's doing well. We've given her several things—"

"Take it out of a man's hands to put it into a woman's!" Alys exclaimed. And Emelene added softly:

"What can a woman be thinking of, to go into a dreadful business like selling real estate and collecting rents!"

"Of course, she was trained by men!" Genevieve threw in, a little anxiously. Alys was so tactless, when George was tired and hungry. She cast about desperately for some neutral topic, but before she could find one the widow spoke again.

"I'll tell you what I'll do, George. I'll bring the books and papers to your office tomorrow morning, and then you can do whatever you think best! Just send me a check every month, and it will be all right!"

"Just gather me up what's there, on the plate," Emelene said, with her nervous little laugh in the silence. "I declare I don't know when I've eaten such a dinner! But that reminds me that you could help me out wonderfully, too, Cousin George – I can't quite call you Mr. Remington! – with those wretched stocks of mine. I'm sure I don't know what they've been doing, but I know I get less money all the time! It's the New Haven, George, that P'pa left me two years ago. I can't understand anything about it, but yesterday I was talking to a young man who advised me to put all my money into some tonic stock. It's a tonic made just of plain earth – he says it makes everything grow. Doesn't it sound reasonable? But if I should lose all I have, I'm afraid I'd *really* wear my welcome out, Genevieve, dear. So perhaps you'll advise me?"

"I'll do what I can!" George smiled, and Genevieve's heart rose. "But upon my word, what you both tell me isn't a strong argument for Betty's cause!" he added good-naturedly.

"P'pa always said," Emelene quoted, "that if a woman looked about for a man to advise her, she'd find him! And as I sit here now, in this lovely home, I think – isn't it sweeter and wiser and better this way? For a while, – because I was a hot-headed, rebellious girl! – I couldn't see that he was right. I had had a disappointment, you know," she went on, her kind, mild eyes watering. Genevieve, who had been gazing in some astonishment at the once hot-headed, rebellious girl, sighed sympathetically. Every one knew about the Reverend Mr. Totter's death.

"And after that I just wanted to be busy," continued Emelene. "I wanted to be a trained nurse, or a matron, or something! I look back at it now, and wonder what I was thinking about! And then dear Mama went, and I stepped into her place with P'pa. He wasn't exactly an invalid, but he did like to be fussed over, to have his meals cooked by my own hands, even if we were in a hotel. And whist – dear me, how I used to dread those three rubbers every evening! I was only a young woman then, and I suppose I was attractive to other men, but I never forgot Mr. Totter. And Cousin George," she turned to him submissively, "when you were talking about a woman's real sphere, I felt – well, almost guilty. Because only that one man ever asked me. Do you think, feeling as I did, that I should have deliberately made myself attractive to men?"

George cleared his throat. "All women can't marry, I suppose. It's in England, I believe, that there are a million unmarried women. But you have made a contented and a womanly life for yourself, and, as a matter of fact, there always *has* been a man to stand between you and the struggle!" he said.

"I know. First P'pa, and now you!" Emelene mused happily.

"I wasn't thinking of myself. I was thinking that your father left you a comfortable income!" he said quickly.

"And now you have asked me here; one of the dearest old places in town!" Emelene added innocently.

Genevieve listened in a stupefaction. This was married life, then? Not since her childhood had Genevieve so longed to stamp, to scream, to protest, to tear this twisted scheme apart and start anew!

She was not a crying woman, but she wanted to cry now. She was not – she told herself indignantly – quite a fool. But she felt that if George went on being martyred, and mechanically polite, and grim, she would go into hysterics. She had been married less than six weeks; that night she cried herself to sleep.

Her guests were as agreeable as their natures permitted; but Genevieve was reduced, before the third day of their visit, to a condition of continual tears.

This was her home, this was the place sacred to George and herself, and their love. Nobody in the world, – not his mother, not hers, had their mothers been living! – was welcome here. She had planned to be such a good wife to him, so thoughtful, so helpful, so brave when he must be away. But she could not rise to the height of sharing him with other women, and saying whatever she said to him in the hearing of witnesses. And then she dared not complain too openly! That was an additional hardship, for if George insulted his guests, then that horrid Penny—

Genevieve had always liked Penny, and had danced and flirted with him aeons ago. She had actually told Betty that she hoped Betty would marry Penny. But now she felt that she loathed him. He was secretly laughing at George, at George who had dared to take a stand for old-fashioned virtue and the purity of the home!

It was all so unexpected, so hard. Women everywhere were talking about George's article, and expected her to defend it! George, she could have defended. But how could she talk about a subject upon which she was not informed, in which, indeed, as she was rather fond of saying, she was absolutely uninterested?

George was changed, too. Something was worrying him; and it was hard on the darling old boy to come home to Miss Emelene and the cat and Eleanor and Alys, every night! Emelene adored him, of course, and Alys was always interesting and vivacious, but – but it wasn't like coming home to his own little Genevieve!

The bride wept in secret, and grew nervous and timid in manner. Mrs. Brewster-Smith, however, found this comprehensible enough, and one hot summer afternoon Genevieve went into George's office with her lovely head held high, her color quite gone, and her breath coming quickly with indignation. "George – I don't care what we do, or where we go! But I can't stand it! She said – she said – she told me—"

Her husband was alone in his office, and Genevieve was now crying in his arms. He patted her shoulder tenderly.

"I'm so worried all the time about dinners, and Lottie's going, and that child getting downstairs and letting in flies and licking the frosting off the maple cake," sobbed Genevieve, "that of *course* I show it! And if I *have* given up my gym work, it's just because I was so busy trying to get some one in Lottie's place! And now they say – they say – that *they* know what the matter is, and that I mustn't dance or play golf – the horrible, spying cats! I won't go back, George, I will not! I—"

Again George was wonderful. He put his arm about her, and she sat down on the edge of his desk, and leaned against that dear protective shoulder and dried her eyes on one of his monogrammed handkerchiefs. He reminded her of a long-standing engagement for this evening with Betty and Penny, to go out to Sea Light and have dinner and a swim, and drive home in the moonlight. And when she was quiet again, he said tenderly:

"You mustn't let the 'cats' worry you, Pussy. What they think isn't true, and I don't blame you for getting cross! But in one way, dear, aren't they right? Hasn't my little girl been riding and driving and dancing a little too hard? Is it the wisest thing, just now? You have been nervous lately, dear, and excitable. Mightn't there be a reason? Because I don't have to tell you, sweetheart, nothing would make me prouder, and Uncle Martin, of course, has made no secret of how *he* feels! You wouldn't be sorry, dear?"

Genevieve had always loved children deeply. Long before this her happy dreams had peopled the old house in Sheridan Road with handsome, dark-eyed girls, and bright-eyed boys like their father.

But, to her own intense astonishment, she found this speech from her husband distasteful. George would be "proud," and Uncle Martin pleased. But it suddenly occurred to Genevieve that neither George nor Uncle Martin would be tearful and nervous. Neither George nor Uncle Martin need eschew golf and riding and dancing. To be sick, when she had always been so well! To face death, for which she had always had so healthy a horror! Cousin Alex had died when her baby came, and Lois Farwell had never been well after the fourth Farwell baby made his appearance.

Genevieve's tears died as if from flame. She gently put aside the sustaining arm, and went to the little mirror on the wall, to straighten her hat. She remembered buying this hat, a few weeks ago, in the ecstatic last days of the old life.

"We needn't talk of that yet, George," she said quietly.

She could see George's grieved look, in the mirror. There was a short silence in the office.

Then Betty Sheridan, cool in pongee, came briskly in.

"Hello, Jinny!" said she. "Had you forgotten our plan tonight? You're chaperoning me, I hope you realize! I'm rather difficile, too. Genevieve, Pudge is outside; he'll take you out and buy you something cold. I took him to lunch today. It was disgraceful! Except for a frightful-looking mess called German Pot Roast With Carrots and Noodles Sixty, he ate nothing but melon, lemon-meringue pie, and pineapple special. I was absolutely ashamed! George, I would have speech with you."

"Private business, Betty?" he asked pleasantly. "My wife may not have the vote, but I trust her with all my affairs!"

"Indeed, I'm not in the least interested!" Genevieve said saucily.

She knew George was pleased with her as she went happily away.

"It's just as well Jinny went," said Betty, when she and the district-attorney-elect were alone. "Because it's that old bore Colonel Jaynes! He's come again, and he says he *will* see you!"

Deep red rose in George's handsome face.

"He came here last week, and he came yesterday," Betty said, sitting down, "and really I think you should see him! You see, George, in that far-famed article of yours, you remarked that 'a veteran of the civil as well as the Spanish war' had told you that it was the restless outbreaking of a few northern women that helped to precipitate the national catastrophe, and he wants to know if you meant him!"

"I named no names!" George said, with dignity, yet uneasily, too.

"I know you didn't. But you see we haven't many veterans of *both* wars," Betty went on, pleasantly. "And of course old Mrs. Jaynes is a rabid suffragist, and she is simply hopping. He's a mild old man, you know, and evidently he wants to square things with 'Mother.' Now, George, who *did* you mean?"

"A statement like that may be made in a general sense," George remarked, after scowling thought.

"You might have made the statement on your own hook," Betty conceded, "but when you mention an anonymous Colonel, of course they all sit up! He says that he's going to get a signed statement from you that *he* never said that, and publish it!"

"Ridiculous!" said George.

"Then here are two letters," Betty pursued. "One is from the corresponding secretary of the Women's Non-partisan Pacific Coast Association. She says that they would be glad to hear from you regarding your statement that equal suffrage, in the western states, is an acknowledged failure."

"She'll wait!" George predicted grimly.

"Yes, I suppose so. But she's written to our Mrs. Herrington here, asking her to follow up the matter. George, dear," asked Betty maternally, "*why* did you do it? Why couldn't you let well enough alone!"

"What's your other letter?" asked George.

"It's just from Mr. Riker, of the *Sentinel*, George. He wants you to drop in. It seems that they want a correction on one of your statistics about the number of workingwomen in the United States who don't want the vote. He says it only wants a signed line from you that you were mistaken—"

Refusing to see Colonel Jaynes, or to answer the Colonel's letter, George curtly telephoned the editor of the *Sentinel*, and walked home at four o'clock, his cheeks still burning, his mind in a whirl. Big issues should have been absorbing him; and his mind was pestered instead with these midges of the despised cause. Well, it was all in the day's work—

And here was his sweet, devoted wife, fluttering across the hall, as cool as a rose, in her pink and white. And she had packed his things, in case they wanted to spend the night at Sea Light, and the "cats" had gone off for library books, and he must have some ginger-ale, before it was time to go for Betty and Penny.

The day was perfection. The motor-car purred like a racing tiger under George's gloved hand. Betty and Penny were waiting, and the three young persons forgot all differences, and laughed and chatted in the old happy way, as they prepared for the start. But Betty was carrying a book: *Catherine of Russia*.

"Do you know why suffragists should make an especial study of queens, George?" she asked, as she and Penny settled themselves on the back seat.

"Well, I'll be interlocutor," George smiled, glancing up at the house, from which his wife might issue at any moment. "Why should suffragists read the lives of queens, Miss Bones?"

"Because queens are absolutely the only women in all history who had equal rights!" Betty answered impassively.

"Do you realize that? The only women whose moral and social and political instincts had full sway!"

"And a sweet use they made of them, sometimes!" said George.

"And who were the great rulers," pursued Betty. "Whose name in English history is like the names of Elizabeth and Victoria, or Matilda or Mary, for the matter of that? Who mended and conserved and built up what the kings tore down and wasted? Who made Russia an intellectual power—"

Again Penny had an odd sense of fear. Were women perhaps superior to men, after all!

"I don't think Catherine of Russia is a woman to whom a lady can point with pride," George said conclusively. Genevieve, who had appeared, shot Betty a triumphant glance as they started. Pudge waved to them from the candy store at the corner.

"There's a new candy store every week!" said Penny, shuddering. "Heaven help that poor boy; it must be in the blood!"

"Women must always have something sweet to nibble," George said, leaning back. "The United States took in two millions last year in gum alone!"

"Men chew gum!" suggested Betty.

"But come now, Betty, be fair!" George said. "Which sex eats more candy?"

"Well, I suppose women do," she admitted.

"You count the candy stores, down Main Street," George went on, "and ask yourself how it is that these people can pay rents and salaries just on candy, – nothing else. Did you ever think of that?"

"Well, I could vote with a chocolate in my mouth!" Betty muttered mutinously, as the car turned into the afternoon peace of the main thoroughfare.

"You count them on your side, Penny, and I will on mine!" Genevieve suggested. "All down the street." "Well, wait – we've passed two!" Penny said excitedly.

"Go on; there's three. That grocery store with candy in the window!"

"Groceries don't count!" objected Betty.

"Oh, they do, too! And drug stores…. Every place that sells candy!"

"Drug stores and groceries and fruit stores only count half a point," Betty stipulated. "Because they sell other things!"

"That's fair enough," George conceded here, with a nod.

Genevieve and Penny almost fell out of the car in their anxiety not to miss a point, and George quite deliberately lingered on the cross-streets, so that the damning total might be increased.

Laughing and breathless, they came to the bridge that led from the town to the open fields, and took the count.

"One hundred and two and a half!" shouted Penny and Geneviève triumphantly. George smiled over his wheel.

"Oh, women, women!" he said. "One hundred and sixty-one!" said Betty. There was a shout of protest.

"Oh, Betty Sheridan! You didn't! Why, we didn't miss *one*!"

"I wasn't counting candy stores," smiled Betty. "Just to be different, I counted cigar stores and saloons. But it doesn't signify much either way, does it, George?"

Chapter VI

Henry Kitchell Webster

Of the quartette who, an hour later, emerged from the bath-houses and scampered across the satiny beech into a discreetly playful surf, Genevieve was the one real swimmer. She was better even than Penny, and she left Betty and George nowhere.

She had an endless repertory of amphibious stunts which she performed with gusto, and in the intervals she took an equal satisfaction in watching Penny's heroic but generally disastrous attempts to imitate them.

The other two splashed around aimlessly and now and then remonstrated.

Now, it's all very well to talk about two hearts beating as one, and in the accepted poetical sense of the words, of course Genevieve's and George's did. But as a matter of physiological fact, they didn't. At the end of twenty minutes or so George began turning a delicate blue and a clatter as of distant castanets provided an obligato when he spoke, the same being performed by George's teeth.

The person who made these observations was Betty.

"You'd better go out," she said. "You're freezing."

It ought to have been Genevieve who said it, of course, though the fact that she was under water more than half the time might be advanced as her excuse for failing to say it. But who could venture to excuse the downright callous way in which she exclaimed, "Already? Why we've just got in! Come along and dive through that wave. That'll warm you up!"

It was plain to George that she didn't care whether he was cold or not. And, though the idea wouldn't quite go into words, it was also clear to him that an ideal wife – a really womanly wife – would have turned blue just a little before he began to.

"Thanks," he said, in a cold blue voice that matched the color of his finger nails. "I think I've had enough."

Betty came splashing along beside him.

"I'm going out, too," she said. "We'll leave these porpoises to their innocent play."

This was almost pure amiability, because she wasn't cold, and she'd been having a pretty good time. Her other (practically negligible) motive was that Penny might be reminded, by her withdrawal, of his forgotten promise to teach her to float – and be sorry. Altogether, George would have been showing only a natural and reasonable sense of his obligations if he'd brightened up and flirted with her a little, instead of glooming out to sea the way he did, paying simply no attention to her at all. So at last she pricked him.

"Isn't it funny," she said, "the really blighting contempt that swimmers feel for people who can't feel at home in the water – people who gasp and shiver and keep their heads dry?"

She could see that, in one way, this remark had done George good. It helped warm him up. Leaning back on her hands, as she did, she could see the red come up the back of his neck and spread into his ears. But it didn't make him conversationally any more exciting. He merely grunted. So she tried again.

"I suppose," she said dreamily, "that the myth about mermaids must be founded in fact. Or is it sirens I'm thinking about? Perfectly fascinating, irresistible women, who lure men farther and farther out, in the hope of a kiss or something, until they get exhausted and drown. I'll really be glad when Penny gets back alive."

"And I shall be very glad," said George, trying hard for a tone of condescending indifference appropriate for use with one who has played dolls with one's little sister, "I shall really be very glad when you make up your mind what you are going to do with Penny. He's just about a total loss down at the office as it is, and he's getting a worse idiot from day to day. And the worst of it is, I imagine you know all the while what you're going to do about it – whether you're going to take him or not."

The girl flushed at that. He was being almost too outrageously rude, even for George. But before she said anything to that effect, she thought of something better.

"I shall never marry any man," she said very intensely, "whose heart is not with the Cause. You know what Cause I mean, George – the Suffrage Cause. When I see thoughtless girls handing over their whole lives to men who..."

It sounded like the beginning of an oration.

"Good Lord!" her victim cried. "Isn't there anything else than that to talk about – *ever*?"

"But just think how lucky you are, George," she said, "that at home they all think exactly as you do!"

He jumped up. Evidently this reminder of the purring acquiescences of Cousin Emelene and Mrs. Brewster-Smith laid no balm upon his harassed spirit.

"You may leave my home alone, if you please."

He was frightfully annoyed, of course, or he wouldn't have said anything as crude as that. In a last attempt to recover his scattered dignity, he caught at his office manner. "By the way," he said, "you forgot to remind me today to write a letter to that Eliot woman about Mrs. Brewster-Smith's cottages."

With that he stalked away to dress. Genevieve and Penny, now shoreward bound, hailed him. But it wasn't quite impossible to pretend he didn't hear, and he did it.

The dinner afterward at the Sea Light Inn was a rather gloomy affair. George's lonely grandeur was only made the worse, it seemed, by Genevieve's belated concern lest he might have taken cold through not having gone and dressed directly he came out of the water. Genevieve then turned very frosty to Penny, having decided suddenly that it was all his fault.

As for Betty, though she was as amiable a little soul as breathed, she didn't see why she should make any particular effort to console Penny, just because his little flirtation with Genevieve had stopped with a bump.

Even the ride home in the moonlight didn't help much. Genevieve sat beside George on the front seat, and between them there stretched a tense, tragic silence. In the back seat with

Penfield Evans, and in the intervals of frustrating his attempts to hold her hand, Betty considered how frightfully silly young married couples could be over microscopic differences.

But Betty was wrong here and the married pair on the front seat were right.

Just reflect for a minute what Genevieve's George was. He was her knight, her Bayard, her thoroughly Tennysonian King Arthur. The basis of her adoration was that he should remain like that. You can see then what a staggering experience it was to have caught herself, even for a minute, in the act of smiling over him as sulky and absurd.

And think of George's Genevieve! A saint enshrined, that his soul could profitably bow down before whenever it had leisure to escape from the activities of a wicked world. Fancy his horror over the mere suspicion that she could be indifferent to his wishes – his comfort – even his health, because of a mere tomboy flirtation with a man who could swim better than he could! Most women were like that, he knew – vain, shallow, inconstant creatures! But was not his pearl an exception? It was horrible to have to doubt it.

By three o'clock the next morning, after many tears and much grave discourse, they succeeded in getting these doubts to sleep – killing them, they'd have said, beyond the possibility of resurrection. It was the others who had made all the trouble. If only they could have the world to themselves – no Cousin Emelene, no Alys Brewster-Smith, no Penfield Evans and Betty Sheridan, with their frivolity and low ideals, to complicate things! An Arcadian Island in some Aeonian Sea.

"Well," he said hopefully, "our home can be like that. It shall be like that, when we get rid of Alys and her horrible little girl, and Cousin Emelene and her unspeakable cat. It shall be our world; and no troubles or cares or worries shall ever get in there!"

She acquiesced in this prophecy, but even as she did so, cuddling her face against his own, a low-down, unworthy spook, whose existence in her he must never suspect, said audibly in her inner ear, "Much he knows about it!" Betty did not forget to remind George of the letter he was to write to Miss Eliot about taking over the agency of Mrs. Brewster-Smith's cottages. In the composition of this letter George washed his hands of responsibility with, you might say, antiseptic care.

He had taken pleasure in recommending Miss Eliot, he explained, and Mrs. Brewster-Smith was acting on his recommendation. Any questions arising out of the management of the property should be taken up directly with her client. Miss Eliot would have no difficulty in understanding that the enormous pressure of work which now beset him precluded him from having anything more to do with the matter.

The letter was typed and inclosed in a big linen envelope, with the mess of papers Alys had dumped upon his desk a few days previously, and it was despatched forthwith by the office boy.

"There," said George on a note of grim satisfaction, "that's done!"

The grimness lasted, but the satisfaction did not. Or only until the return of the office boy, half an hour later, with the identical envelope and a three-line typewritten note from

Miss Eliot. She was sorry to say, she wrote, that she did not consider it advisable to undertake the agency for the property in question. Thanking him, nevertheless, for his courtesy, she was his very truly, E. Eliot.

George summoned Betty by means of the buzzer, and asked her, with icy indignation, what she thought of that. But, as he was visibly bursting with impatience to say what *he* thought of it, she gave him the opportunity.

"I thought you advanced women," he said, "were supposed to stand by each other – stand by all women – try to make things better for them. One for all – all for one. That sort of thing. But it really works the other way. It's just because a woman owns those cottages that Miss Eliot won't have anything to do with them. She knows that women are unreasonable and hard to get on with in business matters, so she passes the buck! Back to a man, if you please, who hasn't any more real responsibility for it than she has."

There was, of course, an obvious retort to this; namely, that business was business, and that a business woman had the same privilege a business man had, of declining a job that looked as if it would entail more bother than it was worth. But Betty couldn't quite bring herself to take this line. Women, if they could ever get the chance (through the vote and in other ways), were going to make the world a better place – run it on a better lot of ideals. It wouldn't do to begin justifying women on the ground that they were only doing what men did. As well abandon the whole crusade right at the beginning.

George saw her looking rather thoughtful, and pressed his advantage. Suppose Betty went and saw Miss Eliot personally,

sometime today, and urged her to reconsider. The business
didn't amount to much, it was true, and it no doubt involved
the adjustment of some troublesome details. But unless Miss
Eliot would undertake it, he wouldn't know just where to turn.
Alys had quarreled with Allen, and Sampson was a skate. And
perhaps a little plain talk to Alys about the condition of the
cottages – "from one of her own sex," George said this darkly
and looked away out of the window at the time – might be
productive of good.

"All right," Betty agreed, "I'll see what I can do. It's kind of
hard to go to a woman you barely know by sight, and talk to her
about her duty, but I guess I'm game. If you can spare me, I'll go
now and get it over with."

There were no frills about Edith Eliot's real estate office,
though the air of it was comfortably busy and prosperous.

The place had once been a store. An architect's presentation
of an apartment building, now rather dusty, occupied the show-
window. There was desk accommodation for two or three of
those bright young men who make a selection of keys and take
people about to look at houses; there was a stenographer's
desk with a stenographer sitting at it; and back of a table in the
corner, in the attitude of one making herself as comfortable
as the heat of the day would permit, while she scowled over a
voluminous typewritten document, was E. Eliot herself. It was
almost superfluous to mention that her name was Edith. She
never signed it, and there was no one, in Whitewater anyway,
who called her by it.

She was a big-boned young woman (that is, if you call the
middle thirties young), with an intelligent, homely face, which

probably got the attraction some people surprisingly found in it from the fact that she thought nothing about its looks one way or the other. It was rather red when Betty came in, and she was making it rapidly redder with the vigorous ministrations of a man's-size handkerchief.

She greeted Betty with a cordial "how-de-doo," motioned her to the other chair at the table (Betty had a fleeting wish that she might have dusted it before she sat down), and asked what she could do for her.

"I'm from Mr. Remington's office," Betty said, "Remington and Evans. He wrote you a note this morning about some cottages that belong to a cousin of his, Mrs. Brewster-Smith."

"I answered that note by his own messenger," said E. Eliot. "He should have got the reply before this." "Oh, he got it," said Betty, "and was rather upset about it. What I've come for, is to urge you to reconsider."

E. Eliot smiled rather grimly at her blotting-pad, looked up at Betty, and allowed her smile to change its quality. What she said was not what she had meant to say before she looked up. E. Eliot was always upbraiding herself for being sentimental about youth and beauty in her own sex. She'd never been beautiful, and she'd never been young – not young like Betty. But the upbraidings never did any good.

She said: "I thought I had considered sufficiently when I answered Mr. Remington's note. But it's possible I hadn't. What is it you think I may have overlooked?"

"Why," said Betty, "George thought the reason you wouldn't take the cottages was because a woman owned them. He used it as a sort of example of how women wouldn't stick together.

He said that you probably knew that women were unreasonable and hard to deal with and didn't want the bother."

It disconcerted Betty a little that E. Eliot interposed no denial at this point, though she'd paused to give her the opportunity.

"You see," she went on a little breathlessly, "I'm for women suffrage and economic independence and all that. I think it's perfectly wonderful that you should be doing what you are – showing that women can be just as successful in business as men can. Of course I know that you've got a perfect *right* to do just what a man would do – refuse to take a piece of business that wasn't worth while. But – but what we hope is, and what we want to show men is, that when women get into politics and business they'll be better and less selfish."

"Which do you mean will be better?" E. Eliot inquired. "The politics and the business, or the women?"

"I mean the politics and the business," Betty told her rather frostily. Was the woman merely making fun of her?

E. Eliot caught the note. "I meant my question seriously," she said. "It has a certain importance. But I didn't mean to interrupt you. Go ahead." "Well," Betty said, "that's about all. George – Mr. Remington – that is – is running for district attorney, and he has come out against suffrage as you know. I thought perhaps this was a chance to convert him a little. It would be a great favor to him, anyway, if you took the cottages; because he doesn't know whom to turn to, if you won't. I didn't come to try to tell you what your duty is, but I thought perhaps you hadn't just looked at it that way."

"All right," said E. Eliot. "Now I'll tell you how I do look at it. In the first place, about doing business for women. It all depends on the woman you're doing business with. If she's had the business training of a man, she's as easy to deal with as a man. If she's never had any business training at all, if business doesn't mean anything to her except some vague hocus-pocus that produces her income, then she's seven kinds of a Tartar.

"She has no more notion about what she has a right to expect from other people, or what they've a right to expect from her, than a white Angora cat. Of course, the majority of women who have property to attend to have had it dumped on their hands in middle life, or after, by the wills of loving husbands. Those women, I'll say frankly, are the devil and all to deal with. But it's their husbands' and fathers' fault, and not their own. Anyhow, that isn't the reason I wouldn't take those cottages.

"It was the cottages themselves, and not the woman who owned them, that decided me. That whole Kentwood district is a disgrace to civilization. The sanitary conditions are filthy; have been for years. The owners have been resisting condemnation proceedings right along, on the ground that the houses brought in so little rental that it would be practical confiscation to compel them to make any improvements. Now, since the war boon struck the mills, and every place with four walls and a roof is full, they're saying they can't afford to make any change because of the frightful loss they'd suffer in potential profits.

"Well, when you agree to act as a person's agent, you've got to act in that person's interest; and when it's a question of the interest of the owners of those Kentwood cottages, whether they're men or women, my idea was that I didn't care for the job."

"I think you're perfectly right about it," Betty said. "I wouldn't have come to urge you to change your mind, if I had understood what the situation was. But," here she held out her hand, "I'm glad I did come, and I wish we might meet again sometime and get acquainted and talk about things."

"No time like the present," said E. Eliot. "Sit down again, if you've got a minute." She added, as Betty dropped back into her chair, "You're Elizabeth Sheridan, aren't you? – Judge Sheridan's daughter? And you're working as a stenographer for Remington and Evans?"

Betty nodded and stammered out the beginning of an apology for not having introduced herself earlier. But the older woman waved this aside.

"What I really want to know," she went on, "if it isn't too outrageous a question, is what on earth you're doing it for – working in that law office, I mean?"

It was a question Betty was well accustomed to answering. But coming from this source, it surprised her into a speechless stare.

"Why," she said at last, "I do it because I believe in economic independence for women. Don't you? But of course you do."

"I don't know," said E. Eliot. "I believe in food and clothes, and money to pay the rent, and the only way I have ever found of having those things was to get out and earn them. But if ever I make money enough to give me an independent income half the size of what yours must be, I'll retire from business in short order."

"Do you know," said Betty, "I don't believe you would. I think you're mistaken. I don't believe a woman like you could live without working."

"I didn't say I'd quit working," said E. Eliot. "I said I'd quit business. That's another thing. There's plenty of real work in the world that won't earn you a living. Lord! Don't I see it going by right here in this office! There are things I just itch to get my hands into, and I have to wait and tell myself 'some day, perhaps!' There's a thing I'd like to do now, and that's to take a hand in this political campaign for district attorney. It would kill my business deader than Pharaoh's aunt, so I've got to let it go. But it would certainly put your friend George Remington up a tall tree."

"Oh, you're a suffragist, then?" Betty exclaimed eagerly. "I was wondering about that. I've never seen you at any of our meetings."

"I'm a suffragist, all right," said E. Eliot, "but as your meetings are mostly held in the afternoons, when I'm pretty busy, I haven't been able to get 'round.

"I'm curious about Remington," she went on. "I've known him a little, for years. When I worked for Allen, I used to see him quite often in the office. And I'd always rather liked him. So that I was surprised, clear down to the ground, when I read that statement of his in the *Sentinel*. I'd never thought he was *that* sort. And from the fact that you work in his office and like him well enough to call him George one might almost suppose he wasn't."

Clearly Betty was puzzled. "Of course," she said, "I think his views about women are obsolete and ridiculous. But I don't see what they've got to do with liking him or not, personally."

E. Eliot's smile became grim again, but she said nothing, so Betty asked a direct question.

"That was what you meant, wasn't it?"

"Yes," the other woman said, "that was what I meant. Why, if you don't mind plain speaking, it's been my observation that the sort of men who think the world is too indecent for decent women to go out into, generally have their own reasons for knowing how indecent it is; and that when they spring a line of talk like that, they're being sickening hypocrites into the bargain."

Betty's face had gone flame color.

"George isn't like that at all," she said. "He's – he's really fine. He's old-fashioned and sentimental about women, but he isn't a hypocrite. He really means those things he says. Why..."

And then Betty went on to tell her new friend about Cousin Emelene and Alys Brewster-Smith, and how George, though he writhed, had stood the gaff.

"A grown-up man," E. Eliot summed up, "who honestly believes that women are made of something fine and fragile, and that they ought to be kept where even the wind can't blow upon them! But good heavens, child, if he really means that, it makes it all the better for what I was thinking of. You don't understand, of course. I hadn't meant to tell you, but I've changed my mind.

"Listen now. That statement in the *Sentinel* has set the town talking, of course, and stirred up a lot of feeling, for and against suffrage. But what it would be worth as an issue to go to the mat with on election day, is exactly nothing at all. You go out and ask a voter to vote against a candidate for district attorney because he's an anti-suffragist, and he'll say, 'What difference does it make? It isn't up to him to give women the vote. It doesn't matter to me what his private opinions are, as long as he makes a good district attorney!' But there is an issue that we *can* go to the mat with, and so far it hasn't been raised at all. There hasn't been a peep." She reached over and laid a hand on Betty's arm.

"Do you know what the fire protection laws for factories are? And do you know that it's against the law for women to work in factories at night? Well, and do you know what the conditions are in every big mill in this town? With this boom in war orders, they've simply taken off the lid. Anything goes. The fire and building ordinances are disregarded, and for six months the mills have been running a night shift as well as a day shift, on Sundays and week-days, and three-quarters of their operatives are women. Those women go to work at seven o'clock at night, and quit at six in the morning; and they have an hour off from twelve to one in the middle of the night.

"Now do you see? It's up to the district attorney to enforce the law. Isn't it fair to ask this defender of the home whether he believes that women should be home at night or not, and if he does, what he's going to do about it? Talk about slogans! The situation bristles with them! We could placard this town with a lot of big black-faced questions that would make it the hottest place for George Remington that he ever found himself in.

"Well, it would be pretty good campaign work if he was the hypocrite I took him to be, from his stuff in the *Sentinel*. But if he's on the level, as you think he is, there's a chance – don't you see there's a chance that he'd come out flat-footed for the enforcement of the law? And if he did!... Child, can you see what would happen if he *did*?"

Betty's eyes were shining like a pair of big sapphires. When she spoke, it was in a whisper like an excited child.

"I can see a little," she said. "I think I can see. But tell me."

"In the first place," said E. Eliot, "see whom he'd have against him. There'd be the best people, to start with. Most of them are stockholders in the mills. Why, you must be, yourself, in the Jaffry-Bradshaw Company! Your father was, anyway."

Betty nodded.

"You want to be sure you know what it means," the older woman went on. "This thing might cut into your dividends, if it went through."

"I hope it will," said Betty fiercely. "I never realized before that my money was earned like that – by women, girls of my age, standing over a machine all night." She shivered. "And there are some of us, I'm sure," she went on, "who would feel the way I do about it."

"Well, – some," E. Eliot admitted. "Not many, though. And then there are the merchants. These are great times for them – town crammed with people, all making money, and buying right and left. And then there's the labor vote itself! A lot of laboring men would be against him. Their women just now are earning as much as they are. There are a lot of these men – whatever they might say – who'd take good care not to vote for a man who would prevent their daughters from bringing in the fifteen, twenty, or twenty-five dollars a week they get for that night work.

"Well, and who would be with him? Why, the women themselves. The one chance on earth he'd have for election would be to have the women organized and working for him, bringing every ounce of influence they had to bear on their men – on all the men they knew.

"Mind you, I don't believe he could win at that. But, win or lose, he'd have done something. He'd have shown the women that they needed the vote, and he'd have found out for himself – he and the other men who believe in fair human treatment for everybody – that they can't secure that treatment without women's votes. That's the real issue. It isn't that women are better than men, or that they could run the world better if they got the chance. It's that men and women have got to work together to do the things that need doing."

"You're perfectly wonderful," said Betty, and sat thereafter, for perhaps a minute and a half, in an entranced silence.

Then, with a shake of the head, a straightening of the spine, and a good, deep, business-like preliminary breath, she turned to her new friend and said, "Well, shall we do it?"

This time it was E. Eliot's turn to gasp.

She hadn't expected to have a course of action put up to her in that instantaneous and almost casual manner. She wasn't young like Betty. She'd been working hard ever since she was seventeen years old. She'd succeeded, in a way, to be sure. But her success had taught her how hard success is to obtain. She saw much farther into the consequences of the proposed campaign than Betty could see. She realized the bitter animosity that it would provoke. She knew it was well within the probabilities that her business would be ruined by it.

She sat there silent for a while, her face getting grimmer and grimmer all the time. But she turned at last and looked into the eager face of the girl beside her, and she smiled, – though even the smile was grim.

"All right," she said, holding out her hand to bind the bargain. "We'll start and we'll stick. And here's hoping! We'd better lunch together, hadn't we?"

Chapter VII

Anne O'Hagan

Mr. Benjamin Doolittle, by profession White-water's leading furniture dealer and funeral director, and by the accident of political fortune the manager of Mr. George Remington's campaign, sat in his candidate's private office, and from time to time restrained himself from hasty speech by the diplomatic and dexterous use of a quid of tobacco.

He found it difficult to preserve his philosophy in the face of George Remington's agitation over the woman's suffrage issue.

"It's the last time," he had frequently informed his political cronies since the opening of the campaign, "that I'll wet-nurse a new-fledged candidate. They've got at least to have their milk teeth through if they want Benjamin Doolittle after this." To George, itchingly aware through all his rasped nerves of Mrs. Herrington's letter in that morning's *Sentinel* asking him to refute, if he could, an abominable half column of statistics in regard to legislation in the Woman Suffrage States, the furniture dealer was drawling pacifically:

"Now, George, you made a mistake in letting the women get your goat. Don't pay no attention to them. Of course their game's fair enough. I will say that you gave them their opening; stood yourself for a target with that statement of yours. Howsomever, you ain't obligated to keep on acting as the nigger head in the shooting gallery.

"Let 'em write; let 'em ask questions in the papers; let 'em heckle you on the stump. All that you've got to say is that you've expressed your personal convictions already, and that you've stood by those convictions in your private life, and that as you ain't up for legislator, the question don't really concern your candidacy. And that, as you're running for district attorney, you will, with their kind permission, proceed to the subjects that do concern you there – the condition of the court calendar of Whitewater County, the prosecution of the racetrack gamblers out at Erie Oval, and so forth, and so forth.

"You laid yourself open, George, but you ain't obligated in law or equity to keep on presenting yourself bare chest for their outrageous slings and arrows."

"Of course, what you say about their total irrelevancy is quite true," said George, making the concession so that it had all the belligerency of a challenge. "But of course I would never have consented to run for office at the price of muzzling my convictions."

Mr. Doolittle wearily agreed that that was more than could be expected from any candidate of the high moral worth of George Remington. Then he went over a list of places throughout the county where George was to speak during the next week, and intimated dolefully that the committee could use a little more money, if it had it.

He expressed it thus: "A few more contributions wouldn't put any strain to speak of on our pants' pockets. Anything more to be got out of Old Martin Jaffry? Don't he realize that blood's thicker than water?"

"I'll speak to him," growled George.

He hated Mr. Benjamin Doolittle's colloquialisms, though once he had declared them amusing, racy, of the soil, and had rebuked Genevieve's fastidious criticisms of them on an occasion when she had interpreted her rôle of helpmeet to include that of hostess to Mr. and Mrs. Doolittle – oh, not in her own home, of course! – at luncheon, at the Country Club!

"Well, I guess that's about all for today."

Mr. Doolittle brought the conference to a close, hoisting himself by links from his chair.

"It takes $3000 every time you circularize the constituency, you know—"

He lounged toward the window and looked out again upon the pleasant, mellow scene around Fountain Square. And with the look his affectation of bucolic calm dropped from him. He turned abruptly.

"What's that going on at McMonigal's corner?" he demanded sharply. "I don't know, I am sure," said George, with indifference, still bent upon teaching his manager that he was a free and independent citizen, in leading strings to no man. "It's been vacant since the fire in March, when Petrosini's fish market and Miss Letterblair's hat st—"

He had reached the window himself by this time, and the sentence was destined to remain forever unfinished.

From the low, old-fashioned brick building on the northeast corner of Fountain Square, whose boarded eyes had stared blindly across toward the glittering orbs of its towering neighbor, the Jaffry Building, for six months, a series of great placards flared.

Planks had been removed from the windows, plate glass restored, and behind it he read in damnable irritation:

"SOME QUESTIONS FOR CANDIDATE REMINGTON."

A foot high, an inch broad, black as Erebus, the letters shouted at him against an orange background. Every window of the second story contained a placard. On the first story, in the show window where Petrosini had been wont to ravish epicurean eyes by shad and red snapper, perch and trout, cunningly imbedded in ice blocks upon a marble slab – in that window, framed now in the hated orange and black, stood a woman.

She was turning backward, for the benefit of onlookers who pressed close to the glass, the leaves of a mammoth pad resting upon an easel.

From their point of vantage in the second story of the Jaffry Building, the candidate and his manager could see that each sheet bore that horrid headline:

"QUESTIONS FOR CANDIDATE REMINGTON."

The whole population of White water, it seemed to George, was crowded about that corner.

"I'll be back in a minute," said Benjie Doolittle, disappearing through the private office door with the black tails of his coat achieving a true horizontal behind him. As statesman and as undertaker, Mr. Doolittle never swerved from the garment which keeps green the memory of the late Prince Consort.

As the door opened, the much-tried George Remington had a glimpse of that pleasing industrial unit, Betty Sheridan, searching through the file for the copy of the letter to the Cummunipaw Steel Works, which he had recently demanded to see. He pressed the buzzer imperiously, and Betty responded with duteous haste. He pointed through the window to the crowd in front of McMonigal's block.

"Perhaps," he said, with what seemed to him Spartan self-restraint, "*you* can explain the meaning of that scene."

Betty looked out with an air of intelligent interest.

"Oh yes!" she said vivaciously. "I think I can. It's a Voiceless Speech."

"A voice l—" George's own face was a voiceless speech as he repeated two syllables of his stenographer's explanation.

"Yes. Don't you know about voiceless speeches? It's antiquated to try to run any sort of a campaign without them nowadays."

"Perhaps you also know who that – female—" again George's power of utterance failed him. Betty came closer to the window and peered out.

"It's Frances Herrington who is turning the leaves now," she said amiably. "I know her by that ducky toque."

"Frances Herrington! What Harvey Herrington is thinking of to allow—" George's emotion constrained him to broken utterance. "And we're dining there tonight! She has no sense of the decencies – the – the – the hospitality of existence. We won't go – I'll telephone Genevieve—"

"Fie, fie Georgie!" observed Betty. "Why be personal over a mere detail of a political campaign?"

But before George could tell her why his indignation against his prospective hostess was impersonal and unemotional, the long figure of Mr. Doolittle again projected itself upon the scene.

Betty effaced herself, gliding from the inner office, and George turned a look of inquiry upon his manager.

"Well?" the monosyllable had all the force of profanity.

"Well, the women, durn them, have brought suffrage into your campaign."

"How?"

"How? They've got a list of every blamed law on the statute books relating to women and children, and they're asking on that sheet of leaves over there, if you mean to proceed against all who are breaking those laws here in Whitewater County. And right opposite your own office! It's – it's damn smart. You ought to have got that Herrington woman on your committee."

"It's indelicate, unwomanly, indecent. It shows into what unsexed degradation politics will drag woman. But I'm relieved that that's all they're asking. Of course, I shall enforce the law for the protection of every class in our community with all the power of the—"

"Oh, shucks! There's nobody here but me – you needn't unfurl Old Glory," counseled Mr. Doolittle, a trifle impatiently. "They're asking real questions, not blowing off hot-air. Oh, I say, who owns McMonigal's block since the old man died? We'll have the owner stop this circus. That's the first thing to do."

"I'll telephone Allen. He'll know."

Allen's office was very obliging and would report on the ownership on McMonigal's block in ten minutes.

Mr. Doolittle employed the interval in repeating to George some of the "Questions for Candidate Remington," illegible from George's desk.

"You believe that 'WOMAN'S PLACE IS IN THE HOME.' Will you enforce the law against woman's night work in the factories? Over nine hundred women of Whitewater County are doing night work in the munition plants of Airport, Whitewater and Ondegonk. What do you mean to do about it?"

"You 'DESIRE TO CONSERVE THE THREATENED FLOWER OF WOMANHOOD.'"

A critical listener would have caught a note of ribald scorn in Mr. Doolittle's drawl, as he quoted from his candidate's statement, via the voiceless speech placards.

"To conserve the threatened flower of womanhood, the grape canneries of Omega and Onicrom Townships are employing children of five and six years in defiance of the Child Labor Law of this State. Are you going to proceed against them?"

"'WOMAN IS MAN'S RAREST HERITAGE.' Do you think man ought to burn her alive? Remember the Livingston Loomis-Ladd collar factory fire – fourteen women killed, forty-eight maimed. In how many of the factories in Whitewater, in which women work, are the fire laws obeyed? Do you mean to enforce them?"

The telephone interrupted Mr. Doolittle's hateful litany.

Alien's bright young man begged to report that McMonigal's block was held in fee simple by the widow of the late Michael McMonigal.

Mr. Doolittle juggled the leaves of the telephone directory with the dazzling swiftness of a Japanese ball thrower, and in a few seconds he was speaking to the relict of the late Michael.

George watched him with fevered eyes, listened with fevered ears. The conversation, it was easy to gather, did not proceed as Mr. Doolittle wished.

"Oh! in entire charge – E. Eliot. Oh! In sympathy yourself. Oh, come now, Mrs. McMonigal—"

But Mrs. McMonigal did not come now. The campaign manager frowned as he replaced the receiver.

"Widow owns the place. That Eliot woman is the agent. The suffrage gang has the owner's permission to use the building from now on to election. She says she's in sympathy. Well, we'll have to think of something—"

"It's easy enough," declared George. "I'll simply have a set of posters printed answering their questions. And we'll engage sandwich men to carry them in front of McMonigal's windows. Certainly I mean to enforce the law. I'll give the order to the *Sentinel* press now for the answers – definite, dignified answers." "See here, George." Mr. Doolittle interrupted him with unusual weightiness of manner. "It's too far along in the campaign for you to go flying off on your own. You've got to consult your managers. This is your first campaign; it's my thirty-first. You've got to take advice—"

"I will not be muzzled."

"Shucks! Who wants to muzzle, anybody! But you can't say everything that's inside of you, can you? There's got to be some choosing. We've got to help you choose.

"The silly questions the women are displaying over there – you can't answer 'em in a word or in two words. This city is having a boom; every valve factory in the valley, every needle and pin factory, is makin' munitions today – valves and needles and pins all gone by the board for the time being. Money's never been so plenty in Whitewater County and this city is feelin' the benefits of it. People are buying things – clothes, flour, furniture, victrolas, automobiles, rum.

"There ain't a merchant of any description in this county but his business is booming on account of the work in the factories. You can't antagonize the whole population of the place. Why, I dare say, some of your own money and Mrs. Remington's is earning three times what it was two years ago. The First National Bank has just declared a fifteen per cent. dividend, and Martin Jaffry owns fifty-four per cent. of the stock.

"You don't want to put brakes on prosperity. It ain't decent citizenship to try it. It ain't neighborly. Think of the lean years we've known. You can't do it. This war won't last forever—" Mr. Doolittle's voice was tinged with regret – "and it will be time enough to go in for playing the deuce with business when business gets slack again. That's the time for reforms, George, – when things are dull."

George was silent, the very presentment of a sorely harassed young man. He had not, even in a year when blamelessness rather than experience was his party's supreme need in a candidate, become its banner bearer without possessing certain political apperceptions. He knew, as Benjie Doolittle spoke, that Benjie spoke the truth – White-water city and county would never elect a man who had too convincingly promised to interfere with the prosperity of the city and county.

"Better stick to the gambling out at Erie Oval, George," counseled the campaign manager. "They're mostly New Yorkers that are interested in that, anyway."

"I'll not reply without due consideration and – er – notice," George sullenly acceded to his manager and to necessity. But he hated both Doolittle and necessity at the moment.

That sun-bright vision of himself which so splendidly and sustainingly companioned him, which spoke in his most sonorous periods, which so completely and satisfyingly commanded the reverence of Genevieve – that George Remington of his brave imaginings would not thus have answered Benjamin Doolittle.

Through the silence following the furniture man's departure, Betty, at the typewriter, clicked upon Georgie's ears. An evil impulse assailed him – impolitic, too, as he realized – impolitic but irresistible. It was the easiest way in which candidate Remington, heckled by suffragists, overridden by his campaign committee, mortifyingly tormented by a feeling of inadequacy, could re-establish himself in his own esteem as a man of prompt and righteous decisions.

He might not be able to run his campaign to suit himself, but, by Jove, his office was his own!

He went into Betty's quarters and suggested to her that a due sense of the eternal fitness of things would cause her to offer him her resignation, which his own sense of the eternal fitness of things would lead him at once to accept.

It seemed, he said, highly indecorous of her to remain in the employ of Remington and Evans the while she was busily engaged in trying to thwart the ambitions of the senior partner. He marveled that woman's boasted sensitiveness had not already led her to perceive this for herself.

For a second, Betty seemed startled, even hurt. She colored deeply and her eyes darkened. Then the flush of surprise and the wounded feeling died. She looked at him blankly and asked how soon it would be possible for him to replace her. She would leave as soon as he desired.

In her bearing, so much quieter than usual, in the look in her face, George read a whole volume. He read that up to this time, Betty had regarded her presence in the ranks of his political enemies as she would have regarded being opposed to him in a tennis match. He read that he, with that biting little speech which he already wished unspoken, had given her a sudden, sinister illumination upon the relations of working women to their employers.

He read the question in the back of her mind. Suppose (so it ran in his constructive fancy) that instead of being a prosperous, protected young woman playing the wage-earner more or less as Marie Antoinette had played the milkmaid, she had been Mamie Riley across the hall, whose work was bitter earnest, whose earnings were not pin-money, but bread and meat and brother's schooling and mother's health – would George still have made the stifling of her views the price of her position?

And if George – George, the kind, friendly, clean-minded man would drive that bargain, what bargain might not other men, less gentle, less noble, drive?

All this George's unhappily sensitized conscience read into Betty Sheridan's look, even as the imp who urged him on bade him tell her that she could leave at her own convenience; at once, if she pleased; the supply of stenographers in Whitewater was adequately at demand.

He rather wished that Penny Evans would come in; Penny would doubtless take a high hand with him concerning the episode, and there was nothing which George Remington would have welcomed like an antagonist of his own size and sex.

But Penny did not appear, and the afternoon passed draggingly for the candidate for the district attorneyship. He tried to busy himself with the affairs of his clients, but even when he could keep away from his windows he was aware of the crowds in front of McMonigal's block, of Frances Herrington, her "ducky" toque and her infernal voiceless speech.

And when, for a second, he was able to forget these, he heard from the outer office the unmistakable sounds of a desk being permanently cleared of its present incumbent's belongings.

After a while, Betty bade him a too courteous good-by, still with that abominable new air of gravely readjusting her old impressions of him. And then there was nothing to do but to go home and make ready for dinner at the Herrington's, unless he could induce Genevieve to have an opportune headache.

Of course Betty had been right. Not upon his masculine shoulders should there be laid the absurd burden of political chagrin strong enough to break a social engagement.

Genevieve was in her room. The library was given over to Alys Brewster-Smith, Cousin Emelene Brand, two rusty callers and the tea things. Before the drawing-room fire, Hanna slept in Maltese proprietorship. George longed with passion to kick the cat.

Genevieve, as he saw through the open door, sat by the window. She had, it appeared, but recently come in. She still wore her hat and coat; she had not even drawn off her gloves. And seeing her thus, absorbed in some problem, George's sense of his wrongs grew greater.

He had, he told himself, hurried home out of the jar and fret of a man's day to find balm, to feel the cool fingers of peace pressed upon hot eyelids, to drink strengthening draughts of refreshment from his wife's unquestioning belief, from the completeness of her absorption in him. And here she sat thinking of something else!

Genevieve arose, a little startled as he snapped on the lights and grunted out something which optimism might translate into an affectionate husbandly greeting. She came dutifully forward and raised her face, still exquisite and cool from the outer air, for her lord's home-coming kiss. That resolved itself into a slovenly peck.

"Been out?" asked George unnecessarily. He tried to quell the unreasonable inclination to find her lacking in wifely devotion because she had been out.

"Yes. There was a meeting at the Woman's Forum this afternoon," she answered. She was unpinning her hat before the pier glass, and in it he could see the reflection of her eyes turned upon his image with a questioning look.

"The ladies seem to be having a busy day of it."

He struggled not quite successfully to be facetious over the pretty, negligible activities of his wife's sex. "What mighty theme engaged your attention?"

"That Miss Eliot – the real estate woman, you know—" George stiffened into an attitude of close attention—" spoke about the conditions under which women are working in the mills in this city and in the rest of the county—" Genevieve averted her mirrored eyes from his mirrored face. She moved toward her dressing-table.

"Oh, she did! and is the Woman's Forum going to come to grips with the industrial monster and bring in the millennium by the first of the year?"

But George was painfully aware that light banter which fails to be convincingly light is but a snarl.

Genevieve colored slightly as she studied the condition of a pair of long white gloves which she had taken from a drawer.

"Of course the Woman's Forum is only for discussion," she said mildly. "It doesn't initiate any action." Then she raised her eyes to his face and George felt his universe reel about him.

For his wife's beautiful eyes were turned upon him, not in limpid adoration, not in perfect acceptance of all his views, unheard, unweighed; but with a question in their blue depths.

The horrid clairvoyance which harassment and self-distrust had given him that afternoon enabled him, he thought, to translate that look. The Eliot woman, in her speech before the Woman's Forum, had doubtless placed the responsibility for the continuation of those factory conditions upon the district attorney's office, had doubtless repeated those damn fool, impractical questions which the suffragists were displaying in McMonigal's windows.

And Genevieve was asking them in her mind! Genevieve was questioning him, his motives, his standards, his intentions! Genevieve was not intellectually a charming mechanical doll who would always answer "yes" and "no" as he pressed the strings, and maintain a comfortable vacuity when he was not at hand to perform the kindly act. Genevieve was thinking on her own account. What, he wondered angrily, as he dressed – for he could not bring himself to ask her aid in escaping the Herringtons and, indeed, was suddenly balky at the thought of the intimacies of a domestic evening – *what* was she thinking? She was not such an imbecile as to be unaware how large a share of her comfortable fortune was invested in the local industry. Why, her father had been head of the Livingston Loomis-Ladd Collar Company, when that dreadful fire—! And she certainly knew that his uncle, Martin Jaffry, was the chief stockholder in the Jaffry-Bradshaw Company.

What was the question in Genevieve's eyes? Was she asking if he were the knight of those women who worked and sweated and burned, or of her and the comfortable women of her class, of Alys Brewster-Smith with her little cottages, of Cousin Emelene with her little stocks, of masquerading Betty Sheridan whose sortie of independence was from the safe vantage-grounds of entrenched privilege?

And all that evening as he watched his wife across the crystal and the roses of the Herrington table, trying to interpret the question that had been in her eyes, trying to interpret her careful silence, he realized what every husband sooner or later awakes to realize – that he had married a stranger.

He did not know her. He did not know what ambitions, what aspirations apart from him, ruled the spirit behind that charming surface of flesh.

Of course she was good, of course she was tender, of course she was high-minded! But how wide-enveloping was the cloak of her goodness? How far did her tenderness reach out? Was her high-mindedness of the practical or impractical variety?

From time to time, he caught her eyes in turn upon him, with that curious little look of re-examination in their depths. She could look at him like that! She could look at him as though appraisals were possible from a wife to a husband!

They avoided industrial Whitewater County as a topic when they left the Herrington's. They talked with great animation and interest of the people at the party. Arrived at home, George, pleading press of work, went down into the library while Genevieve went to bed. Carefully they postponed the moment of making articulate all that, remaining unspoken, might be ignored.

It was one o'clock and he had not moved a paper for an hour, when the library door opened.

Genevieve stood there. She had sometimes come before when he had worked at night, to chide him for neglecting sleep, to bring bouillon or chocolate. But tonight she did neither.

She did not come far into the room, but standing near the door and looking at him with a new expression – patient, tender, the everlasting eternal look – she said: "I couldn't sleep, either.

I came down to say something, George. Don't interrupt me—" for he was coming toward her with sounds of affectionate protest at her being out of bed. "Don't speak! I want to say – whatever you do, whatever you decide – now – always – I love you. Even if I don't agree, I love you."

She turned and went swiftly away.

George stood looking at the place where she had stood, – this strange, new Genevieve, who, promising to love, reserved the right to judge.

Chapter VIII

Mary Heaton Vorse

The high moods of night do not always survive the clear, cold light of day. Indeed it requires the contribution of both man and wife to keep a high mood in married life.

Genevieve had gone in to make her profession of faith to her husband in a mood which touched the high altitudes. She had gone without any conscious expectation of anything from him in the way of response. She had vaguely but confidingly expected him to live up to the moment.

She had expected something beautiful, a lovely flower of the spirit – comprehension, generosity. Living up to the demand of the moment was George's forte. Indeed, there were those among his friends who felt that there were moments when George lived up to things too brightly and too beautifully. His Uncle Jaffry, for instance, had his openly skeptical moments. But George even lived up to his uncle's skepticism. He accepted his remarks with charming good humor. It was his pride that he could laugh at himself.

At the moment of Genevieve's touching speech he lived up to exactly nothing. He didn't even smile. He only stared at her – a stare which said:

"Now what the devil do you mean by that?"

Genevieve had a flicker of bitter humor when she compared her moment of sentiment to a toy balloon pulled down from the blue by an unsympathetic hand.

The next morning, while George was still shaving, the telephone rang. It was Betty.

"Can you have lunch with me at Thorne's, where we can talk?" she asked Genevieve. "And give me a little time tomorrow afternoon?"

"Why," Geneviève responded, "I thought you were a working girl."

There was a perceptible pause before Betty replied.

"Hasn't George told you?" "Told what?" Genevieve inquired. "George hasn't told me anything."

"I've left the office."

"Left! For heaven's sake, why?"

Betty's mind worked swiftly.

"Better treat it as a joke," was her decision. There was no pause before she answered.

"Oh, trouble with the boss."

"You'll get over it. You're always having trouble with Penny."

"Oh," said Betty, "it's not with Penny this time."

"Not with George?"

"Yes, with George," Betty answered. "Did you think one couldn't quarrel with the noblest of his sex? Well, one can."

"Oh, Betty, I'm sorry." Genevieve's tone was slightly reproachful.

"Well, I'm not," said Betty. "I like my present job better. It was a good thing he fired me."

"*Fired* you! George fired *you*?"

"Sure thing," responded Betty blithely. "I can't stand here talking all day. What I want to know is, can I see you at lunch?"

"Yes – why, yes, of course," said Genevieve, dazedly. Then she hung up the receiver and stared into space.

George, beautifully dressed, tall and handsome, now emerged from his room. For once his adoring wife failed to notice that in appearance he rivaled the sun god. She had one thing she wanted to know, and she wanted to know it badly. It was,

"Why did you fire Betty Sheridan?"

She asked this in the insulting "point of the bayonet" tone which angry equals use to one another the world over.

Either question or tone would have been enough to have put George's already sensitive nerves on edge. Both together were unbearable. It was, when you came down to it, the most awkward question in the world.

Why, indeed, had he fired Betty Sheridan? He hadn't really given himself an account of the inward reasons yet. The episode had been too disturbing; and it was George's characteristic to put off looking on unpleasant facts as long as possible. Had he been really hard up, which he never had been, he would undoubtedly have put away, unopened, the bills he couldn't pay. Life was already presenting him with the bill of yesterday's ill humor, and he was not yet ready to add up the amount. He hid himself now behind the austerity of the offended husband.

"My dear," he inquired in his turn, "don't you think that you had best leave the details of my office to me?"

He knew how lame this was, and how inadequate, before Genevieve replied.

"Betty Sheridan is not a detail of your office. She's one of my best friends, and I want to know why you fired her. I dare say she was exasperating; but I can't see any reason why you should have done it. You should have let her leave."

It was Betty, with that lamentable lack of delicacy which George had pointed out to her, who had not been ready to leave.

"You will have to let me be the judge of what I should or should not have done," said George. This piece of advice Genevieve ignored.

"Why did you send her away?" she demanded.

"I sent her away, if you want to know, for her insolence and her damned bad taste. If you think – working in my office as she was – it's decent or proper on her part to be active in a campaign that is against me—"

"You mean because she's a suffragist? You sent her away for *that*! Why, really, that's *tyranny*! It's like my sending away some one working for me for her beliefs—"

They stood staring at each other, not questioningly as they had yesterday, but as enemies, – the greater enemies that they so loved each other.

Because of that each word of unkindness was a doubled-edged sword. They quarreled. It was the first time that they had seen each other without illusion. They had been to each other the ideal, the lover, husband, wife.

Now, in the dismay of his amazement in finding himself quarreling with the perfect wife, a vagrant memory came to George that he had heard that Genevieve had a hot temper.

She certainly had. He didn't notice how handsome she looked kindled with anger. He only knew that the rose garden in which they lived was being destroyed by their angry hands; that the very foundation of the life they had been leading was being undermined.

The time of mirage and glamour was over. He had ceased being a hero and an ideal, and why? Because, forgetting his past life, his record, his achievement, Genevieve obstinately insisted on identifying him with one single mistake. He was willing to concede it was a mistake. She had not only identified him with it, but she had called him a number of wounding things.

"Tyrant" was the least of them, and, worse than that, she had, in a very fury of temper, told him that he "needn't take that pompous" – yes, "pompous" had been her unpleasant word – "tone" with her, when he had inquired, more in sorrow than in anger, if this were really his Genevieve speaking.

There was a pause in their hostilities. They looked at each other aghast. Aghast, they had perceived the same awful truth. Each saw that love in the other's heart was dead, and that things never could be the same again. So they stood looking down this dark gulf, and the light of anger died.

In a toneless voice: "We mustn't let Cousin Emelene and Alys hear us quarreling," said George. And Genevieve answered, "They've gone down to breakfast."

The two ladies were seated at table.

"We heard you two love birds cooing and billing, and thought we might as well begin," said Alys Brewster-Smith. "Regularity is of the highest importance in bringing up a child."

Cousin Emelene was reading the *Sentinel*. George's quick eye glanced at the headlines:

Candidate Remington Heckled by Suffragists. Ask Him Leading Questions.

"Why, dear me," she remarked, her kind eyes on George, "it's perfectly awful, isn't it, that they break the laws that way just for a little more money. But I don't see why they want to annoy dear George. They ought to be glad they are going to get a district attorney who'll put all those things straight. I think it's very silly of them to ask him, don't you, Genevieve?"

"Let me see," said Genevieve, taking the paper.

"All he's got to do, anyway, is to answer," pursued Cousin Emelene.

"Yes, that's all," replied Genevieve, her melancholy gaze on George. Yesterday she would have had Emelene's childlike faith. But this stranger, who, for a trivial and tyrannical reason, had sent away Betty – how would *he* act?

"They showed these right opposite your windows?" she questioned.

"Yes," he returned. "Our friend Mrs. Herrington did it herself. It was the first course of our dinner. If you think that's good taste—"

"I would expect it of her," said Alys Brewster-Smith.

"But it makes it so easy for George," Emelene repeated. "They'll know now what sort of a man he is. Little children at work, just to make a little more money – it's awful!"

"Talking about money, George," said Alys, "have you seen to my houses yet?" "Not yet," replied the harassed George. "You'll have to excuse my going into the reasons now. I'm late as it is."

His voice had not the calm he would have wished for. As he took his departure, he heard Alys saying,

"If you'll let me, my dear, I'd adore helping you about the housekeeping. I don't want to stay here and be a burden. If you'll just turn it over to me, I could cut your housekeeping expenses in half."

"Damn the women," was the unchivalrous thought that rose to George's lips.

One would have supposed that trouble had followed closely enough on George Remington's trail, but now he found it awaiting him in his office.

Usually, Penny was the late one. It was this light-hearted young man's custom to blow in with so engaging an expression and so cheerful a manner that any comment on his unpunctuality was impossible. Today, instead of a gay-hearted young man, he looked more like a sentencing judge.

What he wanted to know was,

"What have you done to Betty Sheridan? Do you mean to say that you had the nerve to send her away, send her out of my office without consulting me – and for a reason like that? How did you think I was going to feel about it?"

"I didn't think about you," said George.

"You bet you didn't. You thought about number one and your precious vanity. Why, if one were to separate you from your vanity, one couldn't see you when you were going down the street. Go on, make a frock coat gesture! Play the brilliant but outraged young district attorney. Do you know what it was to do a thing of that kind – to fire a girl because she didn't agree with you?"

"It wasn't because she didn't agree with me," George interrupted, with heat.

"It was the act of a cad," Penny finished. "Look here, young man, I'm going to tell you a few plain truths about yourself. You're not the sort of person that you think you are. You've deceived yourself the way other people are deceived about you – by your exterior. But inside of that good-looking carcass of yours there's a brain composed of cheese. You weren't only a cad to do it – you were a fool!" "You can't use that tone to me!" cried George.

"Oh, can't I just? By Jove, it's things like that that make one wake up. Now I know why women have a passion for suffrage. I never knew before," Penny went on, with more passion than logic. "You had a nerve to make that statement of yours. You're a fine example of chivalry. You let loose a few things when you wrote that fool statement, but you did a worse trick when you fired Betty Sheridan. God, you're a pinhead – from the point of view of mere tactics. Sometimes I wonder whether you've *any* brain."

George had turned white with anger.

"That'll just about do," he remarked.

"Oh, no, it won't," said Penny. "It won't do at all. I'm not going to remain in a firm where things like this can happen. I wouldn't risk my reputation and my future. You're going to do the decent thing. You're going to Betty Sheridan and tell her what you think of yourself. She won't come back, I suppose, but you might ask her to do that, too. And now I'm going out, to give you time to think this over. And tonight you can tell me what you've decided. And then I'll tell you whether I'm going to dissolve our partnership. Your temper's too bad to decide now. Maybe when you've done that she won't treat me like an unsavory stranger."

He left, and George sat down to gloomy reflection.

To do him justice, the idea of apologizing to Betty had already occurred to him. If he put off the day of reckoning, when the time came he would pay handsomely. He realized that there was no use in wasting energy and being angry with Penny. He looked over the happenings of the last few hours and the part he had played in them, and what he saw failed to please him. He saw himself being advised by Doolittle to concentrate on the Erie Oval. He heard him urging him not to be what Doolittle called unneighborly. The confiding words of Cousin Emelene rang in his ears.

He saw himself, in a fit of ill-temper, discharging Betty. He saw Genevieve, lovely and scornful, urging him to be less pompous. All this, he had to admit, he had brought on himself. Why should he have been so angry at these questions? Again Emelene's remark echoed in his ear. He had only to answer them – and he was going to concentrate on the Erie Oval!

There came a knock on the door, and a breezy young woman demanded,

"D'you want a stenographer?"

George wanted a stenographer, and wanted one badly. He put from him the whole vexed question in the press of work, and by lunch time he made up his mind to have it out with Betty. There was no use putting it off, and he knew that he could have no peace with himself until he did. He felt very tired – as though he had been doing actual physical work. He thought of yesterday as a land of lost content. But he couldn't find Betty.

He bent his steps toward home, and as he did so affection for Genevieve flooded his heart. He so wanted yesterday back – things as they had been. He so wanted her love and her admiration. He wanted to put his tired head on her shoulder. He couldn't bear, not for another moment, to be at odds with her.

He wondered what she had been doing, and how she had spent the morning. He imagined her crying her heart out. He leaped up the steps and ran up to his room. In it was Alys Brewster-Smith. She started slightly.

"I was just looking for some cold cream," she explained.

"Where's Genevieve?" George asked.

"Oh, she's out," Alys replied casually. "She left a note for you."

The note was a polite and noncommittal line informing George that Genevieve would not be back for lunch. He felt as though a lump of ice replaced his heart. His disappointment was the desperate disappointment of a small boy.

He went back to the gloomy office and worked through the interminable day. Late in the afternoon Mr. Doolittle lounged heavily in.

"Have some gum, George?" he inquired, inserting a large piece in his own mouth.

He chewed rhythmically for a space. George waited. He knew that chewing gum was not the ultimate object of Mr. Doolittle's visit.

"Don't women beat the Dutch?" he inquired at last. "Yes sir, mister; they do!"

"What's up now?" George inquired. "The suffragists again?"

"Nope; not on the face of it they ain't. It's the Woman's Forum that's doin' this. They've got a sweet little idea. 'Seein' Whitewater Sweat' they call it.

"They're goin' around in bunches of twos, or mebbe blocks o' five, seein' all the sights; an' you know women ain't reasonable, an' you can't reason with them. They're goin' to find a pile o' things they won't like in this little burg o' ours, all right, all right. An' they'll want to have things changed right off. I want to see things changed m'self. I'd like to, but them things take time, an' that's what women won't understand.

"Jimminee, I've heard of towns all messed up and candidates ruined just because the women got wrought up over tenement-house an' fire laws an' truck like that. Yes sir, they're out seein' Whitewater this minut, or will be if you can't divert their minds. Call 'em off, George, if you can. Get 'em fussy about sumpen else."

"Why, what have I to do with it?" George inquired.

"Well, I didn't know but what you might have sumpen," said Mr. Doolittle mildly. "It's that young lady that works here, Miss Sheridan, an' your wife what's organizin' it. Planning it all out to Thorne's at lunch they was, an' Heally was sittin' at the next table and beats it to me. You can see for yerself what a hell of a mess they'll make!"

Chapter IX
Alice Duer Miller

It was a relief to both men when at this point the door of the office opened and Martin Jaffry entered.

Not since the unfortunate anti-suffrage statement of George's had Uncle Martin dropped in like this. George, looking at him with that first swift glance that often predetermines a whole interview, made up his mind that bygones were to be bygones. He greeted his uncle with the warmest cordiality.

"Well, George," said Uncle Martin, "how are things going?"

"I'm going to be elected, if that's what you mean," answered George.

Doolittle gave a snort. "Indeed, are ye?" said he. "As a friend and well-wisher, I'm sure I'm delighted to hear the news." "Do I understand that you have your doubts, Mr. Doolittle?" Jaffry inquired mildly.

"There's two things we need and need badly, Mr. Jaffry," said Doolittle. "One's money—"

"A small campaign contribution would not be rejected?"

"But there's something we need more than money – and God knows I never expected to say them words – and that's common sense."

"Good," said Uncle Martin, "I have plenty of that, too!"

"Then for the love of Mike pass some of it on to this precious nephew of yours."

"What seems to be the matter?"

"It's them women," said Doolittle.

Uncle Martin turned inquiringly to George: "The tender flowers?" he suggested.

"Look here, Uncle Martin," said George, who had had a good deal of this sort of thing to bear, "I don't understand you. Do you believe in woman suffrage?"

Uncle Martin contemplated a new crumpling of his long-suffering cap before he answered. "Yes and no, George. I believe in it in the same way that I believe in old age and death. I can't avoid them by denying their existence."

"But you fight against them, and put them off as long as you can."

"But I yield a little to them, too, George. What is it? Has Genevieve become a convert to suffrage?"

"Has Genevieve – has my wife—"

Then George remembered that his uncle was an older man and that chivalry is not limited to the treatment of the weaker sex.

"No," he said with a calm hardly less magnificent than the tempest would have been, "no, Uncle Martin, Genevieve has not become a suffragist."

"Well," said Doolittle rising, as if such things were hardly worth his valuable time, "I fail to see the difference between a suffragette an' a woman who goes pokin' her nose into what—"

"You're speaking of my wife, Mr. Doolittle," said George, with a significant lighting of the eye.

"Speakin' in general," said Doolittle.

Uncle Martin was interested. "Has Genevieve been – well, we won't say poking the nose – but taking a responsible civic interest where it would be better if she didn't?"

"It seems," answered George, casting an angry glance at his campaign manager, "that Mr. Doolittle has heard from a friend of his who overheard a conversation between Betty Sheridan and my wife at luncheon. From this he inferred that the two were planning an investigation of some of the city's problems."

Uncle Martin looked relieved.

"Oh, your wife and your stenographer. That can be stopped, I suppose, without undue exertion."

"Betty is no longer my stenographer."

"Left, has she?" said Jaffry. "I had an idea she would not stay with you long."

This intimation was not agreeable to George. He would have liked to explain that Miss Sheridan's departure had been dictated by the will of the head of the firm; in fact he opened his mouth to do so. But the remembrance that this would entail a long and wearisome exposition of his reasons caused him to remain silent, and his uncle went on: "Well, anyhow, you can get Genevieve to drop it."

If Doolittle had not been there, George would have been glad to discuss with his uncle, who had, after all, a sort of worldly shrewdness, how far a man is justified in controlling his wife's opinions. But before an audience now a trifle unsympathetic, he could not resist the temptation of making the gesture of a man magnificently master in his own house.

He smiled quite grandly. "I think I can promise that," he said.

Doolittle got up slowly, bringing his jaws together in a relentless bite on the unresisting gum.

"Well," he said, "that's all there is to it." And he added significantly as he reached the door, "If you kin *do* it!"

When the campaign manager had gone, Uncle Martin asked very, very gently: "You don't feel any doubt of being able to do it, do you, George?"

"About my ability to control – I mean influence, my wife? I feel no doubt at all."

"And Penfield, I suppose, can tackle Betty? You won't mind my saying that of the two I think your partner has the harder job."

A slight cloud appeared upon the brow of the candidate.

"I don't feel inclined to ask any favor of Penny just at present," he said haughtily. "Has it ever struck you, Uncle Martin, that Penny has an unduly emotional, an almost feminine type of mind?"

"No," said the other, "it hasn't, but that is perhaps because I have never been sure just what the feminine type of mind is."

"You know what I mean," answered George, trying to conceal his annoyance at this sort of petty quibbling. "I mean he is too personal, over-excitable, irrational and very hard to deal with."

"Dear me," said Jaffry. "Is Geneviève like that?"

"Geneviève," replied her husband loyally, "is much better poised than most women, but – yes, – even she – all women are more or less like that."

"All women and Penny. Well, George, you have my sympathy. An excitable partner, an irrational stenographer, and a wife that's very hard to deal with!"

"I never said Geneviève was hard to deal with," George almost shouted.

"My mistake – thought you did," answered his uncle, now moving rapidly away. "Let me know the result of the interview, and we'll talk over ways and means." And he shut the door briskly behind him.

George walked to the window, with his hands in his pockets. He always liked to look out while he turned over grave questions in his mind; but this comfort was now denied to him, for he could not help being distracted by the voiceless speech still relentlessly turning its pages in the opposite window.

The heading now was:

DOES THE FIFTY-FOUR-HOUR-A-WEEK LAW APPLY TO FLOWERS?

He flung himself down on his chair with an exclamation. He knew he had to think carefully about something which he had never considered before, and that was his wife's character.

Of course he liked to think about Geneviève; of her beauty, her abilities, her charms; and particularly he liked to think about her love for him.

A week ago he would have met the present situation very simply. He would have put his arm about her and said: "My darling, I think I'd a little rather you dropped this sort of thing for the present." And that would have been enough.

But he knew it would not be enough now. He would have to have a reason, a case.

"Heavens," he thought, "imagine having to talk to one's wife as if she were the lawyer for the other side."

He did not notice that he was reproaching Geneviève for being too impersonal, too unemotional and not irrational enough.

When he went home at five, he had thought it out. He put his head into the sitting-room, where Alys was ensconced behind the tea-kettle.

"Come in, George dear," she called graciously, "and let me give you a really good cup of tea. It's some I've just ordered for you, and I think you'll find it an improvement on what you've been accustomed to." George shut the door again, pretending he had not heard; but he had had time enough to note that dear little Eleanor was building houses out of his most treasured books.

The memory of his quarrel with his wife had been partly obliterated by memories of so many other quarrels during the day that it was only when he was actually standing in her room that he remembered how very bitter their parting had been.

He stood looking at her doubtfully, and it was she who came forward and put her arms about him. They clung to each other like two children who have been frightened by a nightmare.

"We mustn't quarrel again, George," she said. "I've had a real, true, old-fashioned pain in my heart all day. But I think

I understand better now than I did. I lunched with Betty and she made me see."

"What did Betty make you see?" asked George nervously, for he had not perfect confidence in Miss Sheridan's visions.

"That it was all a question of efficiency. She said that in business a man's stenographer is just an instrument to make his work easier, and if for any reason at all that instrument does not suit him he is justified in getting rid of it, and in finding one that does."

"Betty is very generous," he said coldly. He wanted to hear his wife say that she had not thought him pompous; it was very hard to be thankful for a mere ethical rehabilitation.

Part of his thought-out plan was that Geneviève must herself tell him of the Woman's Forum's investigation; it would not do for him to let her know he had heard of it through a political eavesdropper. So after a moment he added casually:

"And what else did Betty have to say?"

"Nothing much."

His heart sank. Was Geneviève becoming uncandid?

"Nothing else," he said. "Just to justify me in your eyes?"

She hesitated, "No, that was not quite all, but it is too early to talk about it yet."

"Anything that interests you, my dear, I should like to hear about from the beginning." Perhaps Geneviève was not so unemotional after all, for at this expression of his affection, her eyes filled with tears.

"I long to tell you," she said. "I only hesitated on your account, but of course I want all your help and advice. It's this: There seems to be no doubt that the conditions under which

women are working in our factories are hideous – dangerous
– the law is broken with perfect impunity. I know you can't act
on rumors and hearsay. Even the inspectors don't give out the
truth. And so we are going to persuade the Woman's Forum to
abandon its old policy of mere discussion.

"We – Betty and I – are going to get the members for once
to act – to make an investigation; so that the instant you come
into the office you will have complete information at your
disposal – facts, and facts and facts on which you can act."

She paused and looked eagerly at her husband, who
remained silent. Seeing this she went on:

"I know what you're thinking. I thought of it myself. Am I
justified in using my position in the Woman's Forum to further
your political career? Well, my answer is, it isn't your political
career, only; it's truth and justice that will be furthered."

Here in the home there was no voiceless speech to make
the view intolerable, and George moved away from his wife
and walked to the window. He looked out on his own peaceful
trees and lawn, and on Hanna, like a tiger in the jungle,
stalking a competent little sparrow.

A temptation was assailing George. Suppose he did put his
opposition to this investigation on a high and mighty ground?
Suppose he announced a moral scruple? But no, he cast Satan
behind him.

"Geneviève," he said, turning sharply toward her, "this
question puts our whole attitude to a test. If you and I are two
separate individuals, with different responsibilities, different
interests, different opinions, then we ought to be consistent;
that ought to mean economic independence of each other,

and equal suffrage; it means that husband and wife may become business competitors and political opponents.

"But if, as you know I believe, a man and woman who love each other are one, are a unit as far as society is concerned, why then our interests are identical, and it is simply a question of which of us two is better able to deal with any particular situation."

"But that is what I believe, too, George."

"I hoped it was, dear; I know it used to be. Then you must let me act for you in this matter."

"Yes, in the end; but an investigation—"

"My darling, politics is not an ideal; it is a practical human institution. Just at present, from the political point of view, such an investigation would do me incalculable harm."

"George!"

He nodded. "It would probably lose me the election."

"But why?"

"Geneviève, am I your political representative or not?"

"You are," she smiled at him, "and my dear love as well; but may I not even know why?"

"If you dismissed the cook, and I summoned you before me and bade you give me your reasons for such an action, would you not feel in your heart that I was disputing your judgment?"

She looked at him honestly. "Yes, I should."

"And I would not do such a discourteous thing to you. In the home you are absolute. Whatever you do, whatever you decide, is right. I would not dream of questioning. Will you not give me the same confidence in my special department?"

There was a short pause; then Geneviève held out her hand.

"Yes, George," she said, "I will, but on one condition—"

"*I* did not make conditions, Geneviève."

"You do not have to, my dear. You know that I am really your representative in the house; that I am really always thinking of your wishes. You must do the same as my political representative. I mean, if I am not to do this work myself, you must do it for me."

"Even if I consider it unwise?"

"Unwise to protect women and children?"

"Geneviève," he said seriously, as one who confides something not always confided to women, "enforcing law sometimes does harm."

"But an investigation—"

"That's where you are ignorant, my dear. If an investigation is made, especially if the women mix themselves up in it, then we shall have no choice but enforcement."

She had sunk down on her sofa, but now she sprang up. "And you don't mean to enforce the law in respect of women? Is that why you don't want the investigation?"

"Not at all. You are most unjust. You are most illogical, Geneviève. All I am asking is that the whole question should not be taken up at this moment – just before election."

"But this is the only moment when we can find out whether or not you are a candidate who will do what we want."

"*We*, Geneviève! Who do you mean by 'we'?"

She stared for a second at him, her eyes growing large and dark with astonishment.

"Oh, George," she gasped finally, "I think I meant women when I said 'we.' George, I'm afraid I'm a *suffragist*. And oh," she added, with a sort of wail, "I don't want to be, I don't want to be!"

"Damn Betty Sheridan," exclaimed George. "This is all her doing."

His wife shook her head. "No," she said, "it wasn't Betty who made me see."

"Who was it?"

"It was you, George."

"I don't understand you."

"You made me see why women want to vote for themselves. How can you represent me, when we disagree fundamentally?"

"How can we disagree fundamentally when we love each other?"

"You mean that because we love each other, I must think as you do?"

"What else could I mean, darling?"

"You might have meant that you would think as I do."

George glanced at her in deep offense.

"We have indeed drifted far apart," he said.

At this moment there was a knock at the door, and the news was conveyed to George that Mr. Evans was downstairs asking to see him.

"Oh dear," said Geneviève, "it seems as if we never could get a moment by ourselves nowadays. What does Penny want?"

"He wants to tell me whether he intends to dissolve partnership or not."

Any fear that his wife had disassociated herself from his interests should have been dispelled by the tone in which she exclaimed: "Dissolve partnership! Penny? Well, I never in my life! Where would Penny be without you, I should like to know! He must be crazy."

These words made George feel happier than anything that had happened to him throughout this day. His self-esteem began to revive.

"I think Penny has been a little hasty," he said, judicially but not unkindly. "He lost all self-control when he heard I had let Betty go."

"Isn't that like a man," said Geneviève, "to throw away his whole future just because he loses his temper?"

George did not directly answer this question, and his wife went on. "However, it will be all right. He has seen Betty this afternoon, and she won't let him do anything foolish."

George glanced at her. "You mean that Betty will prevent his leaving the firm?"

"Of course she will."

George walked to the door.

"I seem to owe a good deal to my former stenographer," he said, "my wife, my partner; next, perhaps it will be my election."

Chapter X
Ethel Watts Mumford

Penny, pacing the drawing-room with pantheresque strides, came to a tense halt as Remington entered.

"Well?" he said, his eyes hard, his unwelcoming hands thrust deep into his pockets.

That identical "well" with its uptilt of question had been on George's tongue. It was a monosyllable that demanded an answer. Penny had got ahead of him, forced him, as it were, into the witness chair, and he resented it.

"Seems to me," he began hotly, "that you were the one who was going to make the statements—' whether or no,' I believe, we were to continue in partnership."

"Perhaps," retorted Penny, with the air of allowing no great importance to that angle of the argument, "but what I want to know is, *are* you going to be a square man, and own up you were peeved into being a tyrant? And when you've done that, are you going to tell Betty, and apologize?"

George hesitated, trapped between his irritation and the still small voice.

"Look here," he said, with that amiable suavity that had won him many a concession, "you know well enough I don't want to hurt Betty's feelings. If she feels that way about it, of course I'll apologize."

His partner looked at him in blank amazement.

"Gad!" he exclaimed as if examining a particularly fine specimen of some rare beetle, "what a bounder."

"Meaning me?" snapped George.

"Don't dare to quibble. Look me in the eye."

There was a third degree fatality about the usually debonair Penny that exacted obedience. George unwillingly looked him in the eye, and had a ghastly feeling of having his suddenly realized smallness X-rayed.

"You know damned well you acted like a cad," Penny continued, "and I want to know, for all our sakes, if you're man enough to own it?"

George's fundamental honesty mastered him. Anger died from his eyes. His clenched hands relaxed and began an unconscious and nervous exploration for a cigarette.

"Since you put it that way," he said, "and it happens that my conscience agrees with you – I'll go you. I *was* a cad, and I'll tell Betty so. Confound it!" he growled, "I don't know *what's* come over me these days. I've got to get a grip on myself."

"You *bet* you have," said Penny, hauling his fists from his trousers as if with an effort. Then he grinned. "Betty said you would."

George's eyes darkened.

"And I'll tell you now," Penny went on, "since you've turned out at least half-decent, Betty'll let you off that apology thing.

She wasn't the one who was exacting it – not she. *I* couldn't stand for your highfalutin excuses for being – well, never mind – we all get our off days. But don't you get off again like that if—" Penny hesitated. "If you want me for a partner," which seemed the obvious conclusion, was tame. "If you want to hang on to any one's respect," he finished.

"Say, though," he murmured, "Betty'll give me 'what for' for drubbing you. She actually took your side – said – oh, never mind – tried to make me think of her just as if she was any old Mamie – the stenog – tried to prune out personal feeling."

"By Jove," he ruminated, "that girl's a corker!"

He raised forgiving eyes from his contemplation of the rug.

"Well, old man, blow me to a Scotch and soda, and I'll be going. Dinged if it wouldn't have broken me all up to have busted with you, even if you are a box of prunes. Shake."

George shook, but he was far from happy. What he had gained in peace of mind he had lost in self-conceit. His resentment against the pinch of circumstance was deepening to cancerous vindictiveness.

As Pennington left with a cheery good-by and a final half-cynical word of advice "to get onto himself" George mounted the stairs slowly and came face to face with Geneviève, obviously in wait for him.

"What happened?" she inquired, with an anxious glance at his corrugated brow.

George did not feel in a mood to describe his retreat, if not defeat.

"Oh, nothing. We had a highball. I think I made him – well – it's all right."

"There, I knew Betty'd make him see reason," she smiled. "I'm awfully glad. I've a real respect for Penny's judgment after all, you know."

"Meaning, you have your doubts about mine."

"No, meaning only just what I said – *just* that. By the way, George, I wish you'd take time to look into Alys' real estate. Somebody ought to, and if you're really representing her—"

"Oh, good heavens!" he exclaimed impatiently, angered by her swift transition from his own to another's affairs. "I can't! I simply can't! Haven't you any conception of how busy I am?"

"I know, dear; I *do* know. But something must be done. The Health Department," she explained, "has sent in complaint after complaint, and Miss Eliot simply won't handle the property unless she's allowed to spend a lot setting things to rights. Alys says it's absurd; none of the other property owners out there are doing anything, and *she* won't. So, nobody's looking after it, and somebody should."

"Who told you all this?" he demanded. "Miss E. Eliot, I suppose."

His wife nodded. "And she's right," she added.

"Well, perhaps she is," he allowed. "I'll get Alien to act as her agent again. He's in with all the politicians; he ought to be able to stall off the department."

The words slipped out before he realized their import, but at Genevieve's wide stare of amazement he flushed crimson. "I mean – lots of these complaints are really mere red tape; some self-important employee is trying to look busy. A little investigation usually puts that straight."

"Of course," she acquiesced, and he breathed a sigh of relief. "That happens, too, but Miss Eliot says that the conditions out there are really dreadful."

"I'll talk to Allen," said George with an affectation of easy dismissal of the subject.

But Genevieve's mind appeared to have grown suddenly persistent. At dinner she again brought up the subject, this time directing her troubled gaze and troubling words at her guest.

"Alys," she said abruptly, "I really think you ought to go out to Kentwood – to see about your property out there, I mean."

Mrs. Brewster-Smith looked up, rolling her large eyes in frank amazement.

"Go out there? What for? It isn't the sort of a district a lady cares to be seen in, I'm told; and, besides, George is looking after that for me. *He* understands such matters, and I frankly own *I* don't. Business makes me quite dizzy," she added with a flash of very white teeth.

Geneviève hesitated, then went to the point.

"But you must advise with your agent, Alys. The property is *yours*."

Alys raised sharply penciled brows. "I have utter confidence in George," she answered in a tone of finality that brought an adoring look from Emelene, and her usual Boswellian echo: "Of *course*."

George squirmed uneasily. Such a vote of confidence implied accepted responsibility, and he acknowledged to himself that he wanted to and would dodge the unwelcome burden. He turned a benign Jovian expression on Mrs. Brewster-Smith and condescended to explain.

"I have considered what is best for you, and I will myself see Allen and request him to take your real-estate affairs in charge again. Neither Sampson nor – er – Eliot is, I think, advisable for your best interests."

At the mention of the last name Genevieve's expressive face stretched to speak; then she closed her lips with self-controlled determination. Mrs. Brewster-Smith looked at her host in scandalized amazement.

"But I *told* you," she almost whimpered, "that his wife is simply impossible."

George smiled tolerantly. "But his wife isn't doing the business. It's the business, not the social interests, we have to consider."

"Oh, but she is in the business," Alys explained. "I think it's because she's jealous of him; she wants to be around the office and watch him."

Geneviève interposed. "Mrs. Allen owns a lot of land herself, and she looks after it. It seems quite natural to me."

"But she *has* a husband," Alys rebuked.

"Yes," agreed Geneviève, "but she probably married him for a husband, not a business agent."

George felt the reins of the situation slipping from him, so he jerked the curb of conversation.

"We are beside the issue," he said in his most legal manner. "The fact is that Allen knows more about the Kentwood district and the factory values than any one else, and I feel it my duty to advise Alys to leave her affairs in his hands. I'll see him for you in the morning."

He turned to Alys with a return of tolerantly protective inflection in his voice.

Geneviève shrugged, a faint ghost of a shrug. Had George been less absorbed in his own mental discomforts, he would have discovered there and then that the matter of his speech, not the manner of his delivery, was what held his wife's attention. No longer could rounded periods and eloquent sophistry hide from her his thoughts and intentions.

A telephone call interrupted the meal. He answered it with relief, bowing a hurried, self-important excuse to the ladies. But the voice that came over the wire was not modulated in tones of flattery.

"Say," drawled the campaign manager, "you'd better get a hump on, and come over here to headquarters. There's a couple of gents here who want a word with you."

The tone was ominous, and George stiffened. "Very well, I'll be right over. But you can pretty well tell them where I stand on the main issues. Who's at headquarters?"

A snort of disgust greeted the inquiry. The snort told George that seasoned campaigners did not use the telephone with such casual lack of circumspection. The words were in like manner enlightening. "Well, there might be Mr. Julius Caesar, and then again Mr. George Washington might drop in. What I'm putting you wise to," he added sharply, "is that you'd better get on to your job."

There was a click as of a receiver hung up with a jerk, and a subdued giggle that testified to the innocent attention of the telephone operator.

With but a pale reflection of his usual courtesy the harassed candidate left the bosom of his family. No sooner had he taken his departure than the bosom heaved.

"My dear girl," said Alys, "if you take that tone with your husband you'll never hold him – never. Men won't stand for it. You're only hurting yourself."

"What tone?" Genevieve inquired as she rose calmly and led the way to the drawing-room.

"I mean" – Mrs. Brewster-Smith slipped a firm, white hand across Genevieve's shoulders – "you shouldn't try to force issues. It looks as if you didn't have confidence in your husband, and men, to *do* and *be* their best, must feel perfect trust from the woman they love. You don't mind my being so frank, dear, but we women must help one another – by our experience and our intuitions."

Geneviève looked at her. Oblique angles had become irritatingly fascinating. "I'm beginning to think so more and more," she replied.

"It's for your own good, dear," Alys smiled.

"Yes," Geneviève agreed. "I understand. Things that hurt are often for our good, aren't they? We have to be *made* to realize facts really to know them."

"Coffee, dear?" inquired Alys, assuming the duties of hostess.

Geneviève shook her head. "No. I find I've been rather wakeful of late: perhaps it's coffee. Excuse me. I must telephone."

A moment later she returned beaming.

"I have borrowed a car for tomorrow, and I want you and Emelene to come with me for a little spin. We ought to have a bright day; the night is wonderful. Poor George," she sighed, "I wish he didn't have to be away so much."

"His career is yours, you know," kittenishly bromidic, Emelene comforted her. The following day fulfilled the promise of its predecessor. Clear and balmy, it invited to the outer, world, and it was with pleased anticipation that Genevieve's guests prepared for the promised outing. Geneviève glanced anxiously into her gold mesh bag. The motor was hired, not borrowed.

She had permitted herself this one white lie.

She ushered her guests into the tonneau and took her place beside the chauffeur. Their first few stops were for such prosaic purchases as the household made necessary; there was a pause at the post office, another at the Forum, where Geneviève left two highly disgruntled women waiting for her while with a guilty sense of teasing her prey she prolonged her business. The sight of their stiffened figures and averted faces when she returned to them kindled a new amusement.

At last they were settled comfortably, and the car turned toward the suburbs.

The town streets were passed and lines of villa homes thinned. The ornate colonial gates of the Country Club flashed by. Now the sky to the right was dark with the smoke of the belching chimneys of many factories. For a block or two cottages of the better sort flanked the road; then, grim, ugly and dilapidated, stretched the twin "improved" sections of Kentwood and Powderville. In the air was an acrid odor. Soot begrimed everything. The sodden ground was littered with refuse between the shacks, which were dignified by the title of "Workmen's Cottages."

Amid the confusion, irregular trodden paths led, short-cutting, toward the clattering, grinding munition plants. For a space of at least half an acre around the huge iron buildings the ground, with sinister import, was kept clear of dwellings, but in all directions outside of the inclosure thousands of new yellow-pine shacks testified to the sudden demand for labor. A large weather-beaten signboard at a wired cross-road bore the name of "Kentwood," plus the advice that the office was adjacent for the purchase or lease of the highly desirable villa sites.

The motor drew up and Genevieve alighted. For the first time since their course had been turned toward the unlovely but productive outskirts, Geneviève faced her passengers. Alys' face was pale. Emelene's expression was puzzled and worried, as a child's is worried when the child is suddenly confronted by strange and gloomy surroundings.

"There is some one in the renting office," said Geneviève with quiet determination. "I'll find out. We shall need a guide to go around with us. Emelene, you needn't get out unless you wish to."

Emelene shuffled uneasily, half rose, and collapsed helplessly back on the cushions, like a baby who has encountered the resistance of his buggy strap.

"I – if you'll excuse me, Geneviève, dear, I won't get out. I've only got on my thin kid slippers. I didn't expect to put foot on the pavement this morning, you know."

"Very well, then, Alys!" Genevieve's voice assumed a note of command her mild accents had never before known.

Alys' brilliant eyes snapped. "I have no desire," she said firmly, with all the dignity of an affronted lady, "to go into this matter." "I know you haven't. But I'm going to walk through. *I* am making a report for the Woman's Forum."

Alys' face crimsoned with anger.

"You have no right to do such a thing," she exclaimed. "I shall refuse you permission. You will have to obtain a permit."

"I have one," Geneviève retorted, "from the Health Department. And – I am to meet one of the officers here."

Mrs. Brewster-Smith's descent from the tonneau was more rapid than graceful.

"What are you trying to do?" she demanded. "Geneviève, I don't understand you."

"Don't you?"

The diffident girl had suddenly assumed the incisive strength of observant womanhood.

"I think you *do*. I am going to show you your own responsibilities, if that's a possible thing. I'm not going to let you throw them on George because he's a man and your kin; and I shan't let him throw them on an irresponsible agent because he has neither the time nor the inclination to do justice to himself, to you, nor to these people to whom he is responsible."

She waved a hand down the muddy, jumbled street.

The advent of an automobile had had its effect. Eager faces appeared at windows and doors. Children frankly curious and as frankly neglected climbed over each other, hanging on the ragged fences. Two mongrel dogs strained at their chains, yelping furiously. Geneviève crossed to the little square building bearing a gilt "office" sign. There was no response to her imperative knock, but a middle-aged man appeared on the porch of the adjoining shack and observed her curiously.

"Wanta rent?" he called jëeringly.

"Are you in charge here?" Geneviève inquired.

"Sorter," he temporized. "Watcha want?"

"I want some one who knows something about it to go around Kentwood with us."

"What for?" he snarled. "I got my orders."

"From whom?" countered Geneviève.

"None of your business, as I can see." He eyed her narrowly. "But my orders is to keep every one nosin' around here without no good raison *out* of the place – and I don't think *you're* here to rent, nor your friend, neither. Besides, there ain't nothin' to rent."

Mrs. Brewster-Smith colored. The insult to her ownership of the premises stung her to resentment.

"My good man," she said sharply. "I happen to be the proprietor of North Kent wood."

"Then you'd better beat it." The guardian grinned. "There's a dame been here with one of them fellers from the town office."

"Where are they now?" questioned Genevieve sharply.

"Went up factory way. But if you *ain't* one of them lady nosies, you'd better beat it, I tell you."

Genevieve looked up the street. "Very well, we'll walk on up. This is North Kentwood, isn't it?"

"Ain't much choice," he shrugged, "but it is. You can smell it a mile. Say, you lady owner there—" he laughed at his own astuteness in not being taken in—" you know the monikers, don't you? South Kentwood, 'Stinktown'; North Kentwood, 'Swilltown'?" He grinned, pulled at his hip pocket and, extracting a flat glass flask, took a prolonged swig and replaced the bottle with a leer.

The two incongruous visitors were already negotiating the muddy thoroughfare between the dilapidated dwellings. Presently these gave place to roughly knocked together structures for two and three families.

The number of children was surprising. Now and again a shrill-voiced woman, who seemed the prototype of her who lived in the shoe, came to admonish her young and stare with hostile eyes at the invaders. Refuse, barrels, cans, pigs, dogs, chickens, were on all sides, with here and there a street watering trough, fed, apparently, by an occasional tap at the wide-apart hydrants, installed by the factories for protection in case of fire, as evidenced by the signs staked by the apparatus.

"What do they pay you for these cottages?" Geneviève inquired suddenly.

Mrs. Brewster-Smith, whose curiosity concerning her possessions had been aroused by the physical evidence of the same, balanced on a rut and surveyed her tormentor angrily.

"I'm sure I don't know. I've told you before I don't understand such matters, and I see nothing to be gained by coming here."

Geneviève pushed open a battered gate, walked up to the door and knocked.

"What are you doing?" her companion called, querulously.

A noise of many pattering feet on bare floors, a strident order for silence, and the door swung open. A young girl stood in the doorway. Behind her were a dozen or more children, varying from toddlers to gawky girls and boys of school age.

Genevieve's eyes widened. "Dear me," she exclaimed, "they aren't all *yours*!"

The young woman grinned mirthlessly. "I should say not!" she snapped. "They pays me to look out for 'em – their fathers and mothers in the factory. Watcha want?"

"What do you pay for a house like this?"

The hired mother's brow wrinkled, and her lips drew back in an ugly snarl. "They robs us, these landlords does. We gotter be 'longside the works, so they robs us. What do I pay for this? Thirty a month, and at that 'tain't fit for no dawg to live in. I could knock up a shack like this with tar paper, I could.

"And what do we get? I gotter haul the water in a bucket, and cook on an oil stove, and they hists the price of the ile, 'cause he comes by in a wagon with it. The landlords is squeezing the life out of us, I tell ye."

She paused in her tirade to yell at her charges. Then she turned again to the story of her wrongs.

"And of all the pest holes I ever seen, this is the plum worst. There's chills an' fever an' typhoid till you can't rest, an' them kids is abustin' with measles an' mumps an' scarlet fever. That I ain't got 'em all myself's a miracle."

"You ought to have a district nurse and inspector/' said Geneviève, amused, in spite of her indignation, at the dark picture presented.

"Distric' nothin'," the other sneered. "There ain't nothin' here but rent an' taxes – doggone if I don't quit. There's plenty to do this here mindin' work, an' I bet I could make more at the factory. They're payin' grand for overtime."

Geneviève looked at the thin shoulders and narrow chest of the girl, noted her growing pallor and wondered how long such a physique could withstand the strain of hard work and overtime. She sighed. Something of her thoughts must have shown in her face, for the girl reddened and her lips tightened. Without another word she slammed the door in her visitor's face.

Mrs. Brewster-Smith cackled thin laughter.

"That's what you get for interfering," she jeered, so angry with her hostess for this forced inspection of her source of income that she was ready to sacrifice the comforts of her extended visit to have the satisfaction of airing her resentment.

"Poor soul!" said Geneviève. "Thirty a month!" Her eyes ran over the rows of crowded shacks. "The owners must get together and do something here," she said. "These conditions are simply vile."

"It's probably all these people are used to," Alys snapped, "And, besides, if they went further into town it'd cost them the trolley both ways, and all the time lost. It's the location they pay for. Mr. Alien told me not two months ago he thought rents could be raised."

"If you all co-operate," Genevieve continued her own line of thought, "you could at least clean the place and make it *safe* to live in, even if they haven't any comforts."

Her face brightened. Around the corner came the strong, solid figure of Miss Eliot; behind her trotted a bespectacled young man who carried a pigskin envelope under his arm and whose expression was far from happy.

"Hello!" called Miss Eliot. "So you did come. I'm glad of it. Let me present Mr. Glass to you. The department lent him to me for the day. And what do you think of it, now that you can see it?"

"Glad to meet you," said Genevieve, nodding to the health officer. "What do I think of it? What does Mr. Glass think? That's more important. Oh, let me present you – this is Mrs. Brewster-Smith."

Miss Eliot's face showed no surprise, though her eyes twinkled, but Mr. Glass was frankly taken aback.

"Mrs. Brewster – Smith – Brewster – Smith," he stammered. "Oh – er—" he gripped his pigskin folio as if about to search its contents to verify the name. "The – er – the owner?" he inquired.

Alys stiffened. "My dear husband left me this property. I have never before seen it."

"I'm very glad," beamed Mr. Glass, "to see that we shall have your co-operation in our efforts to do something definite for this section – and measures must be taken quickly. As you see, there is no sanitation, no trenching, no mosquito-extermination plant. Malaria and typhoid are prevalent; it's all very bad, very bad, indeed. And you'd hardly believe, Mrs. Brewster-Smith, what difficulties we are having with the owners as a class. The five biggest have formed an association. I suppose you've heard about it. They must have made an effort to interest you "—he stopped short, remembering that her name appeared on the lists of the "Protective League."

"Really" – Alys had recovered her hauteur and the aloofness becoming the situation – "I know nothing whatever about what measures my agents have thought it advisable to take."

Mr. Glass choked and glanced uneasily at Miss Eliot.

That lady grinned, almost the grin of a gamin. "You needn't look at *me*, Mr. Glass. I don't represent Mrs. Brewster-Smith."

"Oh, I know, I know," Mr. Glass hastened to exonerate his companion.

"I believe Miss Eliot declined the honor," Genevieve's voice was heard.

"I did," the agent affirmed. She laughed shortly. "Otherwise you would hardly find me here in my present capacity. One does not 'run with the hare and hunt with the hounds,' you know."

Alys lost her temper. It seemed to her she was ruthlessly being forced to shoulder responsibilities she had been taught to shirk as a sacred feminine right. Therefore, feeling injured, she voiced her innocence.

"Your husband, my dear Geneviève, has been good enough to administer my little estate. Whatever he has done, or now plans to do, meets with *my* entire approval."

The thrust went home in more directions than one. Miss Eliot turned her frank gaze upon the speaker, while she slowly nodded her head as if studying a perfect specimen of a noxious species. Mr. Glass gasped. There was political material in the statement. He looked anxiously at the wife of the gentleman implicated, but in her was no fear and no manner of trembling. Instead, the light of battle shone in her eyes.

"My dear Alys," she said, "my husband has told you that he is too busy a man to give your affairs his personal attention. He can only advise you and turn the executive side over to another. His experience does not extend to the stock market or to real estate. It is an imposition to throw your burdens upon him. If you derive benefits from ownership, you must educate yourself to accept your duty to society."

"Indeed!" flared Alys, furious at this public arraignment. "May I ask if you intend to continue this insulting attitude?"

"If you mean, do I expect hereafter to be a live woman and not a parasite – I do."

Mrs. Brewster-Smith turned on her heel and walked away, teetering over the ruts and holes of the path.

Genevieve looked distressed. "I'm sorry," she breathed, "I'm ashamed, but it *had* to come out. I – I couldn't stand it any longer. I – beg everybody's pardon. I'm sure, it was awfully bad manners of me. Oh, dear—" she faltered, half turned, and, with a gesture of appeal toward Mrs. Brewster-Smith's slowly retreating back, moved as if to follow.

"I wouldn't go after her," said E. Eliot. "Of course, you haven't had experience. You don't know how much self-restraint you've got to build up, but you're here now, and I'm sure Mr. Glass understands. *He's* got to come up against all sorts of exasperations on *his* job, too. He won't take any stock in Mrs. Brewster-Smith's trying to tie your husband up to these wretched conditions.

"He's looking forward to seeing an honest, public-spirited district attorney get into office – even if your husband doesn't yet see that women have anything to say about it. They may heckle him in order to force him to come out on his intentions about the graft, and the eight-hour day, and the enforcement of the law, but they don't doubt his honesty. When he know's what's what, I guess the public can trust him to do the right thing. Only he's got to be shown."

As she talked, giving Geneviève time to recover from her upheaval, the three investigators were plowing their way up and down byways equally depressing and insanitary. Silence ensued. Occasionally an expression of commiseration or condemnation escaped one or another of the party.

Suddenly a raucous whistle tore the air, followed by another and another, declaring the armistice of the noon hour. Iron gates in the surrounding wall were opened, a stream of men and women poured out, grimed, sweat-streaked and voluble. The two women and their escort paused and watched the oncoming swarm of humanity.

Around the corner, just ahead, strode a giant of a man, followed by a red-faced, unkempt, familiar figure – the man in charge of the renting office. The giant came forward threateningly.

"What youse doing?" he growled. He jerked his jersey, displaying a brass badge, P. A. Guard.

"Git outer here – git," he called.

Mr. Glass stepped forward, displaying his Health Department permit. The giant laughed.

"Say, sonny," he sneered, "that don't go – see. Them tin fakes don't git by. If you're one of them guys, you come here wit' McLaughlin, and youse can rubber. But we've had enough of this stuff. Them dames is no blind, neither. I'm guard for the owners here, and we ain't takin' no chances wit' trouble makers – git. Git a move on!"

"The department," spluttered Glass, "shall hear of this."

"That's all right. McLaughlin's the boss. Tell 'em not to send a kid to do a man's job."

Geneviève was too amazed to protest. It was her first experience of defiance of Law and Order by Law and Order.

Meanwhile, the first stragglers of the released army of toilers were nearly upon them. The giant observed their approach, and the look of menace deepened on his huge, congested face.

"Move on, now – move on," he snarled, and herded them forward in advance of the workers.

Sheepishly the three obeyed, but Miss Eliot was not silent.

"Your name?" she demanded in judicial command.

The very terseness of her question seemed to jerk an unwilling answer from the guard.

"Michael Mehan."

"And you're employed by the Owners' Protective League?"

"Sure."

"Have they given you orders to keep strangers out of the district?"

"I have me orders, and I know what they be. I'm duly sworn in as extra guard – and I'm not the only one, neither."

"Did *he* come after you?" Miss Eliot indicated the ruffian at his side.

"I seen the lady owner blew the bunch," that worthy remarked with a hoarse chuckle. "I wised Mike, all right. Whatcha goin' to do about it?"

"Mrs. Brewster-Smith, the owner," Miss Eliot observed, "didn't seem to know that she had employed you. How about that?"

"I'm put here by the O.P.L. That's good enough fer yer lady owner – now – ain't it? The things them nosey dames thinks they can git by wit'!" he observed to the guard, and swore an oath that made Mr. Glass turn to him with unexpected fury.

"You may pretend to think that I'm not what I represent myself to be, but let me tell you, McLaughlin is going to hear of this. One more insult to these ladies and I'll make it my business to go personally to your employers. Get me?"

"Shut your trap, Jim," snarled Mehan. "Yer ain't got no orders fer no fancy language." He leered at Geneviève. "Now we've shooed the chickens out, we're tru'." With a wave of his huge paw he indicated the highway the turn of the path revealed.

Geneviève looked to the right, where the car should be waiting her. It was gone. Evidently the indignant Mrs. Brewster-Smith had expedited the departure. Miss Eliot read her discomfiture.

"My car is right down here behind that palatial mansion with the hole in the roof and the tin-can extension. Thank you very much for your escort," she added, turning to the two representatives of the Protective League. "My name, by the way, is E. Eliot. I am a real-estate agent and my office is at 22 Braston Street. You might mention it in your report."

The little car stood waiting, surrounded by a group of admiring children. Its owner stepped in briskly, backed around and received her passengers.

"Well," she smiled as they drew out on the traveled highway, "how do you like the purlieus of our noble little city?"

Genevieve was silent. Then she spoke with conviction.

"When George is in power – and he's *got* to be – the Law will be the Law. I know him."

Chapter XI

Marjorie Benton Cook

George Remington walked toward headquarters with more assurance than he felt. He resented Doolittle's command that he appear at once. He was beginning to realize the pressure which these campaign managers were bringing to bear upon him. He was not sure yet how far he could go, in out-and-out defiance of them and their dictates.

He knew that he had absolutely no ambitions, no interests in common with these schemers, whose sole idea lay in party patronage, in manipulating every political opportunity – in short, in reaping where they had sown. The question now confronting him was this: was he prepared to sell his political birthright for the mess of pottage they offered him?

He stood a second at the door of the office, peering through the reeking, smoke-filled atmosphere, to get a bird's-eye view of the situation before he entered.

Mr. Doolittle sat on the edge of a table monologuing to Wes' Norton and Pat Noonan. Mr.

Norton was the president of the Whitewater Commercial Club, composed of the leading merchants of the town, and Mr.

Noonan was the apostle of the liquor interests. Remington felt his back stiffen as he stepped among them.

"Good-evening, gentlemen," he said briskly.

"H'are ye, George?" drawled Doolittle.

"There was something you wanted to discuss with me?"

"I dunno as there's anything to discuss, but there's a few things Wes' an' Pat an' me'd like to say to ye. There ain't no two ways of thinkin' about the prosperity of Whitewater, ye know, George. The merchants in this town is satisfied with the way things is boomin'. The factory workers is gittin' theirs, with high wages an' overtime. The stockholders is makin' no kick on the dividends – as ye know, George, being one of them.

"Now, we don't want nuthin' to disturb all this If the fact'ries is crackin' the law a bit, why, it ain't the first time such things has got by the inspector. The fact'ry managers'd like some assurance from ye that ye're goin' to keep yer hands off before they line up the fact'ry hands to vote for ye."

Doolittle paused here. George nodded.

"When are ye comin' out with a plain statement of yer intentions, George?" inquired Mr. Norton in a conciliatory tone.

"The voters in this town will get a clear statement of my stand on all the issues of this campaign in plenty of time, gentlemen."

"That's all right fer the voter, but ye can't stall *us* wit' that kind of talk—" began Noonan.

"Wait a minute, Pat," counseled Doolittle. "George means all right. He's new to this game, but he means to stand fer the intrusts of his party, don't ye, George?"

"I should scarcely be the candidate of that party if I did not."

"I ain't interested in no oratory. Are ye or are ye not goin' to keep yer hands off the prosperity of Whitewater?" demanded Noonan angrily.

"Look here, Noonan, I am the candidate for this office – you're not. I intend to do as my conscience dictates. I will not be hampered at every turn, nor told what to say and what to think. I must get to these things in my own way."

"Don't ye fergit that ye're *our* candidate, that ye are to express the opinion of the people who will elect ye, and not any dam' theories of yer own—"

"I think I get your meaning, Noonan."

George spoke with a smile which for some reason disconcerted Noonan. He sensed with considerable irritation the social and class breach between himself and Remington, and while he did not understand it he resented it. He called him "slick" to Wes' and Doolittle and loudly bewailed their choice of him as candidate.

"Then there's that P.L. bizness, Pat – don't fergit that," urged Wes'.

"I ain't fergittin' it. There's too much nosin' round Kentwood district by the women, George. Too much talkin'. Ye'd better call that off right now. Property owners down there is satisfied, an' they got *their* rights, ye know." "I suppose you know what the conditions down there are?"

"Sure we know, George, and we want to clean it up down there just as much as you do," said the pacific Doolittle; "but what we're sayin' is, this ain't the time to do it. Later, mebbe, when the conditions is jest right—"

"Somebody has got the women stirred up fer fair. It's up to you to call 'em off, George," said Mr. Norton.

"How can I call them off?" – tartly.

"Ye can put the brakes on Mrs. Remington and that there Sheridan girl, can't ye?"

"Miss Sheridan is no longer in my employ. As for Mrs. Remington, if she is not one in spirit with me, I cannot force her to be. Every human being has a right to—"

"Some change sence ye last expressed yerself, George. Seems like I recall ye sayin', 'I'll settle that!'" remarked Doolittle coldly.

"We will leave my wife's name out of the discussion, please," said George with tardy but noble loyalty. "Well, them two I mentioned can stir up some trouble; but they ain't the brains of their gang, by a long shot. It's this E. Eliot we gotta deal with. She's as smart, if not smarter, than any man in this town. She's smarter than you, George – or me, either," he added consolingly.

"I've seen her about, but I've never talked to her. What sort of woman is she?"

"Quiet, sensible kind. Ye keep thinking, 'How reasonable that woman is,' till ye wake up and find she's got ye hooked on one of the horns of yer own damfoolishness! Slick as they make 'em and straight as a string – that's E. Eliot."

"What do you want me to do about it?" – impatiently.

"Are ye aimin' to answer them voiceless questions?" Pat inquired.

Silence.

"Plannin' to tear down Kentwood and enforce them factory laws?" demanded Wes' Norton.

Still no answer.

"I'm jest callin' yer attention to the fact that this election is gittin' nearer every day."

"What am I to do with her? I can't afford to show we're afraid of her."

"Huh."

"I can't bribe her to stop."

"I'd like to see the fella that would try to bribe E. Eliot," Doolittle chuckled. "Wouldn't be enough of him left to put in a teacup."

"Then we've got to ignore her."

"*We* can ignore her, all right, George; but the women an' some of the voters ain't ignoring her. It's my idea she's got a last card up her sleeve to play the day before we go to the polls that'll fix us."

"Have you any plan in your mind?"

Doolittle scratched his head, wrestling with thought.

"We was thinking that if she could be called away suddenly, and detained till after election—" he began meaningly.

"You mean—"

"Something like that."

"I won't have it, not if I lose the election. I won't stoop to kidnapping a woman like a highwayman. What do you take me for, Doolittle?"

"Georgie, politics ain't no kid-glove bizness. It ain't what *you* want; you're jest a small part of this affair. You're *our* candidate, and we *got* to win this here election. Do you get me?"

He shot out his underjaw, and there was no sign of his usual good humor.

"Well, but—"

"You don't have to know anything about this. We'll handle it. You'll be pertected to the limit; don't you worry," sneered Noonan.

"But you can't get away with this old-fashioned stuff nowadays, Doolittle," protested Remington.

"Can't we? You jest leave it to your Uncle Benjamin. You don't know nothing about this. See?"

"I know it's a dirty, low, underhanded—"

"George," remarked Mr. Doolittle, slowly hoisting his big body on to its short legs, "in politics we don't call a spade a spade. We call it 'a agricultural implument.'"

With this sage remark Mr. Doolittle took his departure, followed by the other prominent citizens.

George sat where they left him, head in hands, for several moments. Then he sprang up and rushed to the door to call them back.

He would not stand it – he would not win at that price. He had conceded everything they had demanded of him up to this point, but here he drew the line. Ever since that one independent fling of his about suffrage they had treated him like a naughty child. What did they think he was – a rubber doll? He would telephone Doolittle that he would rather give up his candidacy. Here he paused.

Suppose he did withdraw, nobody would understand. The town would think the women had frightened him off. He couldn't come out now and denounce the machine methods of his party. Every eye in Whitewater was focused on him; his friends were working for him; the district attorneyship was the next step in his career; Geneviève expected him to win – no, he must go through with it! But after he got into office, then he would show them! He would take orders from no one. He sat down again and moodily surveyed the future.

In the days which followed, another mental struggle was taking place in the Remington family. Poor Genevieve was like a woman struck by lightning. She felt that her whole structure of life had crashed about her ears. In one blinding flash she had seen and condemned George because he considered political expediency. She realized that she must think for herself now and not rely on him for the family celebration. She had conceived her whole duty in life to consist in being George's wife; but now, by a series of accidents, she had become aware of the great social responsibilities, the larger human issues, which men and women must meet together.

Betty and E. Eliot had pointed out to her that she knew nothing of the conditions in her own town. They assured her that it was as much her duty to know about such things as to know the condition of her own back yard.

Then came the awful revelations of Kentwood – human beings huddled like rats; children swarming, dirty and hungry! She could not bear to remember the scenes she had witnessed in Kentwood.

She recalled the shock of Alys Brewster-Smith's indifference to all that misery! The widow's one instinct had seemed to be to fight E. Eliot and the health officer for their interference. Stranger still, the tenants did not want to be moved out, driven on. The whole situation was confused, but in it at least one thing stood out clearly: Geneviève realized, during the sleepless night after her visit to Kentwood, that she hated Cousin Alys!

The following Sunday, when she put on her coat, she found a souvenir of that visit in her pocket, a soiled reminder of poverty and toil. She remembered picking it up and noting that it was the factory pass of one Marya Slavonsky. She had intended to leave it with some one in the district, but evidently in the excitement of her enforced exit she had thrust it into her pocket.

This Marya worked in the factories. She was one of that grimy army Geneviève had seen coming out of the factory gate, and she went home to that pen which Cousin Alys provided. Marya was a girl of Geneviève's own age, perhaps, while she, Geneviève, had this comfortable home, and George! She had been blind, selfish, but she would make up for it, she *would*! She would make a study of the needs of such people; she would go among them like St. Agatha, scattering alms and wisdom. George might have his work; she had found hers! She would begin with the factory girls. She would waken them to what had so lately dawned on her. How could she manage it? The rules of admission in the munition factories were very strict.

Then again her eye fell upon the soiled card and a great idea was born in her brain. Dressed as a factory girl, she would use Marya's card to get her into the circle of these new-found sisters. She would see how and where they worked. She would report it all to the Forum and to George. She could be of use to George at last.

She remembered Betty's statement that at midnight in the factories the women and girls had an hour off. That was the time she chose, with true dramatic instinct.

She rummaged in the attic for an hour, getting her costume ready. She decided on an old black suit and a shawl which had belonged to her mother. She carried these garments to her bedroom and hid them there. Then, with Machiavellian finesse, she laid her plans.

She would slip out of bed at half-past eleven o'clock, taking care not to waken George, and she would dress and leave the house by the side door. By walking fast she could reach by midnight the factory to which she had admission.

It annoyed her considerably to have George announce at luncheon that he had a political dinner on for the evening and probably would not be home before midnight. He grumbled a little over the dinner. "The campaign," he said, "really ended yesterday. But Doolittle thought it was wise to have a last round-up of the business men, and give them a final speech."

Geneviève acquiesced with a sympathetic murmur, but she was disappointed. Merely to walk calmly out of the house at eleven o'clock lessened the excitement. However, she decided upon leaving George a note explaining that she had gone to spend the night with Betty Sheridan.

She looked forward to the long afternoon with impatience. Cousin Emelene was taking her nap. Mrs. Brewster-Smith left immediately after lunch to make a call on one of her few women friends. Genevieve tried to get Betty on the telephone, but she was not at home.

It was with a thrill of pleasure that she saw E. Eliot coming up the walk to the door. She hurried downstairs just as the maid explained that Mrs. Brewster-Smith was not at home.

"Oh, won't you come in and see me for a moment, Miss Eliot?" Genevieve begged. "I do so want to talk to you."

E. Eliot hesitated. "The truth is, I am fearfully busy today, even though it's Sunday. I wanted to get five minutes with Mrs. Brewster-Smith about those cottages—" she began.

Genevieve laid a detaining hand on her arm and led her into the living-room.

"She's hopeless! I can hardly bear to have her in my house after the way she acted about those fearful places."

"Well, all that district is the limit, of course. She isn't the only landlord."

"But she didn't *see* those people."

"She's human, I guess – didn't want to see disturbing things."

"I would have torn down those cottages with my own hands!" burst forth Geneviève.

E. Eliot stared. "No one likes her income cut down, you know," she palliated.

"Income! What is that to human decencies?" cried the newly awakened apostle.

"Your husband doesn't entirely agree with you in some of these matters, I suppose."

"Oh, yes he does, in his heart! But there's something about politics that won't let you come right out and say what you think."

"Not after you've come right out once and said the wrong thing," laughed E. Eliot. "I'm afraid you will have to use your indirect influence on him, Mrs. Remington."

Geneviève threw her cards on the table.

"Miss Eliot, I am just beginning to see how much there is for women to do in the world. I want to do something big – the sort of thing you and Betty Sheridan are doing – to rouse women. What can I do?" E. Eliot scrutinized the ardent young face with amiable amusement.

"You can't very well help us just now without hurting your husband's chances and embarrassing him in the bargain. You see, we're trying to embarrass him. We want him to kick over the traces and tell what he's going to do as district attorney of this town."

"But can't I do something that won't interfere with George? Couldn't I investigate the factories, or organize the working girls?"

"My child, have you ever organized anything?" exclaimed E. Eliot.

"No."

"Well, don't begin on the noble working girl. She doesn't organize easily. Wait until the election is over. Then you come in on our schemes and we'll teach you how to do things. But don't butt in now, I beg of you. Misguided, well-meaning enthusiasts like you can do more harm to our cause than all the anti-suffragists in this world!"

With her genial, disarming smile, E. Eliot rose and departed. She chuckled all the way back to her rooms over the idea of Remington's bride wanting to take the field with the enemies of her wedded lord.

"Women, women! God bless us, but we're funny!" mused E. Eliot.

Genevieve liked her caller immensely, and she thought over her advice, but she determined to let it make no difference in her plans.

She saw her work cut out for her. She would not flinch!

She would do her bit in the great cause of women – no, of humanity. The flame of her purpose burned steadily and high.

At a quarter-past eleven that night a slight, black-clad figure, with a shawl over its head, softly closed the side door of the Remington house and hurried down the street. Never before had Genevieve been alone on the streets after dark. She had not foreseen how frightened she would be at the long, dark stretches, nor how much more frightened when any one passed her. Two men spoke to her. She sped on, turning now this way, now that, without regard to direction – her eyes over her shoulder, in terror lest she be followed.

So it was that she plunged around a corner and into the very arms of E. Eliot, who was sauntering home from a political meeting, where she had been a much-advertised speaker. She was in the habit of prowling about by herself. Tonight she was, as usual, unattended – unless one observed two burly workingmen who walked slowly in her wake.

"Oh, I beg your pardon," came a gently modulated voice from behind the shawl. E. Eliot stared.

"No harm done here. Did I hurt you?" she replied.

She thought she heard an involuntary "Oh!" from beneath the shawl.

"No, thanks. Could you tell me how to get to the Whitewater Arms and Munitions Factory? I'm all turned around."

"Certainly. Two blocks that way to the State Road, and half a mile north on that. Shall I walk to the road with you?"

"Oh, no, thank you," the girl answered and hurried on. E. Eliot stood and watched her. Where had she heard that voice? She knew a good many girls who worked at the factories, but none of them spoke like that. All at once a memory came to her: "Couldn't I investigate something, or organize the working girls?" Mrs. George Remington!

"The little fool," ejaculated the other woman, and turned promptly to follow the flying figure.

The two burly gentlemen in the rear also turned and followed, but E. Eliot was too busy planning how to manage Mrs. Remington to notice them. She had to walk rapidly to keep her quarry in sight. As she came within some thirty yards of the gate she saw Genevieve challenge the gatekeeper, present her card and slip inside, the gate clanging to behind her.

E. Eliot broke into a jog trot, rounded the corner of the wall, pulled herself up quickly, using the stones of the wall as footholds. She hung from the top and let herself drop softly inside, standing perfectly still in the shadow. At the same moment the two burly gentlemen ran round the corner and saw nothing. "I told ye to run—" began one of them fiercely.

"Aw, shut up. If she went over here, she'll come out here. We'll wait."

The midnight gong and the noise of the women shuffling out into the courtyard drowned that conversation for E. Eliot. She stood and watched the gatekeeper saunter indoors, not waiting for the man who relieved him on duty. She watched Genevieve go forward and meet the factory hands.

The newcomer shyly spoke to the first group. The eavesdropper could not hear what she said. But the crowd gathered about the speaker, shuffling, chaffing, finally listening. Somebody captured the gatekeeper's stool and Geneviève stood on it.

"What I want to tell you is how beautiful it is for women to stand together and work together to make the world better," she began.

"Say, what is your job?" demanded a girl, suspicious of the soft voice and modulated speech.

"Well, I – I only keep house now. But I intend to begin to do a great deal for the community, for all of you—"

"She keeps house – poor little overworked thing!"

"But the point is, not what you do, but the spirit you do it in—"

"What is this, a revival meetin'?"

"So I want to tell you what the women of this town mean to do."

"Hear! Hear! Listen at the suffragette!"

"First, we mean to clean up the Kentwood district. You all know how awful those cottages are."

"Sure; we live in 'em!"

"We intend to force the landlords to tear them down and improve all that district."

"Much obliged, lady, and where do we go?" demanded one of her listeners.

"You must have better living conditions."

"But where? Rents in this town has boomed since the war began. Ain't that got to you yet? There ain't no place left fer the poor."

"Then we must find places and make them healthy and beautiful."

"For the love of Mike! She's talkin' about heaven, ain't she?"

"She's talkin' through her hat!" cried another.

"Then, we mean to make the factories obey the laws. They have no right to make you girls work here at night."

"Who's makin' us?"

"We are going to force the factories to obey the letter of the law on our statute books."

A thin, flushed girl stepped out of the crowd and faced her.

"Say, who is 'we'?"

"Why, all of us, the women of Whitewater."

"How are we goin' to repay the women of Whitewater fer tearin' down our homes an' takin' away our jobs? Ain't there somethin' we can do to show our gratitood?" the new speaker asked earnestly.

"Go to it – let her have it, Mamie Flynn!" cried the crowd.

"Oh, but you mustn't look at it that way! We must all make some sacrifices—"

"Cut that slush! What do you know about sacrifices? I'm on to you. You're one of them uptown reformers. What do you know about sacrifices? Ye got a sure place to sleep, ain't ye? Ye've got a full belly an' a husband to give ye spendin' money, ain't ye? Don't ye come down here gittin' our jobs away an' then fergettin' all about us!"

There was a buzz of agreement and an undertone of anger which to an experienced speaker would have been ominous. But Geneviève blundered on: "We only want to help you—"

"We don't want yer help ner yer advice. You keep yer hands off our business! Do yer preachin' uptown – that's where they need it. Ask the landlords of Kentwood and the stockholders in the munition factories to make some sacrifices, an' see where that gits ye! But don't ye come down here, a-spyin' on us, ye dirty—"

The last words were happily lost as the crowd of girls closed in on Geneviève with cries of "Spy!" "Scab!" "Throw her out!"

They had nearly torn her clothes off before E. Eliot was among them. She sprang up on the chair and shouted:

"Girls – here, hold on a minute."

There was a hush. Some one called out: "It's Miss E. Eliot." "Listen a minute. Don't waste your time getting mad at this girl. She's a friend of mine. And you may not believe me, but she means all right."

"What's she pussyfootin' in here for?"

"Don't you know the story of the man from Pittsburgh who died and went on?" cried E. Eliot. "Some kindly spirit showed him round the place, and the newcomer said: 'Well, I don't think heaven's got anything on Pittsburgh.' 'This isn't heaven!' said the spirit."

There was a second's pause, and then the laugh came.

"Now, this girl has just waked up to the fact that Whitewater isn't heaven, and she thought you'd like to hear the news! I'll take the poor lamb home, put cracked ice on her head and let her sleep it off."

They laughed again.

"Go to it," said the erstwhile spokeswoman for the working girls.

E. Eliot called them a cheery good-night. The factory girls drifted away, in little groups, leaving Geneviève, bedraggled and hysterical, clinging to her rescuer.

"They would have killed me if you hadn't come!" she gasped.

E. Eliot thought quickly.

"Stand here in the shadow of the fence till I come back," she said. "It will be all right. I've got to run into the office and send a telephone message. I have a pal there who will let me do it."

"You – you won't be long?"

It was clear that the nerve of Mrs. Remington was quite gone.

"I won't be gone five minutes."

E. Eliot was as good as her word.

When she returned she seized the stool on which her companion had made her maiden speech – ran to the wall, placed it at the spot where she had made her entrance and urged Geneviève to climb up and drop over; as she obeyed, E. Eliot mounted beside her. They dropped off, almost at the same moment – into arms upheld to catch them.

Geneviève screamed, and was promptly choked. "What'll we do with this extra one?" asked a hoarse voice.

"Bring her. There's no time to waste now. If ye yell again, ye'll both be strangled," the second speaker added as he led the way toward the road, where the dimmed lights of a motor car shone.

He was carrying E. Eliot as if she were a doll. Behind him his assistant stumbled along, bearing, less easily but no less firmly, the, wife of the candidate for district attorney!

Chapter XII
William Allen White

As the two gagged women – one comfortably gagged with more or less pleasant bandages made and provided, the other gagged by the large, smelly hand of an entire stranger to Mrs. George Remington – whom she was trying impolitely to bite, by way of introduction – were speeding through the night, Mr. George Remington, ending a long and late speech before the Whitewater Business Men's Club, was saying these things:

"I especially deplore this modern tendency to talk as though there were two kinds of people in this country – those interested in good government, and those interested in bad government. We are all good Americans. We are all interested in good government. Some of us believe good government may be achieved through a protective tariff and a proper consideration for prosperity [cheers], and others, in their blindness, bow down to wood and stone!"

He smiled amiably at the laughter, and continued:

"But while some of us see things differently as to means, our aims are essentially the same. You don't divide people according to trades and callings. I deplore this attempt to set the patriotic merchant against the patriotic saloonkeeper; the patriotic follower of the race track against the patriotic manufacturer.

"Here is my good friend, Benjie Doolittle. When he played the ponies in the old days, before he went into the undertaking and furniture business, was he less patriotic than now? Was he less patriotic then than my Uncle Martin Jaffry is now, with all his manufacturer's interest in a stable government? And is my Uncle Martin Jaffry more patriotic than Pat Noonan? Or is Pat less patriotic than our substantial merchant, Wesley Norton?

"Down with this talk that would make lines of moral and patriotic cleavage along lines of vocation or calling. I want no votes of those who pretend that the good Americans should vote in one box and the bad Americans in another box. I want the votes of those of all castes and cults who believe in prosperity [loud cheers], and I want the votes of those who believe in the glorious traditions of our party, its magnificent principles, its martyred heroes, its deathless name in our history!"

It was, of course, an after-dinner speech. Being the last speech of the campaign it was also a highly important one. But George Remington felt, as he sat listening to the din of the applause, that he had answered rather neatly those who said he was wabbling on the local economic issue and was swaying in the wind of socialist agitation which the women had started in Whitewater.

As he left the hotel where the dinner had been given, he met his partner on the sidewalk.

"Get in, Penny," he urged, jumping into his car. "Come out to the house for the night, and we'll have Betty over to breakfast. Then she and Geneviève and you and I will see if we can't restore the *ante-bellum modus vivendi*! Come on! Emelene and Alys always breakfast in bed, anyway, and it will be no trouble to get Betty over." The two men rode home in complacent silence. It was long past midnight. They sat on the veranda to finish their cigars before going into the house.

"Penny," asked George suddenly, "what has Pat Noonan got in this game – I mean against the agitation by the women and this investigation of conditions in Kentwood? Why should he agonize over it?"

"Is he fussing about it?"

"Is he? Do you think I'd tie his name up in a public speech with Martin Jaffry if Pat wasn't off the reservation? You could see him swell up like a pizened pup when I did it! I hope Uncle Martin will not be offended."

"He's a good sport, George. But say – what did Pat do to give you this hunch?"

Remington smoked in meditative silence, then answered:

"Well, Penny, I had to raise the devil of a row the other day to keep Pat from ribbing up Benjie Doolittle and the organization to a frame-up to kidnap this Eliot person."

"Kidnap E. Eliot!" gasped the amazed Evans. "Kidnap that very pest. And I tell you, man, if I hadn't roared like a stuck ox they would have done it! Fancy introducing 'Prisoner of Zenda' stuff into the campaign in Whitewater! Though I will say this, Penny, as between old army friends and college chums," continued Mr. Remington earnestly, "if a warrior bold with spurs of gold, who was slightly near-sighted and not particular about his love being so damned young and fair, would swoop down and carry this E. Eliot off to his princely donjon, and would let down the portcullis for two days, until the election is over, it would help some! Though otherwise I don't wish her any bad luck!"

The old army friend and college chum laughed.

"Well, that's your end of the story! I'm mighty glad you stopped it. Here's my end. You remember two-fingered Moll, who was our first client? The one who insisted on being referred to as a lady? The one who got converted and quit the game and who thought she was being pursued by the racetrack gang because she was trying to live decent?"

George smiled in remembrance. "Well, she called me up to know if there was any penalty for renting a house to Mike the Goat and his wife and old Salubrious the Armenian, who had a lady friend they were keeping from the cops against her will. She said they weren't going to hurt the lady, and I could see her every day to prove it. I advised her to keep out of it, of course; but she was strong for it, because of what she called the big money. I explained carefully that if anything should happen, her past reputation would go against her. But she kept saying it was straight, until I absolutely forbade her to do it, and she promised not to."

"Mike and his woman, and Old Salubrious!" echoed Remington. "And E. Eliot locked up with them for two days!"

He shivered, partly at the memory of his own mealy-mouthed protest.

"Well," he said, and there was an air of finality in his tone, "I'm glad I stopped the whole infamous business."

Mentally he decided to get Noonan on the telephone the first thing in the morning and make certain that the plan was abandoned. He continued his chat with Evans.

"But, Penny, why this agonizing of Noonan? What has he to lose by the better conditions in Kentwood? Why should he—"

Outside of a neat white dwelling in the suburbs of Whitewater, four figures were struggling in the night toward a vine-covered door – that door which appeared so attractively in the *Welfare Bulletin* of the Toledo Blade Steel Company's publicity program as the "prize garden home of J. Agricola, roller."

A woman stood in the doorway, holding the door open. Two women, who had been carried by two men, from an automobile at the gate, were forced through. There the men left them with their hostess.

"I was only looking for one of yez," she said, hospitably, "but you're bote welcome. Now, ladies, I'm goin' to make you comfortable. It won't do no good to scream, so I'm goin' to take your gags off. And I hope you, lady, haven't been inconvenienced by a handkerchief. We could just as well have arranged for your comfort, too."

"Madam," gasped E. Eliot, who was the first to be released to speech, "it is unimportant who I am. But do you know that this woman with me is Mrs. George Remington, the wife of the candidate for district attorney – Mr. George Remington of Whitewater? There has been a mistake."

The hostess looked at Genevieve, who nodded a tearful confirmation. But the woman only smiled.

"My man don't make mistakes," she said laconically. "And, what's more to the point, miss, he's a friend of George Remington, and why should he be giving his lady a vacation? You are E. Eliot, and your friends think you're workin' too hard, so they're goin' to give you a nice rest. Nothin' will happen to you if you are a lady, as I think you are. And when I find out who this other lady is, we'll make her as welcome as you!"

She went out of the room, locking the door behind her as the two women struggled vainly with their bonds. In an instant she returned.

"My man says to tell the one who thinks she's Mrs. George Remington that she's spendin' the week-end with Mrs. Napoleon Boneypart." My man says he's a good friend of George Remington and is supportin' him for district attorney, and that's how he can make it so pleasant here.

"And I'll tell you something else," she continued proudly. "When George got married, it was my man that went up and down Smoky Row and seen all the girls and got 'em to give a dollar apiece for them lovely roses labeled 'The Young Men's Republican Club.' Mr. Doolittle he seen to that. My man really collected fifty dollars more'n he turned in, and I got a diamond-set wrist watch with it! So, you see, we're real friendly with them Remingtons, and we're glad to see you, Mrs. Remington!"

"Oh, how horrible!" cried Geneviève. "There were eight dozen of those roses from the Young Men's Republican Club, and to think— Oh, to think—"

"Well, now, George," cried Mr. Penfield Evans, "just stop and think. Use your bean, my boy! What is the one thing on earth that puts the fear of God into Pat Noonan? It's prohibition. Look at the prohibition map out West and at the suffrage map out West. They fit each other like the paper on the wall. Whatever women may lack in intelligence about some things, there is one thing woman knows – high and low, rich and poor! She knows that the saloon is her enemy, and she hits it; and Pat Noonan, seeing this rise of women investigating industry, makes common cause with Martin Jaffry and the whole employing class of Whitewater against the nosey interference of women.

"And Pat Noonan is depending on you," continued Evans. "He expects you to rise. He expects you to go to Congress – possibly to the Senate, and he figures that he wants to be dead sure you'll not get to truckling to decency on the liquor question. So he ties you up – or tries you out for a tie-up or a kidnapping; and Benjie Doolittle, who likes a sporting event, takes a chance that you'll stand hitched in a plan to rid the community of a political pest without seriously hurting the pest – a friendless old maid who won't be missed for a day or two, and whose disappearance can be hushed up one way or another after she appears too late for the election.

"Just figure things out, George. Do you think Noonan got Mike the Goat to assess the girls on the row a dollar apiece for your flowers from the Young Men's Republican Club, for his health! You had the grace to thank Pat, but if you didn't know where they came from," explained Mr. Evans cynically, "it was because you have forgotten where all Pat's floral offerings from the Y.M.R.C. come from at weddings and funerals! And Pat feels that you're his kind of people.

"Politics, George, is not the chocolate éclair that you might think it, if you didn't know it! Use your bean, my boy! Use your bean! And you'll see why Pat Noonan lines up with the rugged captains of industry who are the bulwarks of our American liberty. Pat uses his head for something more than a hatrack."

The two puffed for a time in silence. Finally the host said: "Well, let's turn in." Three minutes later George called across the upper hall to Penfield.

"The joke's on us, Penny. Here's a note saying that Geneviève is over with Betty for the night. We'll call her up after breakfast and have them both over to a surprise party."

Penny strolled across to his friend's door. He was disappointed, and he showed it. He found George sitting on the side of his bed.

"Penny," mused the Young Man in Politics, in his finest mood, "you know I sometimes think that, perhaps, way down deep, there is something wrong with our politics. I don't like to be hooked up with Noonan and his gang. And I don't like the way Noonan and his gang are hooked up with Wesley Norton and the silk stockings and Uncle Martin and the big fellows. Why can't we get rid of the Noonan influence? They aren't after the things we're after! They only furnish the unthinking votes that make majorities that elect the fellows the big crooks handle. Lord, man, it's a dirty mess! And why women want to get into the dirty mess is more than I can see." "What a sweet valedictory address you are making for a young ladies' school!" scoffed Penny. "The hills are green far off! Aren't you the Sweet Young Thing. But I'll tell you why the women want to get in, George. They think they want to clean up the mess."

"But would they clean it? Wouldn't they vote about as we vote?"

"Well," answered Mr. Evans with the cynicism of the judicial mind, "let's see. You know now, if you didn't know at the time, that Noonan got Mike the Goat to assess the disorderly houses for the money to buy your wedding roses from the Y.M.R.C. All right. Noonan's bartender is on the ticket with you as assemblyman. Are you going to vote for him or not?"

"But, Penny, I've just about got to vote for him."

"All right, then. I'll tell Geneviève the truth about Noonan and the flowers, and I'll ask her if she would feel that she had to vote for Noonan's bartender!" retorted Mr. Evans. "Giving women the ballot will help at least that much. If the Noonans stay in politics, they'll get no help from the women when they vote!"

"But aren't we protecting the women?"

* * *

"Anyway, Mrs. Remington," said E. Eliot comfortably, "I'm glad it happened just this way. Without you, they would hold me until after the election on Tuesday. With you, about tomorrow at ten o'clock we shall be released. E. Eliot alone they have made every provision for holding. They have started a scandal, I don't doubt, necessary to explain my absence, and pulled the political wires to keep me from making a fuss about it afterward. They know their man in the district attorney's office, and—"

"Do you mean George Remington?" This from his wife, with flashing eyes.

"I mean," explained E. Eliot unabashed, "that for some reason they feel safe with George Remington in the district attorney's office, or they would not kidnap me to prevent his defeat! That is the cold-blooded situation."

"This party," E. Eliot smiled, "is given at the country home of Mike the Goat, as nearly as I can figure it out. Mike is a right-hand man of Noonan. Noonan is a right-hand man of Benjie Doolittle and Wesley Norton, and they are all a part of the system that holds Martin Jaffry's industries under the amiable beneficence of our sacred protective tariff! Hail, hail, the gang's all here – what do we care now, my dear? And because you are here and are part of the heaven-born combination for the public good, I am content to go through the rigors of one night without a nightie for the sake of the cause!"

"But they don't know who I am!" protested Mrs. Remington. "And—"

"Exactly, and for that reason they don't know who you are not. Tomorrow the whole town will be looking for you, and Noonan will hear who you are and where you are. Then! Say, girl – *say, girl,* it *will* be grist for our mill! Fancy the headlines all over the United States:

'GANG KIDNAPS CANDIDATE'S WIFE MYSTERY SHROUDS PLOT CANDIDATE REMINGTON IS SILENT.'"

"But he won't be silent," protested the indignant Geneviève.

"I tell you, he'll denounce it from the platform. He'll never let this outrage—"

"Well, my dear," said the imperturbable E. Eliot, "when he denounces this plot he'll have to denounce Doolittle and Noonan, and probably Norton, and maybe his Uncle Martin Jaffry. Somebody is paying big money for this job! I said the headlines will declare:

'CANDIDATE REMINGTON is SILENT But Still Maintains That Women Are Protected from Rigors of Cruel World by Man's Chivalry.'"

"Oh, Miss Eliot, don't! How can you? Oh, I know George will not let this outrage—"

"Of course not," hooted E. Eliot. "The sturdy oak will support the clinging vine! But while he is doing it he will be defeated. And if he doesn't protest he will be defeated, for I shall talk!"

"George Remington will face defeat like a gentleman, Miss Eliot; have no fear of that. He will speak out, no matter what happens." "And when he speaks, when he tells the truth about this whole alliance between the greedy, ruthless rich and the brutal, vicious dregs of this community – our cause is won!"

* * *

The next morning George Remington reached from his bed for his telephone and called up the Sheridan residence. Two minutes later Penfield Evans heard a shout. At his door stood the unclad and pallid candidate for district attorney.

"Penny," he gasped, "Genevieve's not there! She has not been with Betty all night. And Betty has gone out to find E. Eliot, who is missing from her boarding-house!"

"Are you sure—"

"God – Penny – I thought I had stopped it!"

George was back in his room, flying into his clothes. The two men were talking loudly. From down the hall a sleepy voice – unmistakably Mrs. Brewster-Smith's – was drawling:

"George – George – are you awake? I didn't hear you come in. Dear Geneviève went over to stay all night with Cousin Betty, and the oddest thing happened. About midnight the telephone bell rang, and that odious Eliot person called you up!"

George was in the hall in an instant and before Mrs. Brewster-Smith's door.

"Well, well, for God's sake, what did she say!" he cried.

"Oh, yes, I was coming to that. She said to send your chauffeur with the car down to the – oh, I forget, some nasty factory or something, for Genevieve. She said Genevieve was down there talking to the factory girls. Fancy that, George! So I just put up the receiver. I knew Genevieve was with Betty Sheridan and not with that odious person at all – it was some ruse to get your car and compromise you. Fancy dear Genevieve talking to the factory girls at midnight!"

Penfield Evans and George Remington, standing in the hall, listened to these words with terror in their hearts.

"Get Noonan first," said George. "I'll talk to him."

In five seconds Evans had Noonan's residence. Remington listened to Penny's voice. "Gone," he was saying. "Gone where?" And then: "Why, he was at the dinner last— What's Doolittle's number?" ("Noonan went to New York on the midnight train," he threw at George.) A moment later Remington heard his partner cry, "Doolittle's gone to New York? On the midnight train?"

"Try Norton," snapped George. Soon he heard Penny exclaim. "Albany?" said Penny. "Mr. Norton is in Albany? Thank you!"

"Their alibis!" said Evans calmly, as he hung up the receiver and stared at his partner.

"Well, it – it— Why, Penny, they've stolen Geneviève! That damned Mike and the Armenian! They've got Geneviève with that Eliot woman! God— Why, Penny, for God's sake, what—"

"Slowly, George – slowly. Let's move carefully."

The voice of Penfield Evans was cool and steady.

"First of all, we need not worry about any harm coming to Geneviève. She is with Miss Eliot, and that woman has more sense than a man. She may be depended upon. Now, then," Evans waved his partner to silence and went on: "the next thing to consider is how much publicity we shall give this episode." He paused.

"It's not a matter of publicity; it's a matter of getting Geneviève immediately."

"An hour or so of publicity of the screaming, hysterical kind will not help us to find Geneviève. But when we do find her, our publicity will have defeated you!"

The two men stared at each other. Remington said: "You mean I must shield the organization!"

"If you are to be elected – yes!"

"Do you think Geneviève and Miss Eliot would consent to shield the organization when we find them? Why, Penny, you're mad! We must call up the chief of police! We must scour the country! I propose to go right to the newspapers! The more people who know of this dastardly thing the sooner we shall recover the victims!"

"And the sooner Noonan, when he comes home tonight, will denounce you as an accessory before the fact, with Norton and Doolittle as corroborating witnesses for him! Oh, you're learning politics fast, George!"

The thought of what Genevieve would say when she knew, through Noonan and Doolittle, that he had heard of the plot to kidnap Miss Eliot, and within an hour had talked to his wife casually at luncheon without saying anything about it, made George's heart stop. He realized that he was learning something more than politics. He walked the floor of the room.

"Well," he said at last, "let's call in Uncle Martin Jaffry. He—"

"Yes; he is probably paying for the job. He might know something! I'll get him."

"Paying for the job! Do you think he knew of this plot?" cried George as Evans stood at the telephone.

"Oh, no. He just knew, in a leer from Doolittle, that they had extraordinary need for five thousand dollars or so in your behalf – that they had consulted you. And then Doolittle winked and Noonan cocked his head rakishly, and Uncle Martin put – Hello, Mr. Jaffry. This is Penny. Dress and come down to the office quickly. We are in serious trouble."

Twenty minutes later Uncle Martin was sitting with the two young men in the office of Remington and Evans. When they explained the situation to him his dry little face screwed up.

"Well, at least Geneviève will be all right," he muttered. "E. Eliot will take care of her. But, boys – boys," he squeezed his hands and rocked in misery, "the devil of it is that I gave Doolittle the money in a check and then went and got another check from the Owners' Protective Association and took the peak load off myself, and Doolittle was with me when I got the P. A. check. We've simply got to protect him. And, of course, what he knows, Noonan knows. We can't go tearing up Jack here, calling police and raising the town!"

George Remington rose.

"Then I've got to let my wife lie in some dive with that unspeakable Turk and that Mike the Goat while you men dicker with the scoundrels who committed this crime!" he said.

"My God, every minute is precious! We must act. Let me call the chief of police and the sheriff—"

"All dear friends of Noonan's," Penny quietly reminded him. "They probably have the same tip about what is on as you and Uncle Martin have! Calm down, George! First, let me go out and learn when Noonan and Doolittle are coming home! When we know that, we can—"

"Penny, I can't wait. I must act now. I must denounce the whole damnable plot to the people of this country. I must not rest one second longer in silence as an accessory. I shall denounce—"

"Yes, George, you shall denounce," exclaimed his partner. "But just whom – yourself, that you did not warn Miss Eliot all day yesterday!"

"Yes," cried Remington, "first of all, myself as a coward!"

"All right. Next, then, your Uncle Martin Jaffry, who was earnestly trying to help you in the only way he knew how to help! Why, George, that would be—"

"That would be the least I could do to let the people see—"

"To let the people see that Mrs. Brewster-Smith and all your social friends in this town are associated with Mike the Goat and his gang—"

Before Evans could finish, his partner stopped him.

"Yes, yes – the whole damned system of greed! The rich greed and the poor greed – our criminal classes plotting to keep justice from the decent law-abiding people of the place, who are led like sheep to the slaughter. What did the owners pay that money for? Not for the dirty job that was turned – not primarily. But to elect me, because they thought I would not enforce the factory laws and the housing laws and would protect them in their larceny! That money Uncle Martin collected was my price – my price!"

He was standing before his friends, rigid and white in rage. Neither man answered him.

"And because the moral sense of the community was in the hearts and heads of the women of the community," he went on, "those who are upholding the immoral compact between business and politics had to attack the womanhood of the town – and Genevieve's peril is my share in the shame. By God, I'm through!"

Chapter XIII
Mary Austin

Close on Young Remington's groan of utter disillusionment came a sound from the street, formless and clumsy, but brought to a sharp climax with the crash of breaking glass.

Even through the closed window which Penfield Evans hastily threw up, there was an obvious quality to the disturbance which revealed its character even before they had grasped its import.

The street was still full of morning shadows, with here and there a dancing glimmer on the cobbles of the still level sun, caught on swinging dinner pails as the loosely assorted crowd drifted toward shop and factory.

In many of the windows half-drawn blinds marked where spruce window trimmers added last touches to masterpieces created overnight, but directly opposite nothing screened the offense of the Voiceless Speech, which continued to display its accusing questions to the passer-by.

Clean through the plate-glass front a stone had crashed, leaving a heap of shining splinters, on either side of which a score of men and boys loosely clustered, while further down a ripple of disturbance marked where the thrower of the stone had just vanished into some recognized port of safety.

It was a clumsy crowd, half-hearted, moved chiefly by a cruel delight in destruction for its own sake, and giving voice at intervals to coarse comment of which the wittiest penetrated through a stream of profanity, like one of those same splinters of glass, to the consciousness of at least two of the three men who hung listening in the window above:

"To hell with the – suffragists!"

At the same moment another stone hurled through the break sent the Voiceless Speech toppling; it lay crumpled in a pathetic feminine sort of heap, subject to ribald laughter, but Penny Evans' involuntary cry of protest was cut off by his partner's hand on his shoulder. "They're Noonan's men, Penny; it's a put-up job."

George had marked some of the crowd at the meetings Noonan had arranged for him, and the last touch to the perfunctory character of the disturbance was added by the leisurely stroll of the policeman turning in at the head of the street. Before he reached the crowd it had redissolved into the rapidly filling thoroughfare.

"It's no use, Penny. Our women have seen the light and beaten us to it; we've got to go with them or with Noonan and his – Mike the Goat!"

Recollection of his wife's plight cut him like a knife. "The Brewster-Smith women have got to choose for themselves!" He felt about for his hat like a man blind with purpose.

The street sweeper was taking up the fragments of the shattered windows half an hour later, when Martin Jaffry found himself going rather aimlessly along Main Street with a feeling that the bottom had recently dropped out of things – a sensation which, if the truth must be told, was greatly augmented by the fact that he hadn't yet breakfasted. He had remained behind the two younger men to get into communication with Betty Sheridan and ask her to stay close to the telephone in case Miss Eliot should again attempt to get into touch with her. He lingered still, dreading to go into any of the places where he was known lest he should somehow be led to commit himself embarrassingly on the subject of his nephew's candidacy.

His middle-aged jauntiness considerably awry, he moved slowly down the heedless street, subject to the most gloomy reflections. Like most men, Martin Jaffry had always been dimly aware that the fabric of society is held together by a system of mutual weaknesses and condonings, but he had always thought of himself and his own family as moving freely in the interstices, peculiarly exempt, under Providence, from strain. Now here they were, in such a position that the first stumbling foot might tighten them all into inextricable scandal.

It is true that Penny, at the last moment, had prevailed on George to put off the relief of his feelings by public repudiation of his political connections, at least until after a conference with the police. And to George's fear that the newspapers would get the news from the police before he had had a chance to repudiate, he had countered with a suggestion, drawn from an item in the private history of the chief – known to him through his father's business – which he felt certain would quicken the chief's sense of the propriety of keeping George's predicament from the press.

"My God!" said George in amazement, and Martin Jaffry had responded fervently with "O Lord!"

Not because it shocked him to think that there might be indiscretions known to the lawyer of a chief of police which the chief might not wish known to the world, but because, with the addition of this new coil to his nephew's affairs, he was suddenly struck with the possibility of still other coils in any one of which the saving element of indiscretion might be wanting.

Suppose they should come upon one, just one impregnable honesty, one soul whom the fear of exposure left unshaken. On such a possibility rested the exemption of the Jaffry-Remingtons. It was the reference to E. Eliot in his instructions to Betty which had awakened in Jaffry's mind the disquieting reflection that just here might prove such an impregnability. They probably wouldn't be able to "do anything" with E. Eliot simply because she herself had never done anything she was afraid to go to the public about. To do him justice, it never occurred to him that in the case of a lady it was easily possible to invent something which would be made to answer in place of an indiscretion.

Probably that was Martin Jaffry's own impregnability – that he wouldn't have lied about a lady to save himself. What he did conclude was that it was just this unbending quality of women, this failure to provide the saving weakness, which unfitted them for political life.

He shuddered, seeing the whole fabric of politics fall in ruins around an electorate composed largely of E. Eliots, feeling himself stripped of everything that had so far distinguished him from the Noonans and the Doolittles.

Out of his sudden need for reinstatement with himself, he raised in his mind the vision of woman as the men of Martin Jaffry's world conceived her – a tender, enveloping medium in which male complacency, unchecked by any breath of criticism, reaches its perfect flower – the flower whose fruit, eaten in secret and afar from the soil which nourishes it, is graft, corruption and civic incompetence.

Instinctively his need directed him toward the Remington place.

Mrs. Brewster-Smith was glad to see him. Between George's hurried departure and Jaffry's return several of the specters that haunt such women's lives looked boldly in at the window.

There was the specter of scandal, as it touched the Remingtons, touching that dearest purchase of femininity, social standing; there was the specter of poverty, which threatened from the exposure of the source of her income and the enforcement of the law; nearer and quite as poignant, was the specter of an ignominious retreat from the comfort of George Remington's house to her former lodging, which she was shrewd enough to realize would follow close on the return of her cousin's wife.

All morning she had beaten off the invisible host with that courage – worthy of a better cause – with which women of her class confront the assaults of reality; and the sight of Martin Jaffry coming up the broad front walk met her like a warm waft of security. She flung open the door and met him with just that mixture of deference and relief which the situation demanded.

She was terribly anxious about poor Geneviève, of course, but not so anxious that she couldn't perceive how Genevieve's poor uncle had suffered.

"What, no breakfast! Oh, you poor man! Come right out into the dining-room."

Mrs. Brewster-Smith might have her limitations, but she was entirely aware of the appeasing effect of an open fire and a spread cloth even when no meal is in sight; she was adept in the art of enveloping tenderness and the extent to which it may be augmented by the pleasing aroma of ham and eggs and the coffee which she made herself. And oh, those *poor* women, what *disaster* they were bringing on themselves by their prying into things that were better left to more competent minds, and what pain to *other* minds! So *selfish*, but of course they didn't realize. Really she hoped it would be a lesson to Geneviève. The dear girl was so changed that she didn't see how she was going to go on living with her; though, of course, she would like to stand by dear George – and a woman did so appreciate a home!

At this point the enveloping tenderness of Mrs. Brewster-Smith concentrated in her fine eyes, just brushed the heart of her listener as with a passing wing, hovered a moment, and dropped demurely to the tablecloth.

In the meantime two sorely perplexed citizens were grappling with the problem of the disappearance of two highly respectable women from their homes under circumstances calculated to give the greatest anxiety to faithful "party" men. It hadn't needed Penny's professional acquaintance with Chief Buckley to impress the need of secrecy on that official's soul. "Squeal" on Noonan or Mike the Goat? Not if he knew himself. Naturally Mr. Remington must have his wife, but at the same time it was important to proceed regularly.

"And the day before election, too!" mourned the chief. "Lord, what a mess! But keep cool, Mr. Remington; this will come out all right!"

After half an hour of such ineptitudes, Penfield Evans found it necessary to withdraw his partner from the vicinity of the police before his impatience reached the homicidal pitch.

"Buckley's no such fool as he sounds," Penny advised. "He probably has a pretty good idea where the women are hidden, but you must give him time to tip off Mike for a getaway."

But the suggestion proved ill chosen, at least so far as it involved a hope of keeping George from the newspapers. Shocked to the core of his young egotism as he had been, Remington was yet not so shocked that the need of expression was not stronger in him than any more distant consideration.

"Getaway!" he frothed. "Getaway! While a woman like my wife—" But the bare idea was too much for him.

"They may get away, but they'll not get off – not a damned one of them – of *us*," he corrected himself, and with face working the popular young candidate for district attorney set off almost on a run for the office of the Sentinel.

Reflecting that if his friend was bent upon official suicide, there was still no reason for his being, a witness to it, Penny turned aside into a telephone booth and called up Betty Sheridan. He heard her jump at the sound of his voice, and the rising breath of relief running into his name.

"O-o-oh, Penny! Yes, about twenty minutes ago. Geneviève is with her.... Oh, yes, I'm sure."

Her voice sounded strong and confident.

"They're in a house about an hour from the factory," she went on, "among some trees. I'm sure she said trees. We were cut off. No, I couldn't get her again.... Yes... it's a party line. In the Redfield district. Oh, Penny, do you think they'll do her any harm?"

It was, no doubt, the length of time it took to assure Miss Sheridan on this point that prevented Evans from getting around to the *Sentinel*, whose editor was at that moment giving an excellent exhibition of indecision between his obligation as a journalist and his rôle of leading citizen in a town where he met his subscribers at dinner.

It was good stuff – oh, it was good! What headlines!

PROMINENT SOCIETY WOMEN KIDNAPPED CANDIDATE REMINGTON REPUDIATES PARTY!

It was good for a double evening edition. On the other hand, there was Norton, one of his largest advertisers. There was also the rival city of Hamilton, which was even now basely attempting to win away from Whitewater a recently offered Carnegie library on the ground of its superior fitness.

Finally there was the party.

The *Sentinel* had always been a sound party organ. But *what* a scoop! And suppose it were possible to save the party at the expense of its worst element? Suppose they raised the cry of reform and brought Remington in on a full tide of public indignation?

Would Mike stand the gaff? If it were made worth his while. But what about Noonan and Doolittle? So the editorial mind shuttled to and fro amid the confused outpourings of the amazed young candidate, while with eyes bright and considering as a rat's the editor followed Remington in his pacings up and down the dusty, littered room.

Completely occupied with his own reactions, George's repudiation swept on in an angry, rapid stream which, as it spent itself, began to give place to the benumbing consciousness of a divided hearing.

Until this moment Remington had had a pleasant sense of the press as a fine instrument upon which he had played with increasing mastery, a trumpet upon which, as his mind filled with commendable purposes, he could blow a very pretty tune, – a noble tune with now and then a graceful flourish acceptable to the public ear. Now as he talked he began to be aware of flatness, of squeaking keys....

"Naturally, Mr. Remington, I'll have to take this up with the business management..." dry-lipped, the tune sputtered out. At this juncture the born journalist awaked again in the editorial breast at the entrance of Penfield Evans with his new item of Betty's interrupted message.

Two women shut up in a mysterious house among the trees! Oh, hot stuff, indeed!

Under it George rallied, recovered a little of the candidate's manner.

"Understand," he insisted. "This goes in even if I have to pay for it at advertising rates."

A swift pencil raced across the paper as Remington's partner swept him off again to the police.

Betty's call had come a few minutes before ten. What had happened was very simple.

The two women had been given breakfast, for which their hands had been momentarily freed. When the bonds had been tied again it had been easy for E. Eliot to hold her hands in such a position that she was left, when their keeper withdrew, with a little freedom of movement.

By backing up to the knob she had been able to open a door into an adjoining room, in which she had been able to make out a telephone on a stand against the wall.

This room also had locked windows and closed shutters, but her quick wit had enabled her to make use of that telephone.

Shouldering the receiver out of the hook, she had called Betty's number, and, with Geneviève stooping to listen at the dangling receiver, had called out two or three broken sentences.

Guarded as their voices had been, however, some one in the house had been attracted by them, and the wire had been cut at some point outside the room. E. Eliot and Geneviève came to this conclusion after having lost Betty and failed to raise any answer to their repeated calls. Somebody came and looked in at them through the half-open door, and, seeing them still bound, had gone away again with a short, contemptuous laugh.

"No matter," said E. Eliot. "Betty heard us, and the central office will be able to trace the call."

It was because she could depend on Betty's intelligence, she went on to say, that she had called her instead of the Remington house – for suppose that fool Brewster-Smith woman had come to the telephone!

She and Geneviève occupied themselves with their bonds, fumbling back to back for a while, until Geneviève had a brilliant idea. Kneeling, she bit at the cords which held Miss Eliot's wrists until they began to give.

* * *

What Betty had done intelligently was nothing to what she had done without meaning it. She had been unkind to Pudge. Young Sheridan was in a condition which, according to his own way of looking at it, demanded the utmost kindness.

Following a too free indulgence in *marrons glacés* he had been relegated to a diet that reduced him to the extremity of desperation.

Not only had he been forbidden to eat sweets, but while his soul still longed for its accustomed solace, his stomach refused it, and he was unable to eat a box of candied fruit which he had with the greatest ingenuity secured.

And that was the occasion Betty took – herself full of nervous starts and mysterious recourse to the telephone behind locked doors – to remind him cruelly that he was getting flabby from staying too much in the house and to recommend a long walk for his good.

It was plain that she would stick at nothing to get her brother out of the way, and Pudge was cut to the heart.

Oh, well, he would go for a walk, from which he would probably be brought home a limp and helpless cripple. Come to think of it, if he once got started to walk he was not sure he would ever turn back; he would just walk on and on into a kinder environment than this.

After all, it is impossible to walk in that fateful way in a crowded city thoroughfare. Besides, one passes so many confectioners with their mingled temptation and disgust. Pudge rode on the trolley as far as the city limits. Here there was softer ground underfoot and a hint of melancholy in the fields. A flock of crows going over gave the appropriate note.

Off there to the left, set back from the road among dark, crowding trees, stood a mysterious house. Pudge always insisted that he had known it for mysterious at the first glance. It had a mansard roof and shutters of a sickly green, all closed; there was not a sign of life about, but smoke issued from one of the chimneys.

Here was an item potent to raise the sleuth that slumbers in every boy, even in such well-cushioned bosoms as Pudge Sheridan's.

He paused in his walk, fell into an elaborately careless slouch, and tacked across the open country toward the back of the house. Here he discovered a considerable yard fenced with high boards that had once been painted the same sickly green as the shutters, and a great buckeye tree just outside, spreading its branches over the corner furthest from the house.

Toward this post of observation he was drifting with that fine assumption of aimlessness which can be managed on occasion by almost any boy, when he was arrested by a slight but unmistakable shaking of one of the shutters, as though some one from within were trying the fastenings.

The shaking stopped after a moment, and then, one after another, the slats of the double leaves were seen to turn and close as though for a secret survey of the field. After a moment or two this performance was repeated at the next window on the left, and finally at a third.

Here the shaking was resumed after the survey, and ended with the shutter opening with a snap and being caught back from within and held cautiously on the crack. Pudge kicked clods in his path and was pretentiously occupied with a dead beetle which he had picked up.

All at once something flickered across the ground at his feet, swung two or three times, touched his shoe, traveled up the length of his trousers and rested on his breast. How that bosom leaped to the adventure!

He fished hurriedly in his pocket and brought up a small round mirror. It had still attached to its rim a bit of the ribbon by which it had been fastened to his sister's shopping bag, from which, if the truth must be told, he had surreptitiously detached it.

Pretending to consult it, as though it were some sort of pocket oracle, Pudge flashed back, and presently had the satisfaction of seeing a bright fleck of light travel across the shutter. Immediately there was a responsive flicker from the window: one, two, three, he counted, and flashed back: one, two, three.

Pudge's whole being was suffused with delicious thrills. He wished now he had obeyed that oft-experienced presentiment and learned the Morse code; it was a thing no man destined for adventure should be without. This wordless interchange went on for a few moments, and then a hand, a woman's hand – O fair, imprisoned ladies of all time! – appeared cautiously at the open shutter, waved and pointed.

It pointed toward the buckeye tree. Pudge threw a stone in that direction and sauntered after it, pitching and throwing. Once at the corner, after a suitable exhibition of casualness, he climbed until he found himself higher than the fence, facing the house.

While he was thus occupied, things had been happening there. The shutter had been thrown back and a woman was climbing down by the help of a window ledge below and a pair of knotted window curtains.

Another woman prepared to follow her, gesticulating forcibly to the other not to wait, but to run. Run she did, but it was not until Pudge, lying full length on the buckeye bough, reached her a hand that he discovered her to be his sister's friend, Geneviève Remington.

In the interval of her scrambling up by the aid of the bent bough and such help as he could give her, they had neglected to observe the other woman. Now, as Mrs. Remington's heels drummed on the outside of the fence, Pudge was aware of some commotion in the direction of the house, and saw Miss Eliot running toward him, crying: "Run, run!" while two men pursued her. She made a desperate jump toward the tree, caught the branch, hung for a moment, lost her hold, and brought Pudge ignominiously down in a heap beside her.

If Miss Eliot had not contradicted it, Pudge would have believed to his dying day that bullets hurtled through the air; it was so necessary to the dramatic character of the adventure that there should be bullets. He recovered from the shock of his fall in time to hear Miss Eliot say: "Better not touch me, Mike; if there's so much as a bruise when my friends find me, you'll get sent up for it."

Her cool, even tones cut the man's stream of profanity like a knife. He came threateningly close to her, but refrained from laying hands on either of them.

Meantime his companion drew himself up to the top of the fence for a look over, and dropped back with a gesture intended to be reassuring. Pudge rose gloriously to the occasion.

"The others have gone back to call the police," he announced. Mike spat out an oath at him, but it was easy to see that he was not at all sure that this might not be the case. The possibility that it might be, checked a movement to pursue the fleeing Geneviève. Miss Eliot caught their indecision with a flying shaft.

"Mrs. George Remington," she said, "will probably be in communication with her friends very shortly. And between his wife and his old and dear friend Mike it won't take George Remington long to choose."

This was so obvious that it left the men nothing to say. They fell in surlily on either side of her, and without any show of resistance she walked calmly back toward the house. Pudge lingered, uncertain of his cue.

"Beat it, you putty-face!" Mike snarled at him, showing a yellow fang. "If you ain't off the premises in about two shakes, you'll get what's comin' to you. See?"

Pudge walked with as much dignity as he could muster in the direction of the public road. He could see nothing of Mrs. Remington in either direction; now and then a private motor whizzed by, but there was no other house near enough to suggest a possibility of calling for help.

He concealed himself in a group of black locusts and waited. In about half an hour he heard a car coming from the house with the mansard roof, and saw that it held three occupants, two men and a woman. The men he recognized, and he was certain that the woman, though she was well bundled up, was not E. Eliot.

The motor turned away from the town and disappeared in the opposite direction. Pudge surmised that Mike was making his getaway. He waited another half hour and began to be assailed by the pangs of hunger. The house gave no sign; even the smoke from the chimney stopped.

He was sure Miss Eliot was still there; imagination pictured her weltering in her own gore. Between fear and curiosity and the saving hope that there might be food of some sort in the house, Pudge left his hiding place and began a stealthy approach.

He came to the low stoop and crept up to the closed front door. Hovering between fear and courage, he knocked. But there was no response. With growing boldness he tried the door. It was locked.

The rear door also was bolted; but, creeping on, he found a high side window that the keepers of this prison in their hasty flight had forgotten to close. With the aid of an empty rain barrel, which he overturned and rolled into position, Pudge scrambled with much hard breathing through the window and dropped into the kitchen. Here he listened; his ears could discern no sound. On tiptoe he crept through the rooms of the first floor – but came upon neither furtive enemy nor imprisoned friend. Up the narrow stairway he crept – peeped into three bedrooms – and finally opening the door of what was evidently a storeroom, he found the object of his search.

E. Eliot sat in an old splint-bottomed chair – gagged, arms tied behind her and to the chair's back, and her ankles tied to the chair's legs. In a moment Pudge had the knotted towel out of her mouth, and had cut her bonds. But quick though Pudge was, to her he seemed intolerably slow; just then E. Eliot was thinking of only one thing.

This was the final afternoon of the campaign and she was away out here, far from all the great things that might be going on.

She gave a single stretch of her cramped muscles as she rose. "I know you – you're Betty Sheridan's brother – thanks," she said briskly. "What time is it?"

Pudge drew out his most esteemed possession, a watch which kept perfect time – except when it refused to keep any time at all.

"Three o'clock," he announced.

"Then our last demonstration is under way, and when I tell my story—" E. Eliot interrupted herself. "Come on – let's catch the trolley!"

With Pudge panting after her, she hurried downstairs, unbolted the door, and, running lightly on the balls of her feet, sped in the direction of the street car line.

Chapter XIV
Leroy Scott

In the meantime, concern and suspense and irruptive wrath had their chief abode in the inner room of Remington and Evans. George had received a request, through Penny Evans, from the chief of police to remain in his office, where he could be reached instantly if information concerning Geneviève were received, and where his help could instantly be secured were it required; and Penny had enlarged that request to the magnitude of a command and had stood by to see that it was obeyed, and himself to give assistance.

George had recognized the sense of the order, but he rebelled at the enforced inactivity. Where was Geneviève? – why wasn't he out doing something for her? He strode about the office, fuming, sick with the suspense and inaction of his rôle.

But Geneviève was not his unbroken concern. He was still afire with the high resentment which a few hours earlier had made him go striding into the office of the *Sentinel*. Fragments of his statement to the editor leaped into his mind; and as he strode up and down he repeated phrases silently, but with fierce emphasis of the soul.

Now and again he paused at his window and looked down into Main Street. Below him was a crowd that was growing in size and disorder: the last afternoon of any campaign in Whitewater was exciting enough; much more so were the final hours of this campaign that marked the first entrance of women into politics in Whitewater on a scale and with an organized energy that might affect the outcome of the morrow's voting.

Across the way, Mrs. Herrington, the fighting blood of five generations of patriots roused in her, had reinstated the Voiceless Speech within the plate-glass window broken by the stones of that morning and was herself operating it; and, armed with banners, groups of women from the Woman's Club, the Municipal League and the Suffrage Society were marching up and down the street sidewalks. It was their final demonstration, their last chance to assert the demands of good citizenship – and it had attracted hundreds of curious men, vote-owners, belonging to what, in such periods of political struggle, are referred to on platforms as "our better element."

Also drifting into Main Street were groups of voters of less prepossessing aspect – Noonan's men, George recognized them to be. These jeered and jostled the marching women and hooted the remarks of the Voiceless Speech – but the women, disregarding insults and attacks, went on with their silent campaigning. The feeling was high – and George could see, as Noonan's men kept drifting into Main Street, that feeling was growing higher.

Looking down, George felt an angered exultation. Well, his statement in the *Sentinel*, due upon the street almost any moment, would answer all these and give them something to think about! – a statement which would make an even greater stir than the declaration which he had issued those many weeks ago, when, fresh from his honeymoon, he had begun his campaign for the district attorneyship.

These people below certainly had a jolt coming to them!

George's impatient and glowering meditations – the hour was then near four – were broken in upon by several interruptions, which came on him in quick succession, as though detonated by brief-interval time-fuses. The first was the entrance of that straw-haired misspeller of his letters who had succeeded Betty Sheridan as guardian of the outer office.

"Mr. Doolittle is here," she announced. "He says he wants to see you."

"You tell Mr. Doolittle *I* don't want to see *him*!" commanded the irritated George.

But Mr. Benjamin Doolittle was already seeing his candidate. As political boss of his party, he had little regard for such a formality as being announced to any person on whom he might call – so he had walked through the open door.

"Well, what d'you want, Doolittle?" George demanded aggressively.

Mr. Doolittle's face wore that look of bland solicitude, that unobtrusive partnership in the misfortune of others, which had made him such an admirable and prosperous officiant at the last rites of residents of Whitewater.

"I just wanted to ask you, George—" he was beginning in his soft, lily-of-the-valley voice, when the telephone on George's desk started ringing. George turned and reached for it, to find that Penny had already picked up the instrument.

"I'll answer it, George.... Hello... Mr. Remington is here, but is busy; I'll speak for him – I'm Mr. Evans.... What – it's you! Where are you?... Stay where you are; I'll come right over for you in my car."

"Who was that?" demanded George.

"Geneviève," Penny said rapidly, seizing his hat, "and I'm going—"

"So am I!" exclaimed George.

"Not till we've had a little understanding," sharply put in Doolittle, blocking his way.

"Stay here, George," his partner snapped out—" she's perfectly safe – just a little out of breath – telephoned from a drug store over in the Red-field district. I'll have her back here in fifteen minutes." And out Penny dashed, slamming the door.

But perhaps it was the straw-haired successor of Betty Sheridan who really prevented George from plunging after his partner.

"You ordered the *Sentinel* sent up as soon as it was out," she said. "Here are six copies."

George seized the ink-damp papers, and as the straw-haired one walked out in rubber-heeled silence he turned savagely upon his campaign manager.

"Well, Doolittle?" he demanded.

"I just want to ask you, George—"

George exploded. "Oh, you just want to ask me! Well, everything you want to ask me is answered in that paper. Read it!"

Doolittle took the copy of the *Sentinel* which was thrust into his hands. George watched him with triumphant grimness, awaiting the effect of the bomb about to explode in the other's face. Mr. Doolittle unfolded the *Sentinel* – looked it slowly through – then raised his eyes to George. His face seemed somewhat puzzled, but otherwise it was overspread with that sympathetic concern which, as much as his hearse and his folding-chairs, was a part of his professional equipment.

"Why, George. I don't just get what you're driving at."

Forgetting that he was holding several copies of the Sentinel, George dropped them all upon the floor and seized the paper from Mr. Doolittle. He glanced swiftly over the first page – and experienced the highest voltage shock of his young public career. Feverishly he skimmed the remaining pages. But of all that he had poured out in the office of the *Sentinel*, not one word was in print.

Automatically clutching the paper in a hand that fell to his side, he stared blankly at his campaign manager. Mr. Doolittle gazed back with his air of sympathetic concern, bewildered questioning in his eyes. And for a space, despite the increasing uproar down in the street, there was a most perfect silence in the inner office of Remington and Evans.

Before either of the two men could speak, the door was violently flung open and Martin Jaffry appeared. His clothing was disarranged, his manner agitated – in striking contrast to the dapper and composed appearance usual to that middle-aged little gentleman.

"George," he panted, "heard anything about Geneviève?"

"She's safe. Penny's got charge of her by this time."

His answer was almost mechanical.

"Thank God!" Uncle Martin collapsed in one of the office chairs. "Mind – if sit here minute – get my breath."

George did not reply, for he had not heard. He was gazing steadily at Mr. Doolittle; some great, but as yet shapeless, force was surging up dazingly within him. But he somehow held himself in control.

"Well, Doolittle," he demanded, "you said you came to ask something."

Mr. Doolittle's manner was still propitiatingly bland. "I'll mention something else first, George, if you don't mind. You just remarked I'd find your answer in the *Sentinel*. There must 'a' been some little slip-up somewhere. So I guess I better mention first that the *Sentinel* has arranged to stand ready to get out an extra."

"An extra! What for?"

"Principally, George, I reckon to print those answers you just spoke of."

George still kept that mounting something under his control. "Answers to what?"

"Why, George," the other replied softly, persuasively. "I guess we'd better have a little chat – as man to man – about politics. Meaning no offense, George, stalling is all right in politics – but this time you've carried this stalling act a little too far. As the result of your tactics, George, why here's all this disorder in our streets – and the afternoon before election. If you'd only really tried to stop these messing women—"

"I didn't try to stop them by kidnapping them!" burst from George – and Uncle Martin, his breath recovered, now sat up, clutching his homespun cap.

"Kidnapping women?" queried the bland, bewildered voice of the party boss. "I say, George, I don't know what you're talking about." "Why, you—" But George caught himself. "Speak it out, Doolittle – what do you want?"

"Since you ask it so frankly, George, I'll try to put it plain: You been going along handing out high-sounding generalities. There's nothing better and safer than generalities – usually. But this ain't no usual case, George. These women, stirring everything up, have got the solid interests so unsettled that they don't know where they're at – or where you're at. And a lot of boys in the organization feel the same way. What the crisis needs, George, is a plain statement of your intentions as district attorney, which we can get into that *Sentinel* extra and which will reassure the public – and the organization."

"A plain statement?" There was a grim set to George's jaw.

"Oh, it needn't go into too many details. Just what you might call a ringing declaration about this being the greatest era of prosperity Whitewater has ever known, and that you conceive it to be the duty of your administration to protect and stimulate this prosperity. The people will understand, and the organization will understand. I guess you get what I mean, George."

"Yes, I get what you mean!" exploded George, his fist crashing upon the table. "You mean you want me to be a complacent accessory to all the legal evasions that you and your political gang and the rich bunch behind you may want to get away with! You want me to be a crook in office! By God, Doolittle—"

"Shut up, Remington," snapped the political boss, his soft manner now vanished, his whole aspect now grimly menacing.

"I know the rest of what you're going to say. I was pretty certain what it 'ud be before I came here, but I had to know for sure. Well, I know now, all right!"

His lank jaws snapped again.

"Since you are not going to represent the people that put you up, I demand your written withdrawal as candidate for the district attorney's office."

"And I refuse to give it!" cried George. "I was nominated by a convention, not by you. And I don't believe the party is as crooked as you – anyhow I'm going to give the decent members of the party a chance to vote decently! And you can't remove me from the ballot, either, for the ballot is already printed and—"

"That'll do you no—"

"I thought some time ago I was through with this political mess," George drove on. "But, Doolittle, damn you, I've just begun to get in it! And I'm going to see it through to the finish!"

Suddenly a thin little figure thrust itself between the bellicose pair and began shaking George's hand. It was Martin Jaffry.

"George – I guess I'm my share of an old scoundrel – and a trimmer – but hearing some one stand up and talk man's talk—" He broke off to shake George's hand again. "I thought you were the king of boobs – but, boy, I'm with you to wherever you want to go – if my money will last that far!"

"Keep out of this, Jaffry," roughly growled Doolittle. "It's too late for your dough to help this young pup. Remington, we may not take you off the ballot, but the organization kin send out word to the boys—"

"To knife me! Of course, I expect that! All right – go to it! But I'm on the ballot – you can't deprive people of the chance of voting for me. And I shall announce myself an independent and shall run as one!"

"We may not be able to elect our own nominee," harshly continued Doolittle, "but we kin send out word to back the Democratic candidate. Miller ain't much, but, at least, he's a soft man. And that *Sentinel* extra is going to say that a feeling has spread among the respectable element that it has lost confidence in you, and is going to say that prominent party members feel the party has made a mistake in ever putting you up. So run, damn you – run as a Democrat, a Republican, an Independent – but how are you going to git it across to the public in a way to do yourself any good – without backing? How are you going to git it across to the public?"

His last words, flung out with overmastering fury, brought George up short, and he saw this. Doolittle's wrath had mounted to that pitch which should never be reached by the resentment of a practical politician; it had attained such force that it drove him on to taunt his man. "How are you going to git it before the public?" he again demanded, eyes agleam with triumphant rancor—" with us shutting you off and hammering you on one side? – and them damned messy women across the street hammering you from the other side? Oh, it's a grand chance you have – one little old grand chance! Especially with those dear damned females loving you like they do! Jest take a look at what the bunch over there are doing to you!"

Doolittle followed his own taunting suggestion; and George, too, glanced through his window across the crowded street into the shattered window whence issued the Voiceless Speech. In that jagged frame in the raw November air still stood Mrs. Harvey Herrington, turning the giant leaves of her soundless oratory. The heckling request which then struck George's eyes began: "*Will Candidate Remington answer*—"

George Remington read no more. His already tense figure suddenly stiffened; he caught a sharp breath. Then, without a word to the two men with him, he seized his hat and dashed from his office. The street was even more a turbulent human sea, with violently twisting eddies, than had appeared from George's windows. It seemed that every member of the organizations whom Mrs. Herrington (and also Betty Sheridan, and later E. Eliot, and, at the last, Geneviève) had brought into this fight, were now downtown for the supreme effort. And it seemed that there were now more of the so-called "better citizens." Certainly there were more of Noonan's men, and these were still elbowing and jostling, and making little mass rushes – yet otherwise holding themselves ominously in control.

Into this milling assemblage George flung himself, so dominated by the fiery urge within him that he did not hear Geneviève call to him from Penny's car, which just then swung around the corner and came to a sharp stop on the skirts of the crowd. George shouldered his way irresistibly through this mass; the methods of his football days when he had been famed as a line-plunging back instinctively returned – and, all the fine chivalry forgotten which had given to his initial statement to the voters of Whitewater so noble a sound, he battered aside many of those "fairest flowers of our civilization, to protect whom it is man's duty and inspiration."

His lunging progress followed by curses and startled cries of feminine indignation, he at length emerged upon the opposite sidewalk, and, breathless and disheveled, he burst into the headquarters of the Voiceless Speech.

Some half-dozen of Mrs. Herrington's assistants cried out at his abrupt entrance. Mrs. Herrington, forward beside the speech, turned quickly about.

"Mr. Remington, you here!" she cried in amazement as he strode toward her. "What – what do you want?"

"I want – I want—" gasped George. But instead of finishing his sentence he elbowed Mrs. Herrington out of the way, shoved past her, and stepped forth in front of the Voiceless Speech. There, standing in the frame of jagged plate-glass, upon what was equivalent to a platform raised above the crowd, he sent forth a speech which had a voice. "Ladies and gentlemen!" he called, raising an imperative hand. The uproar subsided to numerous exclamations, then to surprised silence; even Noonan's men checked their disorder at this appearance of their party's candidate.

"Ladies and gentlemen," and this Voiceful Speech was loud, "I'm here to answer the questions of this contrivance behind me. But first let me tell you that though I'm on the ballot as the candidate of the Republican party, I do not want the backing of the Republican machine. I'm running as an Independent, and I shall act as an Independent.

"Here are my answers:

"I want to tell you that I shall enforce all the factory laws.

"I want to tell you that I shall enforce the laws governing housing conditions – particularly housing conditions in the factory district.

"I want to tell you that I shall enforce the laws governing child labor and the laws governing the labor of women.

"And I want to tell you that I shall enforce every other law, and shall try to secure the passage of further laws, which will make Whitewater a clean, forward-looking city, whose first consideration shall be the welfare of all.

"And, ladies and gentlemen—" he shouted, for the hushed voices had begun to rise— "I wish I could address you all as fellow-voters! – I want to tell you that I take back that foolish statement I made at the opening of the campaign.

"I want to tell you that I stand for, and shall fight for, equal suffrage!

"And I want to tell you that what has brought this change is what some of the women of White-water have shown me – and also some of the things our men politicians have done – our Doolittles, our Noonans—"

But George's speech terminated right there. Noise there had been before; now there burst out an uproar, and there came an artillery attack of eggs, vegetables, stones and bricks. One of the bricks struck George on the shoulder and drove him staggering back against the Voiceless Speech, sending that instrument of silent argument crashing to the floor. Regaining his balance, George started furiously back for the window; but Mrs. Herrington caught his arm.

"Let me go!" he called, trying to shake her off.

But she held on. "Don't – you've said enough!" she cried, and pulled him toward the rear of the room. "Look!"

Through the window was coming a heavier fire of impromptu grenades that rolled, spent, at their feet. But what they saw without was far more stirring and important. Noonan's men in the crowd, their hoodlumism now unleashed, were bowling over the people about them; but these really constituted Noonan's outposts and advance guards.

From out of two side streets, though George and Mrs. Herrington could not see their first appearance upon the scene, Noonan's real army now came charging into Main Street, as per that gentleman's grim instructions to "show them messin' women what it means to mess in politics." Hundreds of Whitewater's women were flung about, many sent sprawling to the pavement, and some hundreds of the city's most respectable voters, caught unawares, were hustled about and knocked down by the same ruthless drive.

"My God!" cried George, impulsively starting forward. "The damned brutes!"

But Mrs. Herrington still held his arm. "Come on – they're making a drive for this office!" breathlessly cried the quick-minded lady. "You can do no good here. Out the rear way – my car's waiting in the back street."

Still clutching his sleeve, Mrs. Herrington opened a door and ran across the back yard of McMonigal's building in a manner which indicated that that lady had not spent her college years (and similarly spent the years since then propped among embroidered cushions consuming marshmallows and fudge.)

The lot crossed, she hurried through a little grocery and thence into the street. Here they ran into a party that, seeing the riot on Main Street and the drive upon the window from which George had spoken, had rushed up reinforcements from the rear – a party consisting of Penny, E. Eliot, Betty Sheridan and Geneviève. "Geneviève!" cried George, and caught her into his arms.

"Oh, George," she choked. "I – I heard it all – and it – it was simply wonderful!"

"George," cried Betty Sheridan, "I always knew, if you got the right kind of a jolt, you'd be – you'd be what you are!"

E. Eliot gripped his hand in a clasp almost as strong as George's arm. "Mr. Remington, if I were a man, I'd like to have the same sort of stuff in me."

"George, you old roughneck—" began Penny.

"George," interrupted Geneviève, still chokingly, her protective, wifely instinct now at the fore, "I saw you hit, and we're going to take you straight home—"

"Cut it all out," interrupted the cultured Mrs. Herrington. "This isn't Mr. Remington's honeymoon – nor his college reunion – nor the annual convention of his maiden aunts. This is Mr. Remington's campaign, and I'm his new campaign manager. And his campaign manager says he's not going away out to his home on Sheridan Road. His campaign headquarters are going to be in the center of town, at the Commercial Hotel, where he can be reached – for there's quick work ahead of us. Come on."

Five minutes later they were all in the Commercial Hotel's best suite.

"Now, to business, Mr. Remington," briskly began Mrs. Herrington. "Of course, that was a good speech. But why, in heaven's name, didn't you come out with it before?"

"I guess I really didn't know where I stood until today," confessed George, "and today I tried to come out with it."

And George went on to recount his experience with the *Sentinel* – his scene with Doolittle – and Doolittle's plan for an extra of the Sentinel, which was doubtless then in preparation.

"So they've got the *Sentinel* muzzled, have they – and are going to get out an extra repudiating you," Mrs. Herrington repeated. There came a flash into her quick, dark eyes. "I want our candidate to stay right here – rest up – get his thoughts in order. There are a lot of things to be done. I'll be back in an hour, Mr. Remington. The rest of you come along – you, too, Mrs. Remington."

Mrs. Herrington did not altogether keep her word in the matter of time. It was two hours before she was back. To George she handed a bundle of papers, remarking: "Thought you'd like to see that *Sentinel* extra."

"I suppose Doolittle has done his worst," he remarked grimly. He glanced at the paper. His face went loose with bewilderment at what he saw – headlines, big black headlines, bigger and blacker than he had ever before seen in the politically and typographically conservative *Sentinel*. He read through a few lines of print, then looked up.

"Why, it's all here!" he gasped. "The kidnapping of Miss Eliot and Geneviève by Noonan's men – my break with Doolittle, my denunciation of the party's methods, my coming out as an independent candidate – that riot on Main Street! How on earth did that ever get into the *Sentinel*?"

"Some straight talk, and quick talk, and the exercise of a little of the art of pressure they say you men exercise," was the prompt reply. "I telephoned Mr. Ledbetter of the *Sentinel* advising him to hold the extra Mr. Doolittle had threatened until he heard from Mr. Wesley Norton, proprietor of the Norton Dry Goods Store. You know, Mr. Norton is the *Sentinel*'s largest single advertiser and president of the Whitewater Business Men's Club.

"Then a committee of us women called on Mr. Norton and told him that we'd organize the women of the city and would carry on a boycott campaign against his store – we didn't really put it quite as crudely as that – unless he'd force the *Sentinel* to stop Mr. Doolittle's lying extra and print your statement.

"Mr. Norton gave in, and telephoned the *Sentinel* that if it didn't do as he said he'd cancel his advertising contract. Then, to make sure, we got hold of Mr. Jaffry, called on Mr. Ledbetter, who called in the business manager – and your Uncle Martin told them that unless they printed the truth, and every bit of it, and printed it at once, he was going to put up the money to start an opposition paper that *would print the truth*. That explains the extra 'Well'," ejaculated George, still staring, "you certainly are a wonder as a campaign manager!"

"Oh, I only did my fraction. That Miss Eliot did as much as I – she's a find – she's going to be one of Whitewater's really big women. And Betty Sheridan, you can't guess how Betty's worked – and your wife, Mr. Remington, she's turning out to be a marvel!"

"But that's not all," Mrs. Herrington continued rapidly. "We bought ten thousand copies of that extra for ourselves – your uncle paid for them – and we're going to distribute them in every home in town. When the best element in Whitewater read how the women were trampled down by Noonan's mob – well, they'll know how to vote! Mr. Noonan will never guess how much he has helped us."

"You seem to have left nothing for me to do," said George.

"You'll find out there'll be all you'll want," replied the brisk Mrs. Herrington. "We're organizing meetings – one in every hall in the city, one on almost every other street corner, and we're going to rush you from one to the next – most of the night – and there'll be no letup for you tomorrow, even if it is election day. Yes, you'll find there'll be plenty to do!"

The next twenty-four hours were the busiest that George Remington had ever known in his twenty-six years.

But at nine o'clock the next evening it was over – the tumult and the shouting and the congratulations – and all were gone save only Martin Jaffry; and District-Attorney-Elect Remington sat in his hotel suite alone in the bosom of his family.

He was still dazed by what had happened to him – at the part he had unexpectedly played – dazed by the intense but well-ordered activity of the women: their management of his whirlwind tour of the city; their organization of parades with amazing swiftness; their rapid and complete house-to-house canvass – the work of Mrs. Herrington, of Betty, of that Miss Eliot, of hundreds of women – and especially of Geneviève. He marveled especially at Geneviève because he had never thought of Geneviève as doing such things. But she *had* done them – he felt that somehow she was a different Geneviève: he didn't know what the difference was – he was in too much of a whirl for analysis – but he had an undefined sense of *aliveness*, of a spirited, joyous initiative in her.

She and all the rest seemed so strange as to be unbelievable. And yet, she – and all of it – true!...

From dramatic events and intangible qualities of the spirit, his consciousness shifted to material things – his immediate surroundings. Not till this blessed moment of relaxation did he become aware of the discomforts of this suite – nor did Geneviève fully appreciate the flamboyantly flowered maroon wall-paper and the jig-saw furniture.

"George," she sighed, "now that you're not needed down here, can't we go home?"

"Home!" The word came out half snort, half growl – hardly the tone becoming one whose triumph was so exultingly fresh. With a jar he had come back to a present which he fully understood. "Damn home! I haven't any home!"

Geneviève stared. Uncle Martin snickered, for Uncle Martin had the gift of understanding.

"You mean those flowers of womanhood whom chivalrous man—"

"Shut up," commanded George. He thought for a brief space; then his jaw set. "Excuse me a moment."

Drawing hotel stationery toward him, he scribbled rapidly and then sealed and addressed what he had written.

"Uncle Martin, your car's outside doing nothing; would you mind going on ahead and giving this little note to Cousin Alys Brewster-Smith, and then staying around and having a little supper with Geneviève and me? We'll be out soon, but there are a few things I want to talk over with Geneviève alone before we come."

Uncle Martin would oblige. But when he had gone, there seemed to be nothing of pressing importance that George had to communicate to Geneviève. Nor half an hour later, when he led his bride of four months up to their home, had he delivered himself of anything which seemed to require privacy.

As they stepped up on the porch, softly lighted by a frosted bulb in its ceiling, Cousin Emelene, her cat under her arm, came out of the front door and hurried past them, without speech.

"Why, Cousin Emelene!" George called after her.

She paused and half turned.

"You – you—" she half choked upon expletives that would not come forth. "The man will come for my trunks in the morning." Thrusting a handkerchief to her face, she hurried away.

"George, what can have happened to her?" cried the amazed Geneviève.

But George was saved answering her just then. Another figure had emerged from the front door – a rather largish figure, all in black – her left hand clutching the right hand of a child, aged, possibly, five. And this figure did not cower and hurry away. This figure halted, and glowered.

"George Remington," exclaimed Cousin Alys, "after your invitation – you – you apostate to chivalry! That outrageous letter! But if I am leaving your home, thank God I'm leaving it for a home of my own! Come on, Martin!"

With that she stalked away, dragging the sleepy Eleanor.

Not till then did George and Geneviève become aware that Uncle Martin was before them, having until now been obscured by Mrs. Brewster-Smith's outraged amplitude. His arms were loaded with coats, obviously feminine.

"Uncle Martin!" exclaimed George.

"George," gulped his uncle— "George—" And then he gained control of a dazed sort of speech. "When I gave her that letter I didn't know it was a letter of eviction. And the way she broke down before me – a woman, you know – I – I – well, George, it's my home she's going to."

"You don't mean—"

"Yes, George, that's just what I mean. Though, of course, I'm taking her back now to Mrs. Gallup's boarding-house until – until – good-night, George; good-night, Geneviève." The little man went staggering down the walk with his burden of wraps; and after a minute there came the sound of his six-cylinder roadster buzzing away into the darkness.

"I didn't tell 'em they had to go tonight," said George doggedly. "But I did remark that even if every woman had a right to a home, every woman didn't have the right to make my home her home. Anyhow," his tone becoming softer, "I've at last got a home of my own. Our own," he corrected.

He took her in his arms. "And, sweetheart – it's a better home than when we first came to it, for now I've got more sense. Now it is a home in which each of us has the right to think and be what we please."

* * *

At just about this same hour just about this same scene was being enacted upon another front porch in Whitewater – there being the slight difference that this second porch was not softly illuminated by any frosted globule of incandescence. Up the three steps leading to this second porch Mr. Penfield Evans had that moment escorted Miss Elizabeth Sheridan.

"Good-night, Penny," she said.

He caught her by her two shoulders.

"See here, Betty – the last twenty-four hours have been mighty busy hours – too busy even to talk about ourselves. But now – see here, you're not going to get away with any rough work like that. Come across, now. Will you?"

"Will I what?"

"Say, how long do you think you're a paid-up subscriber to this little daily speech of mine?... Well, if I've got to hand you another copy, here goes. You promised me, on your word of honor, if George swung around for suffrage, you'd swing around for me. Well, George has come around. Not that I had much to do with it – but he surely did come around! Now, the point is, Miss Betty Sheridan, are you a woman of your promise – are you going to marry me?"

"Well, if you try to put it that way, demanding your pound of flesh—"

"One hundred and twenty pounds," corrected Penny.

"I'll say that, of course, I don't love you, but I guess a promise is a promise – and – and—" And suddenly a pair of strong young arms were flung about the neck of Mr. Penfield Evans. "Oh, I'm so happy, Penny dear!"

"Betty!"

After that there was a long silence... silence broken only by that softly sibilant detonation which belongs most properly to the month of June, but confines itself to no season... to a long, long silence born of and blessed by the gods... until one Percival Sheridan, coming stealthily home from a late debauch at Humphrey's drug store, and mounting the steps in the tennis sneakers which were his invariable wear on dry and non-state occasions, bumped into the invisible and unhearing couple.

"Say, there—" gasped the startled youth, backing away.

Betty gave an affrighted cry – it was a long swift journey down from where she had just been. Her right hand, reaching drowningly out, fell upon a familiar shoulder.

"It's Pudge!" she cried. "Pudge" – shaking him – "snooping around, listening and trying to spy—"

"You stop that – it ain't so!" protested the outraged Pudge, his utterance throttled down somewhat by the chocolate cream in his mouth.

"Spying on people! And, besides, you've been stuffing yourself with candy again! You're ruining your stomach with that sticky sweet stuff – you're headed straight for a candy-fiend's grave. Now, you go upstairs and to bed!"

She jerked him toward the door, opened it, and as he was thrust through the door Pudge felt something, something warm, press impulsively against a cheek. Not until the door had closed upon him did he realize what Betty had done to him. He stood dazed for a moment – unbalanced between impulses. Then the sturdy maleness of fourteen rewon its dominance.

"Guess I know what they was doing, all right – aw, wouldn't it make you sick!" And, in disgust which another chocolate cream alleviated hardly at all, he mounted to his bed.

Outside there was again silence... faintly disturbed only by that softly sibilant, almost muted percussion which recalls inevitably the month of June....

The End

The End

Lives & Works

Samuel Merwin
Harry Leon Wilson
Fannie Hurst
Dorothy Canfield
Kathleen Norris
Henry Kitchell Webster
Anne O'Hagan
Mary Heaton Vorse
Alice Duer Miller
Ethel Watts Mumford
Marjorie Benton Cook
William Allen White
Mary Austin
Leroy Scott

Elizabeth Jordan (editor)

Renowned author, journalist and editor, Elizabeth Jordan (1865–1947) edited *Harper's Bazaar* magazine between 1900 and 1913. As a journalist, she covered famous murder trials such as the suspected axe murderer Lizzie Borden, and wrote about social issues such as the conditions of New York tenements. As a book editor, Jordan worked with Sinclair Lewis on his first two novels, and organized the writing and production of *The Whole Family* (1908), a collaborative novel featuring authors such as William Dean Howells and Henry James. An enthusiastic suffragist, Jordan deplored the image of women as a 'clinging vine' and edited *The Sturdy Oak* in 1917, with all proceeds going to the suffrage cause.

Samuel Merwin

Playwright and author Samuel Merwin (1874–1936) was born in Evanston, Illinois. After attending Northwestern University, he edited *Success* magazine, an American business publication which promoted 'New Thought Philosophy', an approach based on positive thinking and taking control of one's own life and development. Merwin also wrote novels, plays and short stories, collaborating on some of his novels with his friend from childhood, the writer Henry Kitchell Webster. Perhaps influenced by his aunt, Frances E. Willard, the suffragist and reformer, Merwin was a staunch supporter of the women's rights movement. Married with two sons, Merwin died of a stroke while dining at the Players club in New York City.

Harry Leon Wilson

Born in Oregon, Illinois, the novelist Harry Leon Wilson (1867–1939) began his working life as a stenographer before becoming a private secretary. His first published work was a story for the December 1886 issue of *Puck* magazine. Wilson regularly contributed to this publication before becoming its editor in 1890. In 1902, on the publication of his first novel, *The Spenders*, he left *Puck* to become a full-time novelist. Moving to an artist's and writer's colony in Carmel-by-the-Sea, California, Wilson became briefly notorious in the American press after fighting the artist Theodore Morrow Criley. Their long-standing feud about a suspected romance with Wilson's third wife, Helen MacGowan Cooke, ended in embarrassment for Wilson when – despite three months' training – he was soundly beaten by Morrow Criley. Wilson died of a brain haemorrhage at the age of 72.

Fannie Hurst

Popular and topical American writer, Fannie Hurst (1889–1968) was born in Hamilton, Ohio. She moved to New York City in 1911 to become a writer and, struggling at first to find a publisher, she supported herself by waitressing and shop work. These roles gave her an insight into social issues, including gender and class inequality, which she would later explore in her novels and short stories. Following the First World War, Hurst published several short stories and novels, her first being published in the *Saturday Evening Post* in 1912. Hurst's works grew in popularity and by 1925, when she had published five short story compilations and two novels, she was one of the most highly paid authors in the United States. Hurst explored issues such as class, poverty, gender and race. She was also an active campaigner for women's rights.

Dorothy Canfield

The celebrated performer and author Dorothy Canfield (1879–1958) was an advocate for women's rights and the importance of education. She was instrumental in introducing the Montessori education method to the United States, and managed its first adult education programme. She was also active in developing education and rehabilitation, especially in women's prisons. Born in Lawrence, Kansas, Canfield received her BA from Ohio State University and her doctoral degree from Columbia University, New York. Canfield married John Redwood Fisher in 1907 and travelled with him to France during the First World War, where she worked to provide convalescent homes for refugee children. Canfield wrote 22 novels, six short story compilations and 18 non-fiction books, which give readers a glimpse into the life of this remarkable woman.

Kathleen Norris

Kathleen Norris (1880–1966), was one of the highest paid women writers in the US between 1911 and 1959. Norris wrote an incredible 93 novels focusing on themes such as family values and the importance of motherhood and marriage. She began her literary career by writing short stories, with her husband, the novelist Charles Gilman Norris, becoming her literary agent. To allow her to work as a writer, Charles shared responsibility for many household tasks which would usually have fallen to the female. Her works often reflected her traditional and Catholic views, but – to the surprise of some of her admirers – she was also a supporter of suffrage and pacifism, actively campaigning for these and other causes. Many of her best-selling novels were adapted into films and radio broadcasts.

Henry Kitchell Webster

Born in Evanston, Illinois, Henry Kitchell Webster (1875–1932) became one of the most popular serial writers of early twentieth century America. Co-writing *The Short Line War* (1899), among other novels, with friend and author Samuel Merwin, Webster published what he saw as his best works under his own name and used the pseudonym O.C. Cabot (which spells 'tobacco' when read backwards) for less weighty, pulp publications. Novels, which straddled the genres of family drama, science fiction and mysteries, were often first published as serials and he became known for his skill in producing popular, profitable books. Webster died of cancer at the age of 57, leaving behind a wife and three sons.

Anne O'Hagan

American writer and feminist, Anne O'Hagan (1869–1933) was born in Washington, DC. An active suffragist, O'Hagan was a board member of the Equal Suffrage League of New York, as well as several other organizations in the city which worked to prevent prohibition and support her church, the Protestant Church of St Luke in the Fields in Greenwich, also attended by Eleanor Roosevelt. She wrote periodicals and short stories for magazines, such as *Harper's*, *Vanity Fair* and *Collier's*, and was particularly concerned with the mistreatment of female shop clerks. O'Hagan also participated in a number of collaborative projects, including *The Sturdy Oak*, which was first serialized in *Collier's*.

Mary Heaton Vorse

Novelist, activist and journalist, Mary Heaton Vorse (1874–1966) was born in New York. Her concern for the plight of female and immigrant textile workers led to her becoming involved with suffragism and civil rights causes. She was a witness to the tragic fire at the Triangle Shirtwaist Textile Factory in 1911, which led to the deaths of 146 workers who were unable to escape the flames, as they had been locked in. Of this number, 123 were women and girls, the youngest being 14 years of age. A suspected anarchist, Vorse was regularly under surveillance by the US Department of Justice in J. Edgar Hoover's government. She died of a heart attack in Amherst, Massachusetts.

Alice Duer Miller

Poet, author and activist Alice Duer Miller (1874–1942) began her writing career by publishing satirical poetry highlighting the suffrage cause. Hailing from a wealthy family, Miller was educated at Barnard College of Columbia University, New York, where she studied Mathematics and Astronomy. She helped fund her studies by writing for magazines such as *Harper's*. The title of a collection of her poems, *Are Women People?*, became a popular suffrage slogan. Miller wrote several stories and novels which were adapted into film screenplays, and she also wrote directly for films. Her novel, *The White Cliffs* (1940), which was written in verse, was the basis of the 1944 film *The White Cliffs of Dover*.

Ethel Watts Mumford

Ethel Watts Mumford (c. 1876–1940), the successful New York author and playwright, divorced her first husband, George D. Mumford, after seven years of marriage because he refused to support her writing career. Leaving him and taking their son whom she raised alone, Mumford vowed to never remarry unless her future husband agreed to support her career. Her next marriage in 1906 to Peter Geddes Grant was more successful and she went on to publish novels, short stories, plays, songs, poems and articles, with her writing often reflecting the experiences of her extensive travels. Mumford also pursued a successful career as an artist and illustrator. She died in New York.

Marjorie Benton Cooke

Marjorie Benton Cooke (1876–1920) was born in Richmond, Indiana. Following her graduation from the University of Chicago in 1899, Cooke worked as a journalist and monologist, performing as well as publishing many of her monologues. These often focused on the suffrage cause of which Cooke was an active supporter, as did several of her popular novels. A member of the National

American Woman Suffrage Association and the Heterodoxy group, a feminist debating society in New York City, Cooke's novels often focused on the place of women in the home, marriage and in the working world. She died in Manila, the Philippines, while on a world cruise.

William Allen White

Pulitzer Prize-winning politician, editor and author, William Allen White (1868–1944) began his writing and editing career at the *Kansas City Star* in his home state. In 1912, he formed the Kansas Republican League, a progressive party which supported Theodore Roosevelt in the 1912 US presidential election. White's abhorrence of the Ku Klux Klan led to him running for Governor of Kansas in 1924. While he was unsuccessful, he was instrumental in leading a criticism, which resulted in local public opinion turning against the Klan. Married with two children, White published over 20 works during his lifetime, including collections of short stories, articles, biographies and speeches. His fictional works expounded on ideals of middle American small-town values in which members of the community looked out for one another.

Mary Austin

Illinois-born Mary Austin (1868–1934) spent a significant part of her career studying the lives of the indigenous Mojave people. Her novels, plays and poems express the knowledge gained from her intensive studies, with one of her most famous works, *The Land of Little Rain* (1903), exploring the inhabitants and landscape of the

Mojave Desert. A staunch defender of Native American people's rights, Austin was also an active feminist. She died in Santa Fe, New Mexico at the age of 65, and a mountain, Mount Mary Austin, in the Sierra Nevada was named after her.

Leroy Scott

Born in Fairmount, Indiana, Leroy Scott (1875–1929) worked as a reporter and editor before writing novels and screenplays. An active socialist, Scott was one of the founders of the Intercollegiate Socialist Society, a student organization that ran from 1905–21 before expanding to become the League for Industrial Democracy. He married Miriam Finn, a Russian-born Jew, in 1904, with whom he had one daughter. The couple supported the Russian author and socialist Alexei Maximovich Peshkov, known as Maxim Gorky, when he visited the United States while exiled from Russia. Scott drowned in Lake Chateaugay, near New York.

Other Contributors

Ruth Robbins (Series Foreword) is Professor of English Literature and Director of Research for Cultural Studies at Leeds Beckett University. She has published widely on both feminism and the literature of the period 1870–1940. Her books include *Literary Feminisms, Pater to Forster, Subjectivity, Oscar Wilde* and *The British Short Story*. She is currently working on *Virginia Woolf: A Writer's Life*.

June Purvis (Introduction and Further Reading) is Professor Emerita of Women's and Gender History at the University of Portsmouth. She has published extensively on the British women's suffrage campaigns, especially two highly acclaimed biographies of suffragette leaders, Emmeline Pankhurst and Christabel Pankhurst. Other publications include *Votes for Women and The British Women's Suffrage Campaign: National and International Perspectives*. June is also the Founding and Managing Editor of the journal *Women's History Review*.

Judith John (Life & Works and Glossary) is a writer and editor specializing in literature and history. A former secondary school English Language and Literature teacher, she has subsequently worked as an editor on major educational projects, including *English A: Literature* for the Pearson International Baccalaureate series. Judith's major research interests include Romantic and Gothic literature, and Renaissance drama.

Victorian, Gothic, Sci-Fi & Dystopian Fiction

A Glossary of Terms

abbess: nun in charge of a convent; female brothel keeper, a madame

abhorrence: feeling of loathing or revulsion

abode: place where people live; period of living somewhere

abominable: causing revulsion or disgust

aggrandizement: self-promotion; increase in power or status

air-blebs: air heads, empty-headed people

afterlife: existence after death; eternal life

alchemy: mythical practice of turning base metals into gold, prolonging life or finding a universal remedy for disease

alderman: term for a half-Crown; senior local government official

ale: alcoholic drink made from hops and fermented malt, stronger and heavier than beer

almanac: annual calendar which contains information on important dates, tides, astronomical data, etc.

almshouse: lodgings for the poor, privately funded (often by the church), as opposed to the workhouse, which was publicly funded

amorphous: undefined, without clear shape

anatomical: relating to the structure of the body

antagonist: enemy or adversary

antinomianism: policy which allows Christians freedom from moral obligations

apoplexy: a crippling cerebral stroke, sometimes fatal; a fit of anger

apothecary: pharmacist; one who prepares drugs and medicines and gives medical advice; lowest order of medical man

apprentice: someone who works under a skilled professional for a specific amount of time (usually seven years) in order to learn a trade. When one finished his apprenticeship, he became a journeyman and would get paid for work himself

Armageddon: the final battle between good and evil

asylum: institution for people with mental health problems, often referred to as lunatic asylums

athwart: across; in opposition to

atone: to make amends for a crime or offence

automaton: someone who resembles a machine by going through motions repetitively, but without feeling or emotion

B

Babylonian finger: that which spells out the writing on the wall; delivering a judgement

balderdash: nonsense, senseless or exaggerated speech or writing

banns: announcement or notice of a forthcoming marriage in a parish church, proclaimed on three consecutive Sundays

beak: magistrate

bearer up: thief with a female accomplice who would distract the victim so the crime could be performed

beating: repeatedly hitting someone; scaring birds from bushes out into the open for shooting parties

Bedlam: nickname for the Hospital of St Mary of Bethlehem, a London psychiatric hospital; place or situation full of noise, frenzy and confusion

beg to: wish to

berserker: traditionally an ancient and ferocious Norse warrior known for savagery

bizarre: unusual or strange

blackleg: someone who works during a strike, often criticized by those who obey the strike (also known as a 'scab')

blag: to steal something, often by smash-and-grab; to trick or con someone

blasphemy: sacrilegious talk concerning God or religion

blighter: annoying or contemptible person

bloodletting: reducing the volume of blood in the body by either opening a vein or applying leeches as a way of restoring health, used from ancient times up to the nineteenth century

bloofer: vampire, usually female; term possibly comes from the mispronunciation of 'beautiful'

bludger: violent criminal who often used a bludgeon or heavy, stout weapon

blue bottle: policeman

blunderbuss: musket, used at close-range; clumsy or awkward person

boarder: person paying rent for a bed, a room and usually meals in a private home or boarding house

bob: cockney slang for a shilling or five-pence piece

Boche: German person; the term was often used to describe soldiers

body-snatching: the act of stealing corpses from graves, tombs or morgues, usually for dissection or scientific study

borough: town that had been given the right to self-govern by royal charter; in Victorian London, Southwark was referred to as 'the borough'

Bow Street Runners: detective force in London who pre-dated the police, organized by novelist Henry Fielding and his brother John in 1750 up to 1829, when Robert Peel founded London's first police force

brackish: slightly salty, usually refers to water

buck cabbie: dishonest cab driver

bug hunting: stealing from or cheating drunks, especially at night in drinking dens

bull: cockney slang for five shillings

C

calamity: accident or distressing event

cant: a free meal; language or vocabulary spoken by thieves or groups of people perceived to be common

caper: criminal act; dangerous activity

caravanserai: roadside inn for travellers, often found along the Asian trade routes

cash carrier: pimp or whore's minder, who would literally hold the money earned by soliciting

casuist: skilled orator, who uses clever but potentially deceptive reasoning

cavalier: Royalist soldier; often used to describe a chivalrous man or gentleman

census: official list of the British population, including address and details of age, gender, occupation and birthplace, carried out every ten years since 1841

charlatan: person who assumes false skills or knowledge; also known as a mountebank

charnel-house: vault containing the remains of dead bodies or skeletons

cherubim: winged celestial beings (singular: cherub)

chilblains: red, itchy swelling to parts of face, fingers and toes caused by exposure to cold and damp

chimera: something wished for but impossible; a fire-breathing monster from Greek mythology

chink: money (from the noise coins make when they knock against each other)

chiv/shiv: knife, razor or sharpened stick used as a weapon

chivvied: harassed or annoyed by attacks; to be encouraged to do something

choker: clergyman, referring to the clerical collar worn around the neck

cholera: disease of the small intestine, often fatal, marked by symptoms of thirst, cramps, vomiting and diarrhoea, caused by drinking water tainted with human waste. Victorians were hit with several cholera epidemics before sanitation conditions were improved

choused: to have been cheated

christen: to remove identifying marks from; to use for the first time; to make something like new again

chronometer: tool for measuring accurate time

claustrophobia: abnormal dread of being imprisoned or confined in a close or narrow space

cly faking: to pick someone's pocket

coal scuttle: metal pail for carrying and pouring coal

colonial: native of a colony; something characteristic of or relating to a colony

commencement: the beginning or start of something

comrade: term used for someone with shared interests or beliefs, commonly used among communist or socialist parties

confabulation: to cause confusion on purpose by filling in memory gaps with untruths

connubial: conjugal; relating to marriage

contagion: spread of disease caused by close contact

cop/copper: policeman

costermonger: street peddler, usually selling fruits or vegetables

cracksman: safecracker, someone who cracks or breaks locks

cravat: scarf or band of fabric worn around the neck and tied in a bow

creator: someone who makes something come alive

crib: building, house or lodging; location of a gaol

crossgrained: bad tempered or stubborn

crow: lookout during criminal activities; doctor

crusher: policeman

cudgel: heavy stick used as a weapon

cursory: quick, superficial and not very thorough

cypher: coded message; secret way of writing

D

daguerreotype: photograph taken by an early process, now obsolete

dandy: a man very concerned with his appearance and clothing; something excellent or agreeable

daresay: venture to say; think probable

day boarder: someone who spends the day at school but lives at home, as opposed to someone who boards at the school

deadlurk: empty premises

deaner: shilling

debouchment: narrow, confined opening or area; the act of moving from a confined area into an open space

deformity: disfigurement or malformation, often of a body part but can also refer to morals or the mind

deity: god or goddess; supreme being

depraved: wicked, immoral or corrupt

deputation: group of people charged with a mission or to represent other people

despatch: send something; to send someone to carry out a task

despotism: oppressive and often tyrannical rule or authority

deuce: euphemism for 'devil', used to express annoyance; the two on a die or playing card

deuce hog: two shillings

device: tuppence; an emblem or motto

Devil: the Devil, as depicted in Christianity and some other religions, stands as the enemy or opposite to God and tempts people to sin so that they go to Hell; the actual term 'Devil' comes from the Latin *diabolus*, meaning slanderous. Gothic characters are often tempted by agents of the Devil

dewskitch: a beating (bodily assault)

diligence: public stagecoach; taking care or attention over something

ding: to throw something away; to take something that has been thrown away

diphtheria: infectious disease caused by germs in the throat, causing difficulty in breathing, fever and damage to the heart and nervous system

dirge: funeral hymn, mournful lament for the dead

dispatches: loaded dice; sends someone to carry out a task

do down: to beat someone with fists, especially as a punishment

dogmatism: emphatic belief presented as fact without consideration of truth or others' opinions

dollyshop: unlicensed, often cheap, loan or pawn shop

don: eminent, professional or clever person; leader or head of a group

Doppelgänger: literally translated from German as 'doublegoer'; the ghostly apparition of another, living person; double or alter ego

double-knock: applied to the door by a confident visitor, one who was known to the family and comfortable with the purpose of his visit (a single-knock signified a more timid caller, often of an inferior class)

dowager: widow with an inherited title or property from her deceased husband; distinguished, respected older woman

down: cause suspicion or doubt; to inform on a person, when used in the expression 'to put down on someone'

dragsman: someone who steals from carriages or coaches

draught: cheque or bill of exchange; a small quantity of liquid drunk in one mouthful

duckett: street dealer or vendor's licence

duffer: someone who sells allegedly stolen or worthless goods, also known as a 'hawker'

E

ecod: mild curse, most likely derived from 'My God'

economy: cheapness; giving better value

eldritch: ghostly or sinister

Elysian Fields: from Greek mythology, term for the afterlife of the blessed; blissful or heavenly place

employ: to hire someone to work for you; if you were in the employ of or employed by someone, you worked for them

entrapment: imprisoning someone; incarcerating or trapping someone, often in dark, strange or claustrophobic surroundings

epidemic: illness that spreads rapidly and extensively, affecting most of the people who come in contact with it

epoch: period of time marked by particular events

equinoctial: occurring at the time of or near to the equinox, a twice-yearly event when the sun crosses the celestial equator

erethism: extreme excitement or stimulation

escop/eslop: policeman

establishment: shop, place of business

exculpation: exoneration; being cleared from guilt

exorcism: act of forcing the Devil, a demon or evil spirits from the body of someone who is possessed, done through religious prayer or rituals

expectations: chance of coming into an inheritance, property or money

extant: living or existing

extermination: destruction of an entire group or civilization

extra-terrestrial: existing outside of the earth's atmosphere

F

fadge: slang term for farthing

fakement: sham or trick, often used when begging

fan: to feel surreptitiously under someone's clothing while they are wearing it, searching for objects to steal

fanatical: zealous or single-minded

farthing: monetary unit worth a quarter of a penny; something almost worthless or of the lowest value

fawney-dropping: trick where a criminal pretends to find a ring (which has no actual value) and sells it as an item of possible worth

fiend: evil demon; evil or wicked person

finny: slang term for five-pound note

flam: lie or deception

flash: to show off or try to impress; something special or expensive-looking

flash house: public house with criminals as clientele

flimp: snatch stealing or pickpocketing from a crowd

flue faker: chimney sweep, usually young boys

footman: servant in livery, usually in a mansion or palace; a servant who serves at table, tends the door or carriage, runs errands

forebodings: feelings of apprehension or anxiety

forfeits: parlour games where each player needs to supply a correct answer and has a forfeit if the answer is not given

fossicking: rummaging or searching, usually for something valuable. The term is often used to describe searching for gold or valuable stones

foundling: orphan or abandoned child raised by someone else

furlong: unit of measurement equal to 201 m (660 ft), the length of the traditional furrow or plough trench on a farm

furtherance: helping or advancing the progress of something

fusillade: volleys of shots fired simultaneously or in rapid succession

G

gable: triangular end of a building where the wall meets the roof

gaff: show or exhibition; cheap, smutty theatre; hoax or trick

gainsay: contradict; deny

galvanize: to shock someone or something into action

gammon: misleading comment, meant to deceive

gammy: someone false who is not to be trusted

gaol: jail

garniture: decorative ornament or embellishment

garret: fob pocket in a waistcoat; room at the top of the house

gattering: public house

general post: mail that was sent from the London Post Office to the rest of England

ghost: phantom or spirit of somebody who has died and who has possibly not gone on to the afterlife, which often inspires fear or terror

gibbet: post with a projecting beam for hanging executed criminals, often done publicly as a warning to the public

gig: light, open, two-wheeled carriage drawn by a single horse

gill: unit of liquid equalling a quarter of a pint

gimlety: piercing, sharp-eyed

glim: light or fire; a source of light; begging by saying you are homeless due to fire; venereal disease

gloaming: dusk or twilight

glock: slow, half-witted person

gonoph: petty, small-time criminal

Gordian knot: an impossible or extremely complex problem; from the legend of Gordius, king of Phrygia, who tied a knot that could only be cut by the future ruler of Asia and which was cut by Alexander the Great

Gorgon: female monster from Greek mythology with snakes for hair

gothic: style of architecture, music, art or fiction generally associated with strange, frightening occurrences and mysterious or supernatural plots, characters or locations

gout: disease mainly affecting men, causing inflammation and swelling of the hands and feet, arthritis and deformity; caused by excess uric acid production

governess: woman employed to teach and care for children in a school or home

greatcoat: long, heavy overcoat worn outdoors, often with a short cape worn over the shoulders

grog: mixture of alcohol, often rum, and water, named after an English admiral who diluted sailors' rum

grotesque: misshapen or mutated character; something or someone unexpected, monstrous or bizarre

gruel: watery, unappetizing porridge, popular with the owners of the workhouse or orphanage due to its cheapness

guinea: gold coin, monetary value of twenty-one shillings or one pound and one shilling

gulpy: someone gullible or easy to fool

H

haberdasher: someone who sells personal items, often accessories such as thread or ribbons

habiliments: clothing

hackney coach: carriage for hire

hagiology: literature about the lives of saints or venerated people

hansom cab: two-wheeled, horse-drawn carriage where the driver sat on a high seat at the back so that the passengers had a clear view of the road

harbinger: something that signals or foreshadows an event or person

haybag: derogatory term for a woman

hedonism: the pursuit of pleasure

heliograph: signalling device that works by moving a mirror to reflect sunlight

heresy: belief that contradicts generally accepted or official religious teaching

hob: metal shelf or rack over a fireplace where the pans or kettle could be warmed

hoisting: shoplifting; to lift something up

hopping: picking hops, used for making beer

humbug: something insincere or nonsensical, meant to deceive or cheat people; used to express disbelief or disgust; a hoax or fraud

hykey: pride, arrogance

I

inchoate: partly or imperfectly formed; not fully in existence

incubus: name for a male demon, thought to be a fallen angel, who forces himself sexually upon sleeping women, which often resulted in the birth of a demon or deformed, half-human child

infusoria: single-celled organisms

indefatigable: tirelessly persistent; not giving in to fatigue

influenza/flu: viral illness causing aching joints, fever, headaches, sore throat, cough and sneezing, even followed by death in Victorian times

inmate: someone confined to an institution such as a lunatic asylum or prison

Inquisition: organization founded by the Catholic Church charged with the eradication of heresy or acting against God, by which those found guilty were often put to death; (lowercase) period of extended questioning, often associated with violence and torture

insensate: lacking understanding, sense or reason; without sensitivity or feeling

insurrection: uprising in revolt or rebellion, usually against an
    established government or authority
integument: tough, protective outer layer
interred: buried
invidious: unpleasant or undesirable
ironclad: armoured warship
ironmonger: someone who sells metal goods, tools and hardware
irons: guns, usually pistols or revolvers

J

jolly: disturbance or brawl; cheerful or happy
journeyman: skilled worker who has finished an apprenticeship
    and is qualified to hire himself out for work
Judgement Day: the end of the world when God judges humanity
    and the dead come back to life; also known as doomsday
Judy: term for a woman, usually a prostitute
juggernaut: massive and destructive force that is almost
    impossible to stop
jump: ground-floor window, or a burglary committed by
    entering through the window

K

kecks: slang term for trousers
ken: house, lodging or public house
keystone: wedge-shaped stone placed at the summit of an arch, which
    locks the other stones in place; a central principle or policy
kidsman: organizer of child thieves
kismet: fate or destiny
kith: someone's friends, neighbours or relatives

knacker: someone who disposes of injured, unwanted or dead animals, often turning their carcasses into by-products such as animal food, fat or glue

knaves: jacks in a deck of cards

knee breeches: trousers that reach the knee

knock up: to bang loudly on someone's door to wake them up

know life: to be familiar with criminal ways; to be street-wise

kopjes: small hill, South African term meaning 'little head'

L

lag: convict; someone sentenced to transportation or gaol

lassitude: feeling of weariness, lack of energy

laudanum: solution of opium and alcohol used as pain relief or to aid sleep, highly addictive

lavender, lay in: to hide from the police; to pawn something for money; to be dead

league: group or association with mutual interests, such as individuals, states or countries

leg: dishonest person, cheat

Lethean: forgetfulness or oblivion; from the river Lethe, one of the rivers of Hades in Greek mythology. Drinking from the river Lethe made people completely forget their past

leviathan: sea monster; large and powerful object or thing

liberal: generous; tolerant or open-minded

link boy: boy who carries a torch to light a person's way through the dark streets

liverish: feeling unwell, especially bilious; feeling disagreeable or peevish

lodger: person paying rent to stay in a room (or bed) in somebody else's house

logbook: book in which a teacher would comment on pupils' attendance, behaviour, learning progress, etc.

lumber: wood used for building or woodworking, often second-hand furniture; to pawn something; to go to gaol

Lunnun: slag term for London

lurker: criminal; beggar or someone who dresses as a beggar for money

lush: alcoholic drink; someone who drinks too much alcohol; luxurious

M

macaroni: term used to describe young men dressed in the fashionable continental style

macer: cheat

mag: slang term for a ha'pence piece

magistrate: judge over trials of misdemeanours; civil officer who upholds the law

maid-of-all-work: usually a young girl, hired as the only servant in the house and required to do any job asked of her

mail coach: carrier of the mail and a limited number of passengers, replaced in the mid-nineteenth century by the railroad

malefactor: someone who commits a crime or wrongdoing

malignity: malevolence, bad feeling towards someone

malt: grain, such as barley, that has been allowed to ferment, used for brewing beer and sometimes whisky

mandrake: homosexual; type of plant

mania: mental obsession or abnormality which can cause mood swings

manifestation: a sign or visual proof of existence

manifesto: declaration of policy or intent, often published by a political party

mark: the victim of a crime

market day: the regular day each week when country people would bring their livestock and goods to sell in town

market town: town that regularly held a market, usually the largest town of a farming area

masochism: psychosexual perversion where someone gains erotic pleasure by having pain, abuse or humiliation inflicted on them

materially reduced: having your circumstances and/or finances reduced or lessened

maxim: statement or saying

mead: fermented alcoholic drink made of water, honey, malt, yeast and sometimes spices

mecks: alcohol, usually wine or spirits

mesmeric: causing someone to be entranced or rendered unaware of their surroundings

Messrs: plural of Mr., used when referring to more than one man

metamorphosis: change or complete transformation in physical form, shape or structure, thought to be caused by supernatural powers

miasma: unpleasant smell or vapour, often related to disease or death

Michaelmas: Christian festival celebrating the archangel Michael, celebrated on 29 September, one of the four quarters of the year

middle class: people who earn enough money to live comfortably, often in a skilled profession, such as doctors and lawyers

misanthropy: hatred of humankind

mist: cloud of water particles that condense in the atmosphere, often used in Gothic literature to obscure objects or to prelude something or someone terrifying

mizzle: steal or disappear; fine rain

moniker/monniker: signature; first name

monolithic: something huge and impenetrable, often describing a building or an organization

mortality: death rate; the number of deaths in a given time or given group

moucher/moocher: rural vagrant or beggar, someone who lives on the road

mourning clothes: black garments worn after a relative dies, the length of which depended on your relationship to the deceased

muck snipe: someone down on their luck

muffler: scarf

mug-hunter: street thief or pickpocket, from which the modern term 'mugger' comes

mutcher: pickpocket who usually steals from drunks

myrmidons: loyal follower or acolyte, often someone who follows orders blindly or who acts with few scruples

N

nail: steal; to catch someone who is guilty of a crime

narcissism: egotism or self-idolatry; term comes from Greek mythology where the boy Narcissus fell in love with his own reflection in a lake

natural philosophy: the science of nature

nebulous: hazy; vague

necromancy: black art of conversing with the spirits of the dead, usually done to predict or influence the future, also for making the dead perform tasks for you; witchcraft or sorcery

nethers: charges or rent for lodgings

netherskens: cheap, unsavoury lodging houses, flophouses

new-fangled: new or original, not necessarily an improvement over a previous version

nib: point of a pen, often a fountain pen

nibbed: arrested

nickey: slow or simple-minded

nightmare: frightening or unsettling dream, often used in Gothic literature to heighten drama or fear; a malign spirit thought to haunt or suffocate people during sleep

nobble: to inflict severe pain or bodily harm

nocturne: romantic or reflective musical composition; night scene

nonpareil: unequalled or unsurpassed, often used to describe the most popular person of the season

nose: informant or spy; to try to find something out

O

occult: relating to the supernatural, witchcraft or magic; something not capable of being understood by ordinary people, but known only by the initiated

occupation: job, means of earning a living

odour: smell

Old Country: country of origin or of ones' ancestors, usually used to describe European countries

omen: sign or portent of a future event

omnibus: single or double-decker bus which was pulled by horses, capable of carrying lots of people

omnipotent: having unlimited power, god-like, infinite

on the fly: while in motion, moving quickly; done quickly or spontaneously

opium: drug extracted from the dried juice and seeds of the opium poppy which is highly addictive

orthodox: following established rules of religion or society; proper way of behaving

outdoor relief: charity for the poor which did not require them to enter the workhouse, eliminated in 1834 by the New Poor Law to stop people playing the system

outsider: instrument used for opening a lock from the wrong side; stranger or interloper

P

pacifist: someone who is against war or violence for any reason

page: boy or young man working as a servant or running errands

palanquin: box-shaped travelling conveyance, usually carrying one person and borne on horizontal poles by four or six others

pall: detect; become dull or fade; gloomy atmosphere or mood

palmer: shoplifter; someone who 'palms' items to steal them

palsy: medical condition producing uncontrollable shaking of the muscles

pandemonium: wild disorder, chaos

panegyric: impassioned speech or text praising something or someone

parlour: living room, usually for guests

patterer: someone who earns a living by recitation or hawker's sales talk, convincing people to buy goods

peach: inform against someone or give information against someone, often leading to imprisonment

pea-coat: short, heavy, double-breasted overcoat worn by seamen, usually dark blue or black

peelers: nickname for the new London police force, organized by Sir Robert Peel in 1829

perdition: eternal damnation following death; loss of the soul

pertaining to: concerning or to do with

phantasm: ghost or apparition

phenomenon: fact or occurrence that is out of the ordinary or hard to believe, even though it can be seen, felt, heard, etc.

phonograph: gramophone; machine for recording or playing sound

picnic: any informal social gathering for which each guest provided a share of the food; informal meal eaten outside

pidgeon: victim; also known as a plant

pig: policeman, usually a detective

pig in a poke: something for sale at more than its true value

pile: a fortune; large amount of money

pistoles: Spanish gold coin, used until the late 1800s

pleurisy: inflammation of the lungs producing a fever, hacking cough, sharp chest pain and difficulty in breathing

polyglot: someone who can speak or understand several languages

poorhouse: place where poor, old or sick people lived, where anyone able was put to work; also known as the workhouse

portrait: likeness of an individual or group created through photography or in paintings

possession: being controlled by an evil, demonic or supernatural force

post chaise: enclosed, four-wheeled, horse-drawn carriage, used to transport mail and passengers

post-human: class of humans who have evolved or changed to be beyond human, such as the Eloi and Morlocks in *The Time Machine*

premonitory: premonition or warning

prig: self-righteous or superior person

proctor: court officer who manages the affairs of others, answering to an attorney or solicitor

prodigious: great in amount or size; a lot

profane: disrespectful of religious beliefs

prognathous: projecting chin or lower jaw

prolixities: speeches or utterances of tedious or unnecessary length

Prometheus: a Titan who stole fire from the Greek god, Zeus, in order to give it to humankind

proprietor: owner of a commercial or business enterprise

puckering: jabbering; speaking in an incomprehensible manner

pugilistic: relating to the practice of boxing or fist fighting

punishers: men hired to give beatings or 'nobblings'

pursuit: the act of chasing after someone, usually to attack or catch them, often inspiring fear

push: slang term for money

putrefactive: causing decay or putrefaction

Q

quadrille: card game for four players using forty cards; dance

quarter days: four days of the year when quarterly payments were made: Lady Day (25 March), Midsummer (24 June), Michaelmas (29 September) and Christmas (25 December)

quay: wharf or platform in a port or harbour where ships are loaded or unloaded

quick-lime: white, corrosive, alkaline substance consisting of calcium oxide, acquired by heating limestone

quid: slang term for pound

quidnunc: gossip or busy body

quixotic: something unrealistic or improbable

R

racket: illicit or dishonest occupation or activity

ream: someone superior, real or genuine

rebellion: resistance and overthrow of authority, such as a leader or government, in order to change the way things are run

red planet: name for the planet Mars, given due to its red colour

remembrance: memory

repeater: pocket watch that chimed on the hour or quarter past the hour, making it easier to tell the time in the dark

republic: state or country in which the people elect representatives via elections rather than being run by a monarchy

reservist: reserve member of the military

resurrectionist: body snatcher; someone who steals corpses from graves, usually to sell to medical students. Legally, only the bodies of criminals could be used, but demand for corpses was so high that resurrectionists dug up the graves of the recently dead

revenant: dead person who has returned to terrorize or to avenge a score with someone living

revenge: act of avenging or repaying someone for a harm that the person has caused; to punish someone in retaliation for something done to them or to a loved one, carried out by humans or by spirits; a popular theme in Gothic literature

revery: daydream or musing; state of abstraction, also spelt reverie

ribald: description for vulgar, lewd humour, often involving jokes about sex

roller: thief who robs drunks; prostitute who steals from her (usually drunk) customers

Romanticism: arts and literature of the Romantic movement, characterized by the passion, emotion and often danger of love and associated feelings

Romany: gypsy or traveller; language spoken by gypsies

rookery: urban slum or ghetto; nesting place for rooks

rozzers: policemen

ruffles: slang term for handcuffs

ruin: to go out of business; lose all your money or possessions

runic: inscriptions on runes; written in the runic alphabet

S

saddle: loaf; cut of meat

sadism: perversion where one person gains sexual gratification by causing others physical or mental pain, first coined to describe the writings of the Marquis de Sade; delight in torment or excessive cruelty

salubrity: health or well-being

Salvation Army: worldwide religious organization founded by William Booth in 1865; it provided aid to the poor, helped those in need and sought to bring people back to God

sanctum sanctorium: holiest of holy places; place of secret or vital work, also spelt sanctum sanctorum

sapper: military engineer

savan: scientist or learned person

sawbones: physician or surgeon

scarlet fever: infection usually suffered by children, causing a red rash and high fever; also called Scarlatina

screever: forger; writer of fake documents

sealing wax: wax that is soft when heated, used to seal letters – red for business letters, black for mourning and other colours for general correspondence

sentient: able to feel and respond to sensations

sentinel: guard or soldier who keeps watch

sepulture: act of burial or interment

servant's lurk: public house used primarily by crooked or dismissed servants

sharp: conman, card swindler

shilling: unit of money equal to five pence in today's money

shirkster: layabout, work-shy

shofulman: someone who makes or passes bad money

silicious: consisting of silica, a crystalline compound

slap-bang job: public house frequented by thieves, where no credit is given

slate: used to teach children to write; they would write on black slates with white chalk, instead of the paper used today

slum: ghetto; false or faked document; to cheat someone or pass money you know to be bad or false

smasher: someone who passes bad or false money

snakesman: small boy used for housebreaking, as they could enter a house through a small gap

snoozer: someone who steals from sleeping guests in hotels

snowing: stealing clothes that have been hung out on a washing line to dry

somnambulism: sleepwalking, a dissociated mental state that occurs during deep sleep during which, in Gothic literature, people would do things they would not normally do

spectroscope: tool for recording and measuring spectra of light or radiation

spike: slang term for the workhouse

sponging-house: temporary prison for those who cannot pay their debts, prior to them being sent to a prison such as the Marshalsea in London

srew: skeleton key, for use in burglaries

stratagem: scheme or plan that has been carefully worked out

stricken: affected by; suffering or struck by

sublime: the concept of being awed, moved or transported by something, such as religion, beauty or emotions; used in Gothic literature for the thrill of being terrified, because fear inspires such strong emotions

substratum: underlying layer

succubus: female demon, counterpart of the incubus (*q.v.*)

supernatural: used to describe phenomena or events that seem unbelievable or cannot be explained by natural laws or occurrences relating to magic or the occult

superstition: deep-seated but often irrational belief in something, such as an action or ritual, that is thought to bring good or bad luck

supplication: asking for or begging humbly, often to a deity

surreal: bizarre or fantastical

sweetmeat: sweet treat, such as candy or candied fruit, often served at the end of a meal

swell: elegantly or stylishly dressed gentleman; expensive dress

T

tallow: hard, fatty substance from sheep or oxen, used to make candles or soap

taper: small, slim wax candle, narrower at the top than at the bottom

taproom: bar room in a public house where working-class people ate and drank, as opposed to the parlour, used by the middle classes

terrestrial: an inhabitant of, or relating to, the earth

thick 'un: slang term for sovereign

thicker: slang for sovereign or pound

thriving: to be profitable or successful; flourishing

thwart: to prevent someone from doing something

timorous: timid or nervous

Titan: name for the giants from Greek mythology; one of Saturn's moons

tocsin: warning signal or bell

toff: elegant or stylish gentleman; someone rich or upper-class

toffken: house in which well-to-do, upper-class people lived

tonneau: rear compartment of a car, usually consisting of the back seats

topped: to be hung

torpidity: mental inactivity; feeling sluggish or lacking in vigour

tradesman: man in a skilled trade, such as a carpenter or plumber; shopkeeper; someone who buys and sells goods

transfigure: to transform

transportation: when exiled British criminals were sent to the colonies, usually Australia, as punishment

trephining: surgery on the skull to remove sections of bone, sometimes used to treat mental illness

troglodytic: to describe a cave-dweller; bestial or brutal of character

turnkey: jailor; keeper of keys

typhoid: serious, often fatal, illness caused by drinking polluted water (contaminated by sewage)

U

ululation: howling or crying out, often from pain

ulster: long, heavy coat with a cape covering the shoulders and upper arms

umbrageous: providing or creating shade; also describes someone who is angry or has taken offense

unanimity: consensus or agreement

uncanny: something or someone too strange, weird or eerie to be natural or human; supernatural

unclean: dirty, impure

union workhouse: workhouse for the poor, which parishes were obligated to provide after the 1834 New Poor Law

unhallowed: unholy or not consecrated ground

unprovided for: left with no money or security

upper class: people from rich, moneyed families, such as landowners or aristocracy

utopia: imaginary society, place or period in which everything is perfect

V

vamp: to steal; to pawn something; to brazenly seduce or manipulate someone

vampire: supernatural being of a malignant nature, believed to leave its coffin at night to suck the blood of the living for sustenance, from European folklore

vapour: steam

vaporize: to convert something or someone into vapour; to destroy someone or something

veld: open country or grassland in southern Africa

venal: corrupt, capable of being bribed

vespers: evening church service, prayers

vicissitude: contrast or change, often unwelcome

vintner: wine maker or merchant

vivisection: surgery performed upon living organisms for scientific research or investigation

volplaning: gliding

W

watch: men chosen to guard the streets at night, periodically calling out the time and ensuring that no crimes were being committed

werewolf: someone who is human by day and turns into a wolf at night, living off humans, animals or even corpses, from European folklore

whist: popular card game, a variant of which developed into contract bridge

witchcraft: spells and magic performed by a witch; in Gothic fiction the witch is usually depicted as an old, hag-like crone or a beautiful, seductive young woman

without: outside, usually referring to outside the house in which someone is

woe-begone: sad or miserable in appearance

worldling: sophisticated or worldly person

work capitol: crime punishable by death

workhouse: place where the sick, poor, old and those in debt went or were sent for food and shelter. The New Poor Law (1834) made the workhouse almost a prison for the poor, who had to work hard in miserable conditions, often fed on gruel only and separated from their families

working class: those in heavy manual labour, usually for low, hourly wages, such as farm labourers, factory workers and builders

worrit: worry; worry-wort

wretch: miserable or unhappy person

Y

yack: slang term for a watch

Z

zenith: peak; most powerful or successful point

zombie: corpse, believed by voodoo followers to be reanimated by witchcraft; often presented as a monster who bites living people to infect them and spread the disease

zoophagous: carnivorous, feeding on animal flesh

A Selection of
Fantastic Reads

A range of Gothic novels, horror, crime,
mystery, fantasy, adventure, dystopia,
utopia, science fiction and more: available
and forthcoming from Flame Tree 451

Categories: Bio = Biographical, BL = Black Literature, C = Crime,
F = Fantasy, FL = Feminist Literature, G = Gothic, H = Horror, L = Literary,
M = Mystery, MF = Myth & Folklore, P = Political, SF = Science Fiction,
TH = Thriller. Organized by year of first publication.

1764	*The Castle of Otranto*, Horace Walpole	G
1786	*The History of the Caliph Vathek*, William Beckford	G
1768	*Barford Abbey*, Susannah Minifie Gunning	G
1783	*The Recess Or, a Tale of Other Times*, Sophia Lee	G
1791	*Tancred: A Tale of Ancient Times*, Joseph Fox	G
1872	*In a Glass Darkly*, Sheridan Le Fanu	C, M
1794	*Caleb Williams*, William Godwin	C, M
1794	*The Banished Man*, Charlotte Smith	G
1794	*The Mysteries of Udolpho*, Ann Radcliffe	G
1795	*The Abbey of Clugny*, Mary Meeke	G
1796	*The Monk*, Matthew Lewis	G
1798	*Wieland*, Charles Brockden Brown	G
1799	*St. Leon*, William Godwin	H, M
1799	*Ormond, or The Secret Witness*, Charles Brockden Brown	H, M
1801	*The Magus,* Francis Barrett	H, M
1807	*The Demon of Sicily*, Edward Montague	G
1811	*Undine*, Friedrich de la Motte Fouqué	G
1814	*Sintram and His Companions*, Friedrich de la Motte Fouqué	G
1818	*Northanger Abbey*, Jane Austen	G
1818	*Frankenstein*, Mary Shelley	H, G
1820	*Melmoth the Wanderer*, Charles Maturin	G
1826	*The Last Man*, Mary Shelley	SF
1828	*Pelham*, Edward Bulwer-Lytton	C, M
1831	*Short Stories & Poetry*, Edgar Allan Poe (to 1949)	C, M
1838	*The Amber Witch*, Wilhelm Meinhold	H, M

1842	*Zanoni*, Edward Bulwer-Lytton	H, M
1845	*Varney the Vampyre*, Thomas Preskett Prest	H, M
1846	*Wagner, the Wehr-wolf*, George W.M. Reynolds	H, M
1847	*Wuthering Heights*, Emily Brontë	G
1850	*The Scarlet Letter*, Nathaniel Hawthorne	H, M
1851	*The House of the Seven Gables*, Nathaniel Hawthorne	H, M
1852	*Bleak House*, Charles Dickens	C, M
1859	*The Woman in White*, Wilkie Collins	C, M
1859	*Blake, or the Huts of America*, Martin R. Delany	Bl.
1860	*The Marble Faun*, Nathaniel Hawthorne	H, M
1861	*East Lynne*, Ellen Wood	C, M
1861	*Elsie Venner*, Oliver Wendell Holmes	H, M
1862	*A Strange Story*, Edward Bulwer-Lytton	H, M
1862	*Lady Audley's Secret*, Mary Elizabeth Braddon	C, M
1864	*Journey to the Centre of the Earth*, Jules Verne	SF
1868	*The Huge Hunter*, Edward Sylvester Ellis	SF
1868	*The Moonstone*, Wilkie Collins	C, M
1870	*Twenty Thousand Leagues Under the Sea*, Jules Verne	SF
1872	*Erewhon*, Samuel Butler	SF
1874	*The Temptation of St. Anthony*, Gustave Flaubert	H, M
1874	*The Expressman and the Detective*, Allan Pinkerton	C, M
1876	*The Man-Wolf and Other Tales*, Erckmann-Chatrian	H, M
1878	*The Haunted Hotel*, Wilkie Collins	C, M
1878	*The Leavenworth Case*, Anna Katharine Green	C, M
1886	*The Mystery of a Hansom Cab*, Fergus Hume	C, M
1886	*Robur the Conqueror*, Jules Verne	SF
1886	*The Strange Case of Dr Jekyll & Mr Hyde*, R.L. Stevenson	SF
1887	*She*, H. Rider Haggard	F
1887	*A Study in Scarlet*, Arthur Conan Doyle	C, M

1890	*The Sign of Four*, Arthur Conan Doyle	C, M
1891	*The Picture of Dorian Gray*, Oscar Wilde	G
1892	*The Big Bow Mystery*, Israel Zangwill	C, M
1894	*Martin Hewitt, Investigator*, Arthur Morrison	C, M
1895	*The Time Machine*, H.G. Wells	SF
1895	*The Three Imposters*, Arthur Machen	H, M
1897	*The Beetle*, Richard Marsh	G
1897	*The Invisible Man*, H.G. Wells	SF
1897	*Dracula*, Bram Stoker	H
1898	*The War of the Worlds*, H.G. Wells	SF
1898	*The Turn of the Screw*, Henry James	H, M
1899	*Imperium in Imperio*, Sutton E. Griggs	BL, SF
1899	*The Awakening*, Kate Chopin	FL
1899	*The Conjure Woman*, Charles W. Chesnutt	H
1902	*The Hound of the Baskervilles*, Arthur Conan Doyle	C, M
1902	*Of One Blood: Or, The Hidden Self*, Pauline Hopkins	FL, BL
1903	*The Jewel of Seven Stars*, Bram Stoker	H, M
1904	*Master of the World*, Jules Verne	SF
1905	*A Thief in the Night*, E.W. Hornung	C, M
1906	*The Empty House & Other Ghost Stories*, Algernon Blackwood	G
1906	*The House of Souls*, Arthur Machen	H, M
1907	*Lord of the World*, R.H. Benson	SF
1907	*The Red Thumb Mark*, R. Austin Freeman	C, M
1907	*The Boats of the 'Glen Carrig'*, William Hope Hodgson	H, M
1907	*The Exploits of Arsène Lupin*, Maurice Leblanc	C, M
1907	*The Mystery of the Yellow Room*, Gaston Leroux	C, M
1908	*The Mystery of the Four Fingers*, Fred M. White	SF
1908	*The Ghost Kings*, H. Rider Haggard	F
1908	*The Circular Staircase*, Mary Roberts Rinehart	C, M

1908	*The House on the Borderland*, William Hope Hodgson	H, M
1909	*The Ghost Pirates*, William Hope Hodgson	H, M
1909	*Jimbo: A Fantasy*, Algernon Blackwood	G
1909	*The Necromancers*, R.H. Benson	SF
1909	*Black Magic*, Marjorie Bowen	H, M
1910	*The Return*, Walter de la Mare	H, M
1911	*The Lair of the White Worm*, Bram Stoker	H
1911	*The Innocence of Father Brown*, G.K. Chesterton	C, M
1911	*The Centaur*, Algernon Blackwood	G
1912	*Tarzan of the Apes*, Edgar Rice Burroughs	F
1912	*The Lost World*, Arthur Conan Doyle	SF
1913	*The Return of Tarzan*, Edgar Rice Burroughs	F
1913	*Trent's Last Case*, E.C. Bentley	C, M
1913	*The Poison Belt*, Arthur Conan Doyle	SF
1915	*The Valley of Fear*, Arthur Conan Doyle	C, M
1915	*Herland*, Charlotte Perkins Gilman	SF, FL
1915	*The Thirty-Nine Steps*, John Buchan	TH
1917	*John Carter: A Princess of Mars*, Edgar Rice Burroughs	F
1917	*The Terror*, Arthur Machen	H, M
1917	*The Job*, Sinclair Lewis	L
1917	*The Sturdy Oak*, Ed. Elizabeth Jordan	FL
1918	*Brood of the Witch-Queen*, Sax Rohmer	H, M
1918	*The Land That Time Forgot*, Edgar Rice Burroughs	F
1918	*The Citadel of Fear*, Gertrude Barrows Bennett (as. Francis Stevens)	FL, TH
1919	*John Carter: A Warlord of Mars*, Edgar Rice Burroughs	F
1919	*The Door of the Unreal*, Gerald Biss	H
1919	*The Moon Pool*, Abraham Merritt	SF
1919	*The Three Eyes*, Maurice Leblanc	SF
1920	*A Voyage to Arcturus*, David Lindsay	SF
1920	*The Metal Monster*, Abraham Merritt	SF

1920	*Darkwater*, W.E.B. Du Bois	BL
1922	*The Undying Monster*, Jessie Douglas Kerruish	H
1925	*The Avenger*, Edgar Wallace	C
1925	*The Red Hawk*, Edgar Rice Burroughs	SF
1926	*The Moon Maid*, Edgar Rice Burroughs	SF
1927	*Witch Wood*, John Buchan	H, M
1927	*The Colour Out of Space*, H.P. Lovecraft	SF
1927	*The Dark Chamber*, Leonard Lanson Cline	H, M
1928	*When the World Screamed*, Arthur Conan Doyle	F
1928	*The Skylark of Space*, E.E. Smith	SF
1930	*Last and First Men*, Olaf Stapledon	SF
1930	*Belshazzar*, H. Rider Haggard	F
1934	*The Murder Monster*, Brant House (Emile C. Tepperman)	H
1934	*The People of the Black Circle*, Robert E. Howard	F
1935	*Odd John*, Olaf Stapledon	SF
1935	*The Hour of the Dragon*, Robert E. Howard	F
1935	*Short Stories Selection 1*, Robert E. Howard	F
1935	*Short Stories Selection 2*, Robert E. Howard	F
1936	*The War-Makers*, Nick Carter	C, M
1937	*Star Maker*, Olaf Stapledon	SF
1936	*Red Nails*, Robert E. Howard	F
1936	*The Shadow Out of Time*, H.P. Lovecraft	SF
1936	*At the Mountains of Madness*, H.P. Lovecraft	SF
1938	*Power*, C.K.M. Scanlon writing in *G-Men*	C, M
1939	*Almuric*, Robert E. Howard	SF
1940	*The Ghost Strikes Back*, George Chance	SF
1937	*The Road to Wigan Pier*, George Orwell	P, Bio
1938	*Homage to Catalonia*, George Orwell	P, Bio,
1945	*Animal Farm*, George Orwell	P, F
1949	*Nineteen Eighty-Four*, George Orwell	P, F

| 1953 | *The Black Star Passes*, John W. Campbell | SF |
| 1959 | *The Galaxy Primes*, E.E. Smith | SF |

New Collections of Ancient Myths, Early Modern and Contemporary Stories

2014	*Celtic Myths*, J.K. Jackson (ed.)	MF
2014	*Greek & Roman Myths*, J.K. Jackson (ed.)	MF
2014	*Native American Myths*, J.K. Jackson (ed.)	MF
2014	*Norse Myths*, J.K. Jackson (ed.)	MF
2018	*Chinese Myths*, J.K. Jackson (ed.)	MF
2018	*Egyptian Myths*, J.K. Jackson (ed.)	MF
2018	*Indian Myths*, J.K. Jackson (ed.)	MF
2018	*Myths of Babylon*, J.K. Jackson (ed.)	MF
2019	*African Myths*, J.K. Jackson (ed.)	MF
2019	*Aztec Myths*, J.K. Jackson (ed.)	MF
2019	*Japanese Myths*, J.K. Jackson (ed.)	MF
2020	*Arthurian Myths*, J.K. Jackson (ed.)	MF
2020	*Irish Fairy Tales*, J.K. Jackson (ed.)	MF
2020	*Polynesian Myths*, J.K. Jackson (ed.)	MF
2020	*Scottish Myths*, J.K. Jackson (ed.)	MF
2021	*Viking Folktales*, J.K. Jackson (ed.)	MF
2021	*West African Folktales*, J.K. Jackson (ed.)	MF
2022	*East African Folktales*, J.K. Jackson (ed.)	MF
2022	*Persian Myths*, J.K. Jackson (ed.)	MF
2022	*The Tale of Beowulf*, J.K. Jackson (ed.)	MF
2022	*The Four Branches of the Mabinogi*, J.K. Jackson (ed.)	MF
2022	*American Ghost Stories*, Brett Riley (Intro.)	H, G
2022	*Irish Ghost Stories*, Maura McHugh (Intro.)	H, G
2022	*Scottish Ghost Stories*, Helen McClory (Intro.)	H, G
2022	*Victorian Ghost Stories*, Reggie Oliver (Intro.)	H, G
2023	*Slavic Myths*, Ema Lakinska (Intro.)	MF
2023	*Turkish Folktales*, Nathan Young (Intro.)	MF

A TASTE FOR THE FANTASTIC

Herland by *Charlotte Perkins Gilman*

A lost world fantasy in the tradition of Arthur Conan Doyle and the
Utopianism of William Morris, *Herland* inverted expectations with its
exclusively female society visited by three men from the Edwardian era.
An early example of feminist science fiction, this utopian fantasy explores
miracle births, role reversals and concepts of peace and freedom.

The Job by *Sinclair Lewis*

A statement of female empowerment, and self-determination over societal
expectation. Una Golden gains work in an exclusively male world of
commercial real estate. Golden struggles for the recognition of her male
peers while balancing romantic and work life; she marries, divorces,
continues to work hard and finally emerges triumphant on her own terms.

The Awakening by *Kate Chopin*

Edna Pontellier is a wife and mother of two who struggles to submit to the
prevalent views of women in late nineteenth-century Southern Louisiana.
Her unconventional ideas of motherhood and femininity have got her
in trouble more than once. When she meets Robert and falls in love, it
is the beginning of her journey to stepping away from her life of purely
maternal duties, reclaiming her individuality and finding happiness. This is
a touching story of self-discovery that was very much ahead of its time.

**For information on these as paperbacks and
ebooks please visit flametreepublishing.com**